ACKNOWLEL   .. 1 S

I am indebted to my father and stepmother, Tom and Pansy Gray, for their researches, and for their wonderful reminiscences of Missouri rural life. I must also thank Mrs Mary Ray of Columbia, Missouri, for her invaluable researches in the archives of the Missouri Historical Society. Finally, once again, my thanks to my good friend, Constance Barry, for her excellent preparation of the manuscript, and for her moral support!

1

St Louis, Missouri. 17 May, 1849

Belle opened her eyes, heaved herself over to look at the girl, and nearly fell off the sofa. 'What's all the fuss about this time of night?'

The girl hugged her wrapper tightly around her as she stood in the doorway. 'There's a fire on board the *White Cloud*.'

Belle snuffled. She would have liked to get up and see a steamboat on fire, but her bulk and the whiskey with which she had been whiling away the evening made it seem like an impossible task.

'Look at that!' cried the girl. 'The one next to it's just caught fire! What's the name of that packet, Tone?'

The scraggy man looked over the girl's shoulder. 'By golly, that's the *Eudora!*' He wrapped the belt around his narrow waist and notched it tight. 'Where the hell's my boots? I got to get out there. Them boats is packed together tighter'n a tick. Don't you know river boats is just floating matchboxes? They could all go up! Oti – get your tail out here!'

Belle turned her head and saw Big Oti and the plump girl emerge from the other bedroom.

'Fire?' asked Oti, tucking in his shirt. 'We better try to help. Could be you and me'll end up without no jobs, Tone. You coming, Belle?'

Belle squinted at the four of them through a fog of alcohol. 'Naw, I seen fires before.'

'Well, we're going out to watch,' said the plump girl.

'Yes, sir!' said Tone excitedly. 'The whole place could go up! It's not safe here, Belle. There's hemp and linseed oil and all sorts of cargo stacked around on the landing.

It could all go with a bang. I wouldn't be surprised if there warn't some gunpowder.'

Their noisy talk was irritating Belle. 'I'll go when I have to. Don't y'all bother about me. Just close the door behind you.'

The four of them left, the girls still wearing nothing but their cotton wrappers, rolled-down stockings and shoes. Belle's eyes closed. She meant to stay awake in case it was necessary to get out in a hurry, but couldn't resist the soporific effect of the home-made whiskey. Twenty minutes later, excited voices outside woke her. A red glow lit up the only window, so she knew the fire must have reached the cargo on the levee.

Now she did make the effort to get up, steadying herself with a hand on the sofa back, reaching for the nearby table. She would have leaned against the window glass for support, but the glass was hot, and cracked suddenly with a sound like a gunshot.

'Damned fire!' she muttered, staggering towards the door. 'Gonna lose this place, too. Whole town's going up. Must be two dozen steamboats floating out there in flames. Got to get out of here.'

The brass door handle was surprisingly hot. She yanked her hand away and shook it. She needed something to wrap around her hand so that she could bear to turn the knob. Seeing nothing better than the wrapper she was wearing, she began to gather up the hem. She was sober now, but her body couldn't respond to the urgency of her fear. Heat reddened her sagging cheeks and sucked the sweat from her pores.

The door handle was still too hot to touch, even through the folds of cloth. Any minute now she'd have to take off the whole damned thing, wrap it round the handle, and run out into the night bare-assed naked. Above the sounds of panic on the waterfront, the shouts and crashes, she heard an ominous crackle and looked up at the rafters where fingers of flame were clutching the beams.

*

East St Louis, Illinois, 17 May, 1849.

'Well, Mrs Brocklehurst, I suppose this is where we must part company,' I said. 'I hope I've been of some help to you since we left Chicago.'

'I reckon. When you've got five young'uns you need all the help you can get. Pity you warn't a stronger woman.'

'Yes.'

If I had been stronger, I would have *poled* my way south on a raft rather than travel overland with the Brocklehurst family. I patted young Jeffery on the head – a substitute for what I would have liked to do him – and he called me a rude name.

'Seems to me,' said Mr Brocklehurst, picking his nose, 'that you got the best end of the bargain.'

I hoisted my carpet-bag, ready to move off smoothly. 'But we did agree, didn't we? I was to help your wife with the children on the trek overland from Chicago in exchange for my food and the privilege of sleeping under your wagon at night. No money to change hands.'

'You could of done more, to my way of thinking. I thought you said you was a schoolteacher. The kids didn't take to you at all.'

I began backing away. 'That's fair enough. I didn't take to them. I don't pinch, kick, use bad language or sass my elders, and I don't like children who do. A little discipline would do them no harm.'

Before Mr Brocklehurst could demand money for my food, I turned and walked briskly towards the landing. It was dark; I couldn't cross the Mississipi river tonight. I would have to spend the night on the Illinois side, which meant paying out a few cents for a room somewhere. Since the cheapest rooming houses were on the water-front, and since I was determined to get away first thing in the morning, I took a room in the sort of run-down place I would normally have avoided.

3

The room was small and hot, situated directly over the dining room. It had a decent-sized window overlooking the river, and I could see the lights of St Louis blinking invitingly about half a mile across the water. After all those nights camping out under the Brocklehurst wagon, the lumpy bed looked positively luxurious.

I had started out from Boston several weeks earlier, travelling in comfort at first on some very well-appointed trains and steamboats. By the time I reached Chicago I knew I dare not buy yet another ticket on a packet, because my funds were dangerously low. I was, there-fore, most grateful for the invitation from the Brocklehursts to fall in with them. Those last few hundred miles were so terrible that I prefer not to dwell on them. It is enough to say that I developed a horror of land travel, indulgent mothers and large families.

I had never intended to return to St Louis at all. At the end of April, I had been expecting to marry Carlton Dobbs, a successful businessman of forty-three. He was twenty years older than I, but I loved everything about him: his powerful vocabulary, his ready wit, his capacity to read the most abstruse tome and make sense of it. I especially loved his reputation as an intellectual.

Carlton owned a radical newspaper for which he wrote brilliant editorials. I often visited his printing shop in my spare time, loving the smell of the ink, the skill of the typesetter, and the knowledge that Carlton was challeng-ing the ingrained attitudes of the common man. I learned everything I could on my visit to the newspaper office.

'What intrigues you, my dear?' Carlton used to say. 'The setting of type is a task for menials. It is the writing of editorials and the reporting of events which should attract higher intellects like yours. Study the construc-tion of my sentences, learn about phrasing and the development of an argument. Leave the mechanical details of newspaper production to Thomas O'Malley, who knows his business very well.'

4

I saw his point, but still enjoyed the mechanical details. Setting type was an eye-straining, back-aching, fiddly sort of activity, but I found it relaxing. I often set a paragraph or two for Thomas.

I also studied the construction of Carlton's essays. I did try to learn how he developed an argument, and I was convinced that I would one day be able to play an important part in the publishing of the *Boston Eye*.

Alas, Carlton's views were too advanced even for the citizens of Boston. It has to be said, also, that he was never as interested in financial matters as he was in political issues. The competition from numerous more conservative papers forced him to close down the *Eye* in January.

To make matters worse, established publishers had shown no interest in Carlton's great work, a comprehensive history of Boston. Defiantly, he published it himself in February. To prove my loyalty and trust, I even agreed to lend him my own small savings so that the book could be handsomely bound. I was certain that the sales would soon justify the gamble.

Unfortunately, only twenty prominent citizens responded favourably to Carlton's letter which begged for subscriptions prior to publication. When the book had been printed, his brother bought a further ten copies to distribute among friends and distant relatives. There were no more sales. To my intense disappointment, Carlton lost heart. A month before the wedding date, he impulsively sold the printing business for a pitiful sum. Despite all these financial reverses, I was still under the impression that the wedding would take place as planned. Then I heard he had left for New York in the company of a wealthy widow of his own age.

The news of his departure was given to me bluntly by his older brother. Hamilton Dobbs made no attempt to disguise his relief that Carlton would not, after all, be tied for life to a schoolteacher of unknown family. To give him his due, Hamilton was a decent man and was surprisingly sympathetic when he saw my shock and distress. My tears came to him as a complete surprise. He seemed to have formed the impression that I would not mind at all if my fiancé left town with another woman.

He knew that I had given my savings to Carlton, and also that I had handed in my notice to the owners of the school. With more sensitivity and grace than I had imagined him capable, he offered me twenty-five dollars as 'compensation for a broken heart', which was slightly more than my lost savings. I am ashamed to say I had no hesitation in taking the money. Refusal would have been an expensive and futile gesture. After all, I was already suffering all the pain of rejection that is common to those who have been jilted. Nothing could be done about Carlton's defection. I thought I might as well save myself from ruin.

The next day, I received a curious letter from my mother in St Louis. She wanted to see me again, wanted to talk, she said. Could I possibly come to St Louis? Her invitation provided an avenue of escape, a chance to get over my humiliation. No wonder I was prepared to set off on the long journey so quickly!

The waterfront in East St Louis, as in any city, draws disreputable persons like a magnet. They gather after dark with their whiskey to offer each other the sort of respect and friendship conventional citizens withhold from them. On this particular night, they had turned their eyes towards the distant lights of St Louis and were speculating about the activities on the other side of the Mississippi as if that metropolis of seventy thousand people were situated on the moon. Their slurred voices and frequent high-pitched giggles reached me through my open window. I put my only piece of luggage – a faded carpet-bag – on the bed and went straight away to close the shutters. It was a warm night, but I was

6

prepared to suffer the heat in order to be spared the inane chatter.

I didn't close the shutters, however, because the cry went up of fire on board a steamboat on the far side of the river. I quickly blew out my candle and could then see the packet clearly. At such a distance the fire had an unreal quality, fascinating but not threatening. Distance made it a toy boat.

Within three or four minutes, the packets on either side of the flaming steamboat had caught fire as well. By the light of the flames, I perceived that those on shore were setting loose all the other steamboats, presumably to prevent them from catching fire. As in a dream, I saw the unmanned boats float darkly out to the middle of the river. As in a nightmare, I saw one of the flaming packets sail among them, spreading destruction. At one time, I counted twenty-three boats alight. My mother had moved since I last visited St Louis, but I knew she lived somewhere on the waterfront. Dread engulfed me.

No more than fifteen minutes later, a sharp-eyed lout cried that the fire had reached the shore in St Louis. Now I began to tremble, to clutch the shutters and pray for a swift dousing of the flames as they travelled from Cherry Street, or thereabouts, all the way down to Duncan's Island. Before long, at least a mile of the waterfront was alight; no one knew then how far inland it had spread. A dozen times or more I said it aloud: 'If only I had reached St Louis and my mother before the fire!' Yet what could I have done?

I was too tired to maintain my vigil at the window all night. I went to bed about midnight and fell into a troubled sleep. In the early hours, I was awakened by a blast of gunpowder, and guessed that they were blowing up buildings in the path of the fire. I later learned that the fire had not been brought under control until about seven o'clock in the morning of the eighteenth. That fire was the biggest disaster in the history of St Louis, and is

7

said to have done half a million dollars' worth of damage.

The first ferry of the morning left at ten o'clock and did brisk business. I was fortunate to get on it, but fortune helps those who help themselves. Perhaps this would be an appropriate place to say something about myself. I am a small-boned woman with nothing special about my appearance. When dressed in my brown travelling costume, I look every inch the schoolteacher. I have brown hair and eyes, and too many freckles on my nose. Someone once called me a speckled sparrow. The comparison did not offend me. I was content with the description.

It is not so very bad to be considered dull but respectable, except that I am apt to be elbowed aside in a crowd, jostled on the street and passed over by gentlemen with appreciative eyes. I have just one special quality, if I may be forgiven this small boast. I have a good, commanding voice, clear and not particularly deep – and I know how to use it to good effect. Its use got me on to the ferry that morning ahead of several burly men and two or three grandly-dressed ladies.

I stood by the rail as the squat boat fought the current of the Mississippi, and refused to give up my vantage point to the haughty women on board. They clung to their men and declared that they thought they would die with the horror of it all. Such extravagant behaviour is repugnant to me.

'Excuse me,' I said as the ferry gangplank was slipped into place. 'If you would just let me pass, sir. I have urgent business on shore. Make way, if you please, madam.'

Without knowing why they did it, people stood aside for me, so that I was the first one to set foot on the fire-damaged levee, the first to discover that here and there the cobbles were still hot against the soles of one's shoes.

8

I could hear some of the women behind me exclaiming about it as I threaded my way through the crowd waiting by the gangplank.

Having disembarked with such determination, I now stopped to consult my letter, before walking uncertainly up the incline and along the street until I stood looking down at a heap of smouldering rubble that had recently been, I supposed, a row of single-storey shanties.

I set down my carpet-bag and prodded the debris diffidently with one toe, not at all sure that I was standing before the right dwelling. Then, with a low moan, I bent to retrieve a piece of twisted metal: a pinchbeck picture frame, its picture singed beyond recognition beneath the cracked glass. Ignoring the heat and thick ash which leapt up to cover the lower inches of my skirt. I stepped into the area that had been a home of sorts, stripped off my gloves and began poking around in the charred remains like a scavenger on a dung-heap. Here were the springs of the old sofa, surely there a flatiron and the stove. Metal lumps might be the claw feet of the old standing mirror before which I had preened when I was sixteen. This very mirror had finally convinced me that I would never be a beauty.

Eagerly, I snatched up the strongbox, the object to which I had always taken second place in my mother's heart. It was empty. Since there were no ashes in it, I hoped desperately that its contents were safe in Brown's bank.

The sight of these burnt mementoes acted on me so powerfully that it was a minute or two before I realized that I was not alone. Small boys, both black and white, were prancing from one bare foot to the other in the hot rubble as they moved ever closer to study me. They met my angry gaze unabashed. Looking around, I saw that the many adults wandering about this section of the levee were not quite so bold as the boys, but just as curious. They gaped, they sniggered, they sneered, but

9

they turned away when they caught me looking back at them.

Twenty yards away, a man on a handsome chestnut reined in his horse in order to look down at me. If I am a speckled sparrow he was, that day, a glossy crow. His square shoulders filled out an expensive black frockcoat, beneath which I could just see a red brocade waistcoat with a gold watch-chain looped across it. His grey beaver hat was tilted forward at an arrogant angle. Later in the day its shadow would obscure his features. At that moment, he was turned due east to observe me, so that the morning sun fell full on his face, on the clean-shaven jaw, straight nose and neat dark eyebrows that were drawn together in puzzlement as he tried to remember who I was. At twenty yards, I couldn't possibly see the colour of his eyes, but I knew just the same. Palest blue with black lashes.

I gave no sign of recognition. Still puzzled, he lifted his hat politely and rode on. How beautiful he was! The sight of him squeezed the air from my lungs. I could remember the sound of his deep voice as if I had last heard him speak just five minutes before. Didn't I have enough to contend with, without his arrival to stir painful memories?

I took several quick, deep, head-spinning breaths as I watched him ride away. Then I nearly fainted when I bent down once more, this time to pick up a pathetic scrap of red silk that had somehow defied the flames.

A man with oily hair sidled up to me, leering familiarly. He wore his dirty red shirt open at the throat and had rolled up the sleeves to reveal heavily-muscled forearms, the product of his trade as a heaver of cargo on and off steamboats. I moved back because of the smell of him.

'You lookin' for Belle?' he asked.

'Yes, I am. Do you know where she is?'

'Why, she died last night, lady! Burned up right where

10

you're standing. I helped get her body to the under-takers. Wern't much left of her, but we couldn't leave her here. We put her in a old sack and – say, are you all right?'

I was not all right, of course. Shock chilled my skin on this warm morning as I fought nausea and the desire to wail in anguish. 'I'm fine, just fine. She used to live over on Second and Walnut. Do you know why she moved here?'

'Fell on hard times, maybe. You know what them women is like. What I mean is, she was drinking pretty heavy towards the end. The two girls warn't hurt none. They was out watching the fire and got away in good time when the flames reached the shore.'

'I see. And Brown's bank?'

'Burned down. Warn't much of a bank. Just a old wooden building down on Main. The other banks is all safe.'

'Thank you.' I turned away and pulled my handker-chief from my sleeve to wipe away the tears I could no longer control. If only I had somewhere to sit down! I was incredulous at first. I couldn't believe all this was happening. Belle dead! Then a devastating sense of loss swept over me, catching me completely by surprise. I had thought I hated my mother. Now, I couldn't forgive her for having died before I could say all that was in my heart. I longed for one last chance to clear the air between us. How strange! Carlton's departure had left me angry but relatively unscathed. And I had thought I loved him!

The number of small boys had increased to about twenty. They milled around, pushing and shoving and whispering among themselves. Two of the older ones, sensing my preoccupation, began picking among the ruins of my mother's last home. I rushed over to shove them away.

'I have never seen such a pathetic bunch of useless

11

boys in my life,' I said in a voice loud enough to make them jump. 'Go on about your business, before I take a stick to you.'

I watched them scatter, feeling a little better for my outburst. The roustabout who had so sensitively informed me of my mother's death was striding away up Locust, but other people were just arriving. Every minute more carriages drew up. Well-dressed men got out to walk down among the burnt cargo, shaking their heads in disbelief, conferring with one another, looking up at the skeletons of riverside warehouses. Those who filled the road had come to gape, to witness for themselves the results of the calamitous fire. Some were awed by the damage, others were merely human vultures feeding off the misery of those who had lost so much.

There seemed to be a heap of old clothes down by the water's edge. It moved and I saw that the clothing was worn by a middle-aged woman with greying black hair. She had the pallor of death as she stared at the river, hoping perhaps for deliverance in its depths. Moved by the sight of someone whose grief was greater than my own, I walked down the slope to touch the woman on the shoulder.

'Are you all right, ma'am? Did you lose a loved one last night?'

The woman squinted upwards, tucking a wisp of hair into the tight bun on the top of her head. I thought she might be a farmer's wife; her hands were coarse and red, big-knuckled and blunt-fingered.

'Last night I lost nearly every penny I had in the world,' she said in a flat voice. 'I'm finished, but I don't care. I'm just waiting on the Lord. I lost my only child, a boy, two years ago, and Husband died of the cholera back in March. I've managed somehow, feeding myself as best I could, sleeping anywheres I could pay for and holding on to my savings so's I could buy a few bolts of cloth and maybe go into business. We had to sell the farm in January, you see. Well, I bought some bolts of right nice calico from a company in Chicago. Paid for them, too. They was burned up right here on the levee. If only I'd come down here last night! But what was I to do? They *told* me to come today. If I'd a come yesterday night, maybe I could of saved them. Or died trying. I don't know that I much care which.'

'Didn't you have any insurance?'

The question made her smile. 'I didn't even think of it. Couldn't have afforded it if I did.'

'What are you going to do?'

'Starve, I guess. I don't care, I tell you. It'd be the best thing, I reckon. Wish I'd died alongside Husband. He warn't sick but twenty-four hours. It was terrible, but it was quick. My boy Toby didn't die for three whole weeks after he tooken sick.'

The roustabout was back, full of important news and grinning broadly. 'You Miss Carlotta Schultz?'

'I am.'

'Mr Walkern wants to see you. Right away, he says.'

I frowned. 'Isn't he the hemp and rope merchant?'

'That's the one. Everybody knows Mr Walkern. Over on Third and Laurel. That street there is Locust, then comes Vine and then Laurel, then up three blocks.'

'I remember.' In St Louis, the streets running north to south are numbered – Main, Second and so on. Those running east to west are, for the most part, named after trees. I picked up my bag, murmured goodbye to the woman and began walking towards Laurel. I had to pass through the idling crowd at the levee's edge, and it seemed they all now knew who I was.

Somebody out of sight shouted, 'That's the daughter of Missouri Belle!'

Angrily, I turned my head, looking for the speaker. 'Don't you think that now she's dead, you could show some respect and call her Miss Schultz?'

13

The same voice came from the back of the crowd. I couldn't locate him. 'Who was your daddy, Carlotta?'

It was a question I had been asked as long as I could remember. I always gave the same answer. 'Beelzebub!'

Everyone laughed, some guffawing and slapping their thighs as if they hadn't had so much to laugh about for years. I walked on, holding my head high, remembering how it always was in St Louis. I had been foolish to think it could be any different, even after all these years.

As I moved away from the levee, the fire damage was less. But everywhere people were loitering and looking at the remains of those buildings which had been reduced to rubble. I later heard that fifteen square blocks had been destroyed.

Otis Walkern's office on Third Street was like so much of St Louis property in those days. It had a brick-built basement and foundations, topped by a white-painted wooden structure with small square windows. No attempt had been made to build something of architectural merit. A sycamore shaded it: weeds surrounded it. Paint curled away from the planks in the warm sun, but at least it had escaped the fire.

Mr Walkern was a fat man in his sixties with purple cheeks and an enlarged bulbous nose on which anyone interested enough to bother could have counted the pores. His head was so fat that his small ears were tucked away in the flesh, and his collar was barely visible beneath his chins. He recognized me from long ago, knew of my shameful origins. My mother had always spoken of him with contempt.

He waved me irritably to a chair in his small office. 'You smell of smoke,' was the friendly greeting as he plumped himself down in an armchair behind the desk. 'You been poking around down there on the waterfront? Won't do you any good, Lottie. Your ma died owing everybody in town. I can testify to that.'

I sucked in my breath and began taking off my gloves,

14

finger by finger, to keep him from seeing how shocked I was. I wanted to give myself a second or two to adjust to my changed circumstances. I couldn't remember having ever spoken to the man, yet he hadn't hesitated to call me Lottie. None of the 'Yes, Miss Schultz' and 'No, Miss Schultz' I had worked so hard to deserve in Boston. In St Louis, no matter how hard I tried to be decent, I would always be considered just the low-down daughter of Missouri Belle. I should never have come back home.

'My mother wrote to me many weeks ago, Mr Walkern, asking me to come to St Louis. She said she had business interests which would enable her to retire from her . . . to retire and move to the East or somewhere. Unfortunately, I arrived a day too late.'

Mr Walkern leaned back in his chair and patted his face with a handkerchief. 'Your ma never had any business dealings except with a pack of cards, a jug of whiskey and any man foolish enough to walk into her brothel. She spent every penny she had. I believe she owned that house on Second and Walnut at one time, but she sold it. She drew out whatever savings she had from Brown's bank, too, so don't go thinking some big inheritance burned down with the building. I'm . . . I *was* a director of that bank, so I know what I'm talking about. She even borrowed two thousand dollars from me. What do you think about that?'

I attempted to moisten my lips with a dry tongue. 'I don't know what to think, sir, except that it's a strange businessman who lends two thousand dollars to a woman who owes money all over town.'

The old man stood up and leaned across the desk, bringing his face alarmingly close to mine. 'We had a deal! It was a good investment. I must assume you were to be part of it, if she sent for you. I gave her the two thousand in soft money. Bills. I guess she pushed it down the front of her dress and it burned up with her. I'm going to be a hard money man in the future. Gold or silver.'

15

'I don't know what sort of thing I could possibly do . . .'

'Well, I'll tell you about that, miss. Because that's why I sent for you. You're a pretty woman and you got a respectable look about you. You never liked your ma, I guess, or you would have come back home more often, maybe gone into the business. I don't know what you've been doing all these years back East, but I think I know what you're going to be doing in the future. You're going to be earning money for me just like your ma was going to do. It'll mean laying out more of my money, and I can't hardly afford it, but it's got to be done. A lot of my stock was on the levee and most of it was uninsured. I'm facing ruin, and me with a son to provide for and five daughters to marry off. You're going to do it, do you understand me?'

He was working himself up into a rage and I became afraid that he might actually strike out at me. His eyes were bulging and his face was redder and sweatier than ever. 'What is it you want, Mr Walkern? If I can help you, I surely will.'

'Oh, you can help, all right.' He sat down and fanned his face with his handkerchief. 'You're going to get you some girls together – about three, I reckon – and you're going to go to California. There's hundreds of men out there digging thousands of dollars' worth of gold out of the ground every day. You're going to set up a hurdy-gurdy house and earn me some money. That was the agreement I had with your ma. I gave her two thousand dollars to take three girls to California. She was going to send me back *four* thousand dollars, and then our deal was to be finished. Now, don't go looking at me that way. It was *her* idea. "Give me two thousand dollars to take some girls to California," she said, "and I'll double your money." '

'I won't do it.'

'You could be rich! I hear those fool miners are paying

16

six dollars a dozen for eggs. Think what they'll pay for a woman! And hardly a white woman in the whole of California. I'll give you two thousand dollars and you send me back *six*. I got to recoup my losses.'

'I won't do it.'

'Why not? It's what your ma planned for you. What are you going to do in St Louis? You got any money? I bet you don't. You sure as hell don't look rich. I bet you would just have to set up in the old business within a week. Use your head, girl. You ain't even got a place to do business in! How much could you make at it? Tell me that. Or maybe you're going to ask your pa for some money, whoever *he* is.'

I was calculating feverishly. I had hoped that my mother, for once, had decided to show her love for me by some respectable act of generosity. But it wasn't just a sign of love I needed at the moment. I also needed some money to keep me going, to give me time to find my direction. My situation was indeed desperate, and as I sat in Mr Walkern's office, I hardly cared what I might have to do. At least, I hardly cared what I might have to *promise* to do.

'All right, Mr Walkern. I can see the sense of what you are proposing. Give me two thousand, and I'll see if I can find some girls to go out West.'

A sly expression suffused his flushed face. 'Not so fast, Lottie. I ain't no fool. I trusted your ma because I knew her. I don't know you, so I've got to have me some safeguards. Anyways, I can tell you two of the girls you're going to take. Them two what was working for your ma. I hear they ain't got nothing left but what they had on their backs when they got out last night. They'll go with you for sure. But you'll have to find one more. You just sit right there while I tell you how I'm going to work this thing, so's you don't cheat me. And we'll draw us up a contract!'

I had no choice but to sit and listen to the man. My legs, I was sure, were too weak to bear my weight.

2

Mr Walkern removed a gold toothpick from his waist-coat pocket and began picking his teeth. 'You'll be travelling by way of New Orleans and then over to Panama. When you get there, you get yourselves some mules and a guide and you cross the country to the Pacific coast. There, you get on a boat that's come all the way around South America and you take it up to San Francisco. After that, it's up to you.'

'You can't be expecting four unprotected women to make such a hazardous journey. It's unthinkable.'

Walkern thumped the table. 'No, it's not! Your ma knew it was the easiest way to get to the gold fields. I suppose you could join a wagon train if the wagon-master would have you. Two thousand miles on the Oregon Trail. Now, that really would be impossible for your sort of woman. Or you could sail from New Orleans all the way round the Horn. Up to six months on the high seas, a-heaving and a-rolling until you wished you were dead. It's expensive this way, but it's the best for four females who ain't used to hard times.'

There was no point in arguing. I was merely playing for time, and had no intention of going to California by any route. 'Very well. We'll go by way of Panama.'

'You surely will, and what's more, you won't cheat Otis Walkern. I've got a man who will put you on the packet to New Orleans and another who will see you on to the ship for Panama. He'll give you money for the rest of the journey. You'll provision up in St Louis, of course. That's the best place. You'll need a pretty good-sized tent to live and work in, I suppose. Get yourselves a couple of rooms at the Lacomte Hotel. It's only a dollar a night. Although, come to think of it, what with all the trouble over the fire, there may not be any rooms available.'

'I should think most people will stay at the Estes or the Missouri.'

Walkern shook his head. 'The Estes was razed in the fire last night.'

'The Estes destroyed? Was it insured?'

'The word is it wasn't. Young Estes has been too keen to get himself rich. There's been lots of rumours about that man. Everybody said he'd get his come-uppance one day. He lost some stuff on the levee, too. He deals in linseed oil and canvas, which is good business, what with all the greenhorns coming to St Louis to provision up before going out to the gold fields. I expect Estes has learned his lesson. He thought pretty well of himself for a man of twenty-six. Thought he just about owned the whole of St Louis.'

I changed the subject. 'I will need some money. I must pay for accommodation, supplies, food and clothing for myself and the girls.'

'How much?' asked Walkern suspiciously.

'Fifty dollars.'

'Twenty-five.'

I was determined; Walkern was mean. We settled on thirty-five dollars. I was told that I should get myself over to the hotel, which was over on Hickory, down by the levee. A Mr Boyd, he said, would contact me in a day or two about tickets for the packet to New Orleans. I had no intention of being at the hotel, or even in town when this Mr Boyd came to call. I would have preferred not to sign a contract, but there was nothing I could do about it at the moment. I hoped it didn't matter. I intended to see to it that the contract was torn up when I repaid the thirty-five dollars.

As so often happens in St Louis at this time of year, the day had begun quite chilly, but the temperature was rising by the minute. As I left Mr Walkern's office and turned down Laurel, I felt the sun beating down on my brown costume and rising up around my ankles from the dusty road. I took out the much-folded letter and read it for the thousandth time, looking for some hint of what my mother had intended for me.

'*Come to St Louis,*' she had written. '*I'll see you have enuf money to set yourself up in stile. We will be able to live like ladies in Boston or St Louis or anywhere else you chose. I owe you something. I ain't been able to do much for you all these years, but I'm making it up to you now. Come home to your ma.*'

Could she really have intended to take me to California to be a soiled dove? I supposed she had. My mother had no self-respect, had never cared how decent people lived. 'Gelt and grog' had been her cry, and 'to hell with Martin Luther!' This was such a terrible thing to say that as a young girl I had wondered if she would one day be struck down for her blasphemy.

She had lied and cheated all her life. I knew this, because my grandmother had been at pains to tell me. How Belle Schultz had gone to the bad at fourteen, had set out with a scallywag three times her age to travel all the way to St Louis. How, abandoned and hungry, she had eventually set up a brothel when she was no more than sixteen.

My mother hadn't even cared about the only live child she had given birth to. Grandma Schultz was summoned when I was ten years old, because my mother was tired of having me hanging around the brothel. Grandma took me back to Boston where I was decently brought up in a God-fearing, work-worshipping, German-American home.

My grandmother died suddenly when I was sixteen. Since I had no other relative except my mother, I returned to St Louis. For three traumatic months, I lived in the brothel on Second and Walnut, talking to the girls and watching my mother stagger around, the worse for drink most evenings.

By the time my seventeenth birthday arrived, I knew what I must do. I packed up and spent the last of my slim inheritance from my grandmother on paying my fare back to Boston, where I went into domestic service. Being a maid of all work was hard, but I studied in my few spare hours until I had enough knowledge to teach young children. It was a lonely life, but everyone did say what a hardworking girl I was and what a credit I was to my grandmother. Those words were gold to me, better than friends, and almost powerful enough to cleanse my mind of the stigma of my birth. Someone once said I worshipped God and good manners and clean linen and being called Miss Schultz. That's fair comment. I have learned the hard way the value of my deities.

Now, chaotic emotions clouded my mind. I didn't know what I wanted to do or where I wanted to go. I should have gone directly to Lacomte's Hotel, if only to deposit my carpet-bag. It was heavy, and I was tired of carrying it around. Instead, I headed once more for the levee and the shack where my mother had died. I couldn't stay away. Perhaps I was hoping for some sign from her, a voice from heaven. The excuse I gave myself was much more practical. I thought I should spend some time sifting through the ash for anything that might have escaped the fire.

On top of the shock of her death came the shock of hearing she had wanted me to be a soiled dove in California. How dared she? How dared she strike a deal with that dreadful man? I was pleased to have tricked thirty-five dollars from him. It served him right for having spoken to me so rudely. Tomorrow, perhaps, when I had taken time to consider my position, I could make some sensible plans about earning my living somewhere. Then I would march into Mr Walkern's office and throw the money on his desk with contempt.

During the hour or so I had been away from it, the levee was transformed. Trading had to go on despite the disaster. Dozens of steamboats, up from New Orleans or down from Chicago or from the western border of the state by way of the Missouri river, had crowded to the shore, presenting a forest of tall black smokestacks. Horses, mules, wagons, free men and slaves made a tremendous racket as they went about their usual business. Spaces had been swept clean of debris; cargo was being stacked for removal by wagon. Wheels clattered over the cobbles to the untidy rows of gang-planks. Mules stood incongruously at a thirty degree angle on the sloping levee while their wagons were loaded.

Although the *Sultans* and *Amulets*, *Darts* and *Dakotas* hid the mighty river from view, the huddled form of the widow was still right where I had last seen her, isolated in her misery. Her suffering clutched at my heart. I had a few dollars in my pocket and a terrible dread of being alone at this time, so I walked past my mother's old home and went directly to her.

'What's your name, ma'am?'

She looked up when my shadow fell across her and blinked once or twice as if trying to remember where she had seen me before. 'Name's Minnie Taylor. What difference does it make?'

'I am Carlotta Schultz. Pleased to meet you, Minnie. You can't sit here all day. I've got some money – enough for us to hire a room and get ourselves something to eat. Come on, you must be hungry.'

'Leave me be.'

I took her by the elbow and heaved. She stood up, but was visibly weak, needing my support. 'I am hungry, I guess, but it don't matter. I'm thirty-six year old and I don't want to see thirty-seven. I've had all the sorrowing I can take.'

I had thought she was older. Her breasts were flabby beneath her cotton shift. Her waist was thick above broad but bony hips. Dark eyes set deep in their sockets,

22

a pug nose and pale, thin, lips did not add to her appearance. I doubted that she had ever been pretty, but poverty had aged her beyond her years.

I picked up her bundle of clothing and handed it to her. 'We'll go to Lacomte's Hotel and get a room. Then we'll have something to eat and we'll both feel better. There are a few things I must think through, but I can't do my thinking on an empty stomach.'

'I sure could do with a cup of coffe,' said Minnie, straightening her shoulders and setting her feet unsteadily on the cobbles. 'It's mighty kind of you to help me out. Wish I could do something for you in return. I'm not . . . I don't want you to think I'm destitute. I've got five dollars. I can pay for my own room and food. I just didn't feel . . .'

Her voice thickened, and I gave her arm a friendly squeeze. 'We can pool our resources. It's good that you've got money, too. It's a tough old world, Minnie, but we'll manage. We just need to give each other some support. You see, my mother died down here on the levee last night. I can't face up to being alone today. I don't know anyone in St Louis any more and . . .'

'Your ma died? Last night? Where?'

'Just up there.' I pointed in the direction of the burnt-out shacks. 'She lived in a little house there.'

'*Right up there?*' exclaimed Minnie, and she too pointed to where the shacks had been. 'Then you must be the daughter of . . .'

'Missouri Belle. I guess you've heard of her. Believe me, I'm not proud of my parentage.'

'Well, she was pretty notor . . . well-known in these parts. You don't look a bit the way I'd expect you to.'

'Please don't imagine I'm anything like her. I have been living in Boston for many years. This is my first visit to St Louis since I left town in forty-three. Unfortunately, I arrived too late to save my mother from the fire. I'm a schoolteacher. I lead a respectable life, I assure you.'

23

'Of course,' said Minnie politely. Her cheeks had taken on some colour; there was new animation in her voice. My interesting parent had given her something to think about besides her sorrows. With the resilience I would later learn to expect of her, Minnie was regaining her spirit.

I said I wanted to have one more look at my mother's last home. Minnie readily agreed. I sensed her curiosity. We waded into the fine ash and soon discovered the simple layout of the house: the front door led directly into a central parlour, another door led onto a passage to the primitive kitchen. There were two more doors in the parlour, leading to the two small bedrooms. I saw no signs that water had been laid on. The accommodation would have been primitive, unsanitary, hot in summer and cold in the winter. So far had my mother sunk! The wood-frame beds were reduced to smoking sticks as was a single chest-of-drawers which held clothing, none of it wearable. My mother had always been proud of her linen. She would have hated . . . but then, what was the use of such speculation? She was dead.

'Carlotta!'

At Minnie's cry, I looked up from the large size petticoat I was holding, to see two young women staring at me aggressively. They were respectably shod, but respectability ended with their shoes. I was certain they hadn't a stitch on beneath their wrappers. The younger one was staggeringly pretty. Her dark blonde hair was an uncombed mess at the moment, but when brushed and pinned up would be her finest feature. Wide brown eyes, childishly full cheeks and a generous mouth were at variance with her ageless feral expression. Her slim body was youthful, but it sagged in a pose as old as time; cynical and weary. She couldn't have been more than sixteen or seventeen.

The other girl was older, perhaps all of twenty. She was plump but shapely, her full lips set in a permanent pout, the sort of woman for whom men lusted. I guessed that she was less intelligent than her companion, and that she was lazy. Laziness was what drew girls to brothels, my mother used to say. They were too lazy to find men for themselves. I was in no doubt that I was confronting my mother's two employees, the last in the long line of stupid women who placed no value on themselves.

'I'm Roxanne Bristow,' said the pretty, younger one, 'and this here's Tilda Engleston. I guess you must be Belle's daughter.'

'I am. I suppose you worked for her. There's just the two of you? I don't think there's anything here worth saving.'

'No,' said Tilda. 'It all went up before we knew one thing about it. We ain't got nothing left.'

'Have you any money?'

'Not one red cent. Our gentlemen, the gentlemen we was with last night, paid for us to sleep on the floor of that tavern over there. We ain't even had breakfast.'

'We come down here at sun-up to see what we could save,' said Roxanne. 'Everything was too hot to look real careful, but we could see nothing was spared.'

Their faces registered the shock and hopelessness that I felt so keenly. We were four women whose lives had been turned upside down by the fire. 'What will you do now?'

They shrugged, almost in unison, looking like marionettes operated by an indifferent puppetmaster. I wondered what my mother would have done had she been alive at this moment. She had never seemed nonplussed. She always appeared to have energy for whatever needed to be done. Nevertheless, I felt sure she would have been at least temporarily paralyzed by the calamity of last night's fire. I felt a wave of pity for these two frightened girls. And a sense of shared suffering.

'Why don't you go back to work for whoever you were with before?'

25

Tilda smiled bitterly. Roxanne was not amused. 'We ain't never worked for nobody else! Your ma got us into the trade. Now we're done for. Out on the street without so much as a decent dress to wear.'

'Excuse me a minute,' I said. 'I want a word with my friend.'

Minnie was looking frosty. I pulled her out of earshot of the girls and whispered urgently: 'Did you hear what they said?'

'They'll soon find work. They ain't like you and me. Their sort! I hope you don't think you're responsible for them.'

'But I do! You heard what they said. My mother led them into prostitution. It was bad enough that she employed such women. But actually to start them on the life! To corrupt young girls! I feel deeply ashamed. Maybe you can't understand that. It's different for you. You didn't have a mother like mine. Minnie, I've just got to do what I can to save them.'

'Save them! You won't do it,' she said. 'Oh, you can buy them food and clothing and give them shelter, but you won't save them. They're bad. Your ma just gave them a chance to show their wickedness. She didn't make them wicked. They was *born* that way.'

I introduced the girls to Minnie and told them we would be staying at Lacomte's Hotel. I would buy them some clothes from the old-clothes man and then we could see what the future had to offer us.

I thought I knew Roxanne and Tilda's sort. I was surprised, therefore, when instead of accepting my charity with a sneer, they fell to thanking me for my kindness. They were desperate, they said. I was like an angel from heaven. I shot a glance at Minnie to see her reaction to all this gratitude, and saw a pensive expression on her face. She was reserving judgement.

It occurred to me that although I had managed to get my hands on thirty-five dollars, I now had three women tagging along who looked on me as a provider. Still, I couldn't bring myself to abandon any of them. Besides, I didn't want to be alone with my thoughts. Perhaps I was buying a little company for a few days. What could be the harm in that?

It was a day of shocks. The manager at Lacomte's Hotel was not pleased to see us. No business in the rooms, he said in his most insulting manner, and payment in advance. We were to behave ourselves in the small dark lobby as we passed through. We must not let other residents know there were four whores staying in the attic. Humiliated by his sneering remarks, I gave him the sharp edge of my schoolteacher's tongue, but it didn't have the customary effect. Minnie and I were branded as whores by association. I remembered I hated St Louis.

You don't get much comfort in a waterfront hotel for a dollar a night, especially if the rooms are in the attic. I knew that the Estes Hotel charged a dollar fifty a night, but they probably had towels in the rooms for that money. The Lacomte certainly didn't offer such a luxury. Our two rooms adjoined and had mattresses filled with corn cobs and bed bugs. Only Minnie felt it was an improvement over her previous accommodation. The rest of us had known better days.

A hearty lunch cheered us all, but first we had to buy some decent clothes for Roxanne and Tilda. They were delighted with my purchases from a second-hand store, but I felt the loss of a further ten dollars.

In the afternoon, we went to the undertaker to enquire about my mother, and to see about giving her a modest funeral. We were too late. Believing she had no relatives, the authorities had seen to it that she was immediately buried in a pauper's grave. The undertaker said dead bodies were a health hazard, and there wasn't much left of her anyway.

One minute I was standing talking to the undertaker,

27

the next I was seated in a chair as Minnie fanned me. I didn't know what had happened to the seconds in between.

'I wanted to say goodbye,' I murmured. 'Do the right thing.'

'Of course you did,' said Minnie. 'But you ain't got the money to do the right thing. Sit there a spell until you feel like getting up.'

Roxanne and Tilda were touching in their concern. 'She wouldn't have minded,' said Roxanne. 'Old Belle was a practical woman. If you ain't got the money for a proper funeral or a tombstone, well you ain't, and that's that.'

'It's not right,' said Minnie. 'It ain't fitting. Carlotta won't like leaving her ma this way. Will you, Carlotta?'

I didn't like it, but there was nothing I could do about it at the moment. I made up my mind that I would return one day and put up a handsome granite stone. In the meantime, I asked the undertaker where she was buried, and was told she had been taken all the way out to Bellefontaine.

'Bellyfountain!' said Minnie. 'That's where Husband is buried.'

'There's been a terrible epidemic of cholera,' added Tilda. 'Hundreds of people have died and they ran out of places to bury them. Everybody is scared. It sure has been a bad year for St Louis, and it's only May!'

Strength was seeping away from me, and I realized for the first time just how tired I was. Leading my little party back to Lacomte's, I took them to the room Minnie and I were sharing and told them about Mr Walkern, his proposal and the money he had given me.

'Belle never said anything to us about going to California territory,' said Roxanne. 'Sly old thing. Not that I'd've gone west. I want to get out of this trade. I'm tired of lying on my back for no-account men.'

'Hallelujah!' said Minnie. 'You two are young enough to find a better way of life.'

Tilda stuck out her lower lip as she lolled on the bed. 'That's easy for you to say. I don't want to go with men neither, but being a whore pays good money. I'm going to do what I have to, to keep from starving.'

'If it pays such good money, where's all your gold, rich lady?' crowed Minnie. 'Tell me that if you can.'

Roxanne bent her head to look out of the little window. 'You say you ain't got any money but what old Walkern give you. So what are you going to do when the money runs out? I can tell you Belle wouldn't have left you so much as five cents. After she moved us from Second and Walnut, trade fell off something terrible. Our customers was afraid we'd give them cholera, anyway. They had to be powerful anxious before they'd risk coming to us. Belle didn't care. She would just cuddle up to a jug of whiskey and drink herself to sleep. What I'm trying to say is, when that man you were talking about comes here with the tickets, why don't we just go to New Orleans and see if we can't make a new life for ourselves down there? We don't have to go no farther.'

'They say it's warm all winter long in New Orleans,' mused Minnie. 'It gets powerful cold in St Louis. I just hate the cold winters.'

Tilda approved of the idea. 'I hear they got some real fine houses down there. Velvet curtains and all.' She meant brothels.

It was an idea worth considering, but I didn't wish to go south just yet. Mr Walkern and Roxanne were both convinced that my mother had been poor and in debt. I wanted more proof. She must have put some money away somewhere. I intended to find it.

When evening came, we went out to the tavern next door to have something to eat. We all drank more cider than was good for us and went to bed early.

If the bedroom had been any larger, the hotel manager would have insisted that the four of us share it.

29

On the floors below, whole families were settling themselves in for the night in rooms which could be comfortable only for two. Our attic accommodation really was too small for four, so Minnie and I had it to ourselves. The slope of the roof was so steep that there was room for just one person at a time to stand upright. All day long the sun had pounded down on the roof. Now, after dark, the very walls and beams were giving up that heat. The small window was of little help, although it stood wide open on rusty hinges.

Somewhere a child cried. Steamboat bells clanged dismally as the packets wallowed on their moorings, and in the distance a party of men sang rowdy songs as they approached the tavern next door.

'Good to be lying down,' said Minnie. She had stripped to her shift and braided her hair in a long pigtail. Now she noisily wriggled about on the mattress and arranged her shawl across her shoulders. It was too hot for covers.

I was counting our money, seated cross-legged on the bed in my shift. I had arrived in St Louis with nine dollars. Mr Walkern had given me thirty-five. Ten dollars had gone towards outfitting Tilda, Roxanne and Minnie. And I added a petticoat. A further eight went to the hotel for two nights in advance. We had eaten well today: three dollars' worth. I was left with twenty-three dollars: with Minnie's cash, our combined wealth now came to just twenty-eight dollars. Tomorrow, I would discuss with the others what plans they had for looking out for themselves.

'You know,' said Minnie, 'I just can't think what I would have done if you hadn't come along. I'd just plain lost my *fight*. I'm not saying I've got it back yet, but I feel better. And with you doing the thinking for a while, I reckon I can get my head turned round. You'll come up with something, I just know it. You're a real smart girl, Carlotta.'

'This real smart girl can't think how we're going to feed ourselves next week.'

'You'll think of some plan. I've got faith in you. There's one thing been on my mind almost all day – how come you ain't married?'

I shoved the greasy pillow against the wall, leaned back and told her the whole story about Carlton.

Minnie was silent for a few seconds when I finished, then spoke softly. 'Did he know about your ma?'

'No, of course not.'

'Did you go chasing after him to New York? Did you fight for him?'

'I most certainly did not,' I said indignantly. 'I have my pride. If he wanted to leave me, then I didn't want to marry him.'

With some effort, Minnie battled against the shifting corn cobs and hauled herself up to sit beside me. We both stared at the old door in front of us.

'You know what I think? I think you never really thought you was good enough for the likes of that there Carlton. I think you only wanted him because of his fancy ways and book learning. And what's more, I think you're lucky he got away.'

'That's not true.' I turned to face her. 'I think very well of myself. I'm too proud to beg any man to marry me.'

'Oh, you felt kind of sore at him, but you never really thought he'd marry a whore's daughter, did you?'

'Minnie . . .' I began, but couldn't think what to say next.

Minnie patted my shoulder. 'Don't mind me, dear. I just think you should face facts. Times are hard right now, but at least you're not living a lie. You're the daughter of Missouri Belle and everybody knows it. You'll find your way, and it won't be by lying. Now suppose you blow out that candle. I'm fagged out.'

I did as she asked and slid down on the bed with my

31

back towards her. If she heard me crying in the darkness, she made no sign.

3

The next morning, Roxanne and Tilda flatly refused to get out of bed when I knocked for them at eight o'clock. Minnie and I were ready to be out and about, so I pushed a couple of coins for breakfast under their door before we left; we had hot biscuits and coffee at the tavern.

I had never considered myself to be a sentimental person, but now I felt a strong urge to look once more at the old house that had been my home for the first ten years of my life. I wanted Minnie to see it with me, afraid that the memories it evoked would be too much to bear on my own.

The morning was still cool as we headed over to Second and Walnut, but it promised to be yet another warm, clear day. People were beginning to complain about the dry spell, to speculate on what effect this would have on the summer crops, and to look skywards to see what clouds were hanging about. In fact, there were none. The sky was so blue it was almost black, if you looked straight upwards.

When we got to the corner where the old house should have been, there was not much to see except a tall heap of rubble where a very splendid building had once stood. The walls had collapsed so that the four-gabled roof sat right on top of the ground floor. The fine old staircase was somewhere underneath. The house had always been cool in the heat of summer, because a covered porch had run round all four sides just below the upper windows. The whole building had been set on brick pilings about eighteen inches to two feet high, allowing fresh air to circulate underneath the floors, which helped to prevent the wood from rotting. I used to play under the porch, crawling in there among the spiders, and trying to keep my spotted dog 'Poochie' from running wild, chasing frogs and mice.

All of this I explained to Minnie as we picked our way among the rubble. For all the destruction – the window-glass blown in and the front door torn completely off its hinges – there was no fire damage. My mother's former place of business had been blown up to create a fire-break. Several other houses on Walnut had received the same treatment. I didn't see any fragments of furniture, so I assumed the new owners had been given time to remove the contents before the dynamite did its work.

'Must have been a mighty fine home at one time,' said Minnie. 'I guess your ma's business paid pretty well.'

'I always assumed so. I suppose she made money from her enterprise the way businessmen make money from theirs.'

It was Minnie who found the small sign with ESTES HOTEL in bold letters. 'You didn't tell me somebody turned it into a hotel.'

I felt a surge of helpless anger. 'No one told *me*. My mother was a strange person. She only wrote to me about once a month, but she did tell me there was a new hotel in town called the Estes. She just never mentioned where it was. Come on, I want to look at the backyard.'

The shady plot behind the house was enclosed by a white-painted picket fence and had been my special kingdom during the summer days. At night, lanterns were hung on posts, and the girls came out to walk with their men. My mother would be there in some gaudy gown that heaved her breasts into view. She was a fat woman. I can't recall a time when she was slender. But she always walked with her head up high and her shoulders well back. Sometimes there would be a band of black musicians, and always there was wine or cider. Then the sound of laughter would drift upwards to my

34

second-storey window. When they had all gone inside, I would creep down the back staircase and out into the backyard to chase fireflies, until one of the servants saw me and sent me to bed again.

A huge oak tree had spread its branches over almost the whole garden. Grass wouldn't grow under it. My mother had ordered the ground to be paved around the trunk in concentric circles of red brick extending out for several yards. At the back, the circle poured into a narrow path bordered by half bricks planted at an angle. Every winter, frost would damage some of the bricks but at other times the rain and heavy shade would encourage great green velvet patches of moss. I wanted to see all this again and feel the pain of bitter-sweet memories.

Minnie and I entered by what was left of the picket gate, and immediately saw stacks of furniture. She would have proceeded right on to the back, but I put out a hand to stay her.

The old oak tree had lost a few branches in the blast, and the brickwork was all but covered with fallen green leaves. Two men stood beneath the tree. One, a white man with a beaver hat and a brocade waistcoat, had put his right foot on the seat that surrounded the tree. He had blue eyes with black lashes, and his deep voice carried clearly over the distance.

Before him stood a splendidly-dressed black man in a cutaway coat, white cravat tied in a very neat bow and shoes that gleamed. He was leaning on a silver-topped cane, frowning as he listened.

'You're a damned fool, William,' said the white man.

'Yes, sir. Master.'

'Hell, man, I don't mean to be rude, and don't hand me that "master" talk. But can't you learn by my mistakes? Never brag. Especially don't brag to white men about how well former slaves have done in St Louis, nor how much money y'all have.'

35

'I know it's dangerous, but I'm proud of my people, Mr Estes.'

'And so you should be, but don't say so to white men. What with abolitionists and pro-slavers at each other's throats every day, these are difficult times. What's more, it's the freed slaves who have the most to lose if people get riled.'

'They've been hard enough on us. Can't teach our kids their letters, can't move out of the county without permission, got to send the young'uns out as bond servants, but . . .' He shrugged, lifted the cane and grasped it around the middle. 'Word is, you didn't have no insurance on this place.'

The white man didn't answer. He had seen us. 'Good morning, Carlotta. I didn't recognize you yesterday on the levee. Someone told me later that you were in town. I was sorry to hear what happened to your mother. I don't believe I've spoken to her in the last six years, but I'm sorry just the same. Did you get to visit with her before she died?'

'If you haven't spoken to her in six years, how were you able to buy this house from her a year ago?'

'Ah, I gather you *didn't* get to visit with her before she died. I bought this house from William Davis here.' He indicated the black man, and I heard Minnie gasp.

'I remember you from when you was a little girl, Miss Carlotta,' said William Davis, lifting his hat. 'My sister worked for your ma. You remember Minerva, don't you?'

'Yes, I do. I hope she is well, but I don't understand. How long . . . that is, when did you buy this property?'

William scratched his head. 'It just sort of happened, ma'am. Your ma kept getting into debt. Things got a bit difficult for her. The ladies in town tried to have her closed down, and then, too, she did like a game of cards. I kept lending her money, and then one day she sent for me and said she'd just like to sell out. Said she was tired.

That's why I'm the one who sold the old house to Mr Estes. It made a fine hotel until last night.'

Wick Estes was looking steadily at me. I couldn't meet his eyes as I spoke. 'I'm told she died owing money all over town. I hadn't realized she was in such difficulties.'

'You didn't take much interest in your mother or come home to see her very often, so how could you know?' asked Wick.

'I haven't been home since – ' Wick was smiling, so I left the sentence unfinished. 'It's a shame to see the house in this state. A great financial loss to you, Mr Estes.'

Wick grinned broadly. 'Surely, we know each other well enough to be on first-name terms, Carlotta, and yes, I'm pretty well washed up.'

'From rags to rags in three years,' I said sweetly. I could *feel* Minnie's curiosity.

'My, my, Carlotta. You say you haven't been home in six years, and yet you know so much about me. I'm flattered.'

'I suppose my mother owed *you* some money, William.'

William shook his head. 'Nothing I care to remember, ma'am.'

'Where's your manners, Carlotta? You always were keen on good manners, I believe. Aren't you going to introduce your friend? I'm Wick Estes, ma'am. How do you do?'

'Minnie Taylor.' Minnie stuck out a rough red hand which Wick shook heartily. She didn't offer her hand to William, but they nodded to each other very civilly.

'Well,' I said, backing towards the gate. 'I just wanted to see the house. It looks dreadful, and I don't think I want to see any more. Good day, Wick. Do give my regards to Minerva, William. Where is she now, by the way?'

'Married and living in Canada, ma'am. Very happy, so I hear.'

'Well, if that don't beat all,' said Minnie when we were well away from the house and the men. 'I never did see a black man dressed so fine. And your ma owned his sister?'

'My mother would not have a slave. Minerva was a free woman. I believe William bought her freedom when she was a little girl. He used to be a slave, too. He has apparently done very well.'

'I'll say he has. Just think of that!'

'Minnie, I have to face facts. My mother didn't leave money anywhere. She really was poor. I don't know what the four of us are going to do now.'

'Why don't you get that gentleman we saw to help you out? I bet he would if you asked.'

'Wick? Didn't you hear him say he lost everything in the fire? He's got no money.'

'Well, then, maybe you two could get married. Then you could work together. It would be better than . . .'

My harsh laughter stopped her. 'I assure you, Wick Estes would never consider marrying the daughter of Missouri Belle.'

'Exactly who is he? I think he's stuck on you, and I noticed you looking at him in a funny way.'

'You don't understand. I'd better tell you all about it, but mind you don't say anything to the others. As I told you last night, I was taken to Boston by my grandmother when I was ten. She died when I was sixteen, and I had to come back to St Louis, because there was nowhere else to go. I lived back there in my mother's house. One night, I was sitting on the stairs looking through the banisters at everything that was going on, when this man of about twenty walked through the front door into the hallway. He was so handsome, I thought my heart would break. He looked up the stairs at me and smiled, and I smiled back. We were so young we both blushed. He looked away after that, but I kept staring at him as if I could eat him up.

'My mother came out into the hall – I can still see her as if it happened yesterday. She had on a purple satin dress and her thick blonde hair was piled up on top of her head very attractively. "Well, young sir," she said. "What may I do for you?" Wick Estes pointed up the stairs in my direction without looking at me at all. Too shy, I suppose. He said: "I want that one."

'My mother said I wasn't one of her girls. I was her daughter and not in the business. I blush every time I think of it now, but he *was* beautiful. I said: "It's all right, I'll do it. I don't mind, mother." Wick looked up at me then and smiled so that I could see all his teeth. Did you notice? He's got good teeth. I could have died for him at that moment.

'Anyway, my mother said: "Did you hear that? She calls me mother, not ma. My daughter has been brought up like a lady back East, and she's not going to go into this life. Now, come on into the parlour, young man, and meet the others." She had five beautiful girls in those days, but Wick just said if he couldn't have me, he didn't want anyone.'

'Why, Carlotta!' exclaimed Minnie. 'That was a real good thing to do, considering what she was, and all. *And* it just goes to show what Wick Estes thinks of you.'

'I suppose so. As you may imagine, the next day I bitterly regretted my impetuous offer to Wick. Typically, the next day my mother bitterly regretted her impetuous *refusal*. Especially as Wick never came back. I left St Louis a week later, and didn't return until yesterday. However, when my mother wrote to me, which was not often, she always told me news of Wick. She used to say, if she hadn't stupidly refused to let Wick have me, he'd have set me up in some beautiful establishment of my own. Not that I would have wanted to be a kept woman. The sight of Wick Estes is acutely embarrassing these days. I wish one of us could leave town, and I've got a feeling it ought to be me.'

Not knowing what else to do, we returned to the Lacomte Hotel. Roxanne and Tilda were just emerging from the tavern, having spent all of twenty-five cents on breakfast. They were full of news and anxious to speak to us where no one could overhear. Minnie was all for finding a quiet spot on the levee. We could sit in some shade and enjoy a breeze off the river, she said.

This was not nearly private enough for Tilda and Roxanne, so we went back upstairs to the hot little room I shared with Minnie, it being by far the tidier of the two.

'After y'all went to bed, we went out last night,' Roxanne informed us. 'Not downstairs to the tavern next door, but uptown a piece – Clancy's Tavern, where all the greenhorns go. You remember Clancy, Carlotta? I believe he was a customer of your ma's in the old days before he got married.'

'An Irishman,' I said, surprised to be able to remember him so clearly. 'Thick grey hair and a red face with a scar on one cheek. My mother said he would steal your *skin* if you didn't watch out. He came to the house one night still wearing a long dirty apron that reached his ankles. My mother wouldn't let him in until he took it off. He wouldn't remove it, but insisted on coming in. There was a terrible row in the street. She threatened to have the law on him. He suddenly burst out laughing and took off the apron. I remember he asked her if that was all he had to take off, and she said he could leave his silly grin on the doorstep.'

'His hair's white now, but he still wears a dirty apron. He's working his second wife to death and he's got ten kids. Sends his condolences to you.'

'What's all this about?' asked Minnie. 'Is he offering us work?'

Roxanne and Tilda thought that was very funny. 'Naw,' laughed Tilda. 'We want to tell you about the greenhorns. Tell her, Roxanne.'

'There's sure a lot of them in town, although

everybody says most of them have already taken off for the other side of Missouri, ready to join a wagon train. It don't matter how old they are, they act just like kids. Drinking and cussing and insulting each other. And every once in a while, a couple of them start to fight, and everybody laughs and bets on who will win. They're all dressed up in new boots and blue pants tucked into the tops. And they tie the dandiest little red handkerchiefs around their necks. Clancy says they've got hands like a baby's and no sense at all. But they've got money, and St Louisans are taking it away from them any way they can. Tilda and me took ten dollars.'

'That was after they bought us two glasses of cider,' added Tilda.

Minnie stood up from the bed. 'I don't hold with stealing.'

'They got what they deserved,' said Roxanne. 'And I don't call it stealing at all. Two of them came over to our table – '

'Oh,' said Minnie. 'I think I know how you got the money.'

'No, you don't, so just listen a minute. We told them we get five dollars a time. In advance, but that Clancy don't allow business on the premises and – '

'And,' I finished for her, 'you two left first, and just came on back to the hotel. So now the greenhorns feel cheated and are looking out for you. You'll be in trouble if they find you.'

'I guess you saved them from an act of sin,' muttered Minnie darkly. 'It could have been worse.'

I was grateful for the extra money and said so. Minnie and I were lucky to have heard about the money at all. The girls might have kept it for themselves. I didn't have time to say more, because there was a bold knock on the door. We all assumed it was the greenhorns looking for their money. Roxanne and Tilda were just on their way out through the connecting door, when the door from the

41

hall opened and a huge man walked in. The first thing he did was to hit his head on one of the rafters.

'How do, Roxanne?' said the man, straightening his hat on his head. Roxanne glared back at him.

His dark pants were greasy on the front of each leg where, perhaps for years, he had wiped his hands down them. His shirt was stained by sweat and food, and his open waistcoat was as dirty as the rest of his clothing.

'You must be Miss Carlotta Schultz,' he boomed, looking me up and down crudely. 'I'm Boyd. They call me Bullmouth. I was sorry to hear about Belle. I knowed her real well. Didn't I, Roxanne?'

Roxanne didn't answer, seemingly more interested in the ceiling. Tilda, I noticed, was equally interested in her shoes.

Minnie stepped up to him. He must have been a foot taller and a hundred pounds heavier than she was. 'What y'all want here, mister?'

'You better be nice to me, ladies.' Bullmouth's long chin moved excessively as he spoke, sending his scraggy chin-beard up and down in a way that should have been funny, except that everything about the man was sinister. He had the look of someone with little control of his temper. 'I'm the man who's going to take you folks to New Orleans. I'll be right there on the packet with you. And if y'all don't behave yourselves, I'll tell Mr Walkern. I'm going to see you on to the clipper for San Francisco, too. If I don't like the way you been acting, I just might not give y'all the money Mr Walkern has guv me.' He patted his chest as if the money were in an inside waistcoat pocket.

Minnie backed off a little, not liking the tone of his remarks. 'Mr Boyd,' I said. 'Am I to understand we will be travelling with you all the way to New Orleans?'

'Ain't that what I just said? I'll see nobody bothers you, and I'll see you don't bother nobody. So don't you go getting feisty with me.'

42

Boyd took off his hat and wiped the sweat from his brow with his arm. Dark uncombed hair grew close to his eyebrows, leaving him with small temples and a shallow forehead. The combination of his muscular body and moronic, unstable expression sent a chill through me. He would be a dangerous man to cross.

Boyd told us not to bother purchasing a tent. We wouldn't, he pointed out, know a good tent if it hit us on the head. He would buy it, and the necessary supplies. A bunch of silly women couldn't be trusted to do it. In the meantime, he didn't mind if we enjoyed ourselves, because we would be gone a good long time. The circus was in town and there was a play over at the theatre. Yes sir, St Louis was a big town. Over seventy thousand people, some said. A place where a body could have a real good time. Wasn't that right, he asked Roxanne with a wink.

Of course, the cholera epidemic was terrible, and more people were expected to die when the hotter weather arrived. But in spite of everything, including the fire, there were still some real rich men in St. Louis. While he thought of it, we were not to worry about Mr Walkern being able to pay our fares. Otis Walkern might choose to call himself poor these days, but there was still plenty of money in the pot. The only man who had really been destroyed by the fire was that there Wick Estes. It served him right, Bullmouth reckoned. He could tell a few tales about Mr Estes that would raise eyebrows all over the place.

Throughout his monologue, the four of us remained silent. Bullmouth eventually ran out of words. Receiving no encouragement to stay, he told us he would see us on board the *Daisy Lou* on Friday at four o'clock. 'Y'all take care now,' he said and backed out of the door, plainly baffled by our silence.

We heard him descend the stairs. Roxanne went to the window and didn't speak until she saw him walk away from the hotel. 'I don't want nothing to do with that Bullmouth. He's one mean man, I tell you. I didn't know he had anything to do with this business or I might not have agreed to come along.'

'I didn't know he would have anything to do with us either,' I snapped. 'Do you think I want to travel with that animal? I'll have to see what can be done.'

'He's tall as a grizzly and twice as mean,' said Minnie.

Tilda nervously twisted the ring on her little finger. 'I seen him hit your ma right in the face with his fist.'

I gasped. 'He struck my mother? Whatever did she do?'

'She wasn't afraid of nobody,' laughed Roxanne. 'She just called some of the men what was in the house to come and throw him out. Then when they had him by the arms, she picked up the fire-tongs and cut his head open. Belle always said you couldn't let a man get away with nothing, else he'd think he could always do it.'

'Wish somebody had given me that advice years ago,' said Minnie.

'Well,' I said. 'There goes our dream of travelling to New Orleans. We can't go with Bullmouth Boyd, because he'll see to it that we travel on to Panama. It was a foolish idea anyway. I can't take any more of Mr Walkern's money. I'm already worrying about how I'll repay the thirty-five dollars.'

Roxanne was impatient, bouncing on the bed and waving her arms. 'I didn't get a chance to tell you about the greenhorns. They said it costs about a thousand dollars to sail all the way from New York to San Francisco. But what they're doing is travelling by packet on the Missouri river to Independence or St Joseph. They'll be joining up with a wagon train to cross by land to California territory on the Oregon Trail. It's just a hundred and fifty dollars and a dollar a day to the wagon-master. Only I don't know if that includes buying a wagon and oxen, or not.'

44

'They'd have to buy supplies, too,' said Minnie. 'What's all this got to do with us?'

'We got to go somewhere. It might as well be St Jo.'

'We aren't known in St Jo,' I said. 'I could start a school. We could maybe go into business. How much is it to St Jo?

'They're paying six dollars to Independence. I believe St Jo is quite a-ways farther.'

'Sounds like a good idea, Carlotta,' said Minnie quietly. 'We got to do something. And we got to get out of town.'

I began to pace the floor. 'But why should we go to that particular town? What is there in St Jo? Maybe we should go somewhere closer.'

'There's greenhorns in St Jo!' cried Roxanne. 'Darn fools who think they're going to pick up twenty thousand dollars' worth of gold right off the ground. And they've got money to spend. Can't wait, in fact.'

'They must need a lot of supplies,' I mused.

'I know!' said Minnie. 'We could open a restaurant. Folks has got to eat. Or a tavern. Now there's a good business. Or no, I'd rather open a laundry. I'm really good at bringing clothes up with a hot iron. And my whites *are* white.'

'We could open a house like your ma's,' suggested Tilda. 'We could all be rich.'

It was time to put an end to this dreaming. 'I haven't enough money to get us to St Jo on the packet, much less keep us in bed and board until we're on our feet.'

Roxanne's lips curved into an evil little smile. 'Bullmouth's got the money, and I know how to get it offen him.'

'No!' I cried. 'Do you want to go to the penitentiary?'

'I'm for it,' said Minnie quietly.

'*What?* I didn't think you'd hold with stealing.'

'I don't hold with men giving money to starving women only if they'll take up a life of sin. Besides, we could maybe pay it back one day soon.'

45

They begged and cajoled. They told me how evil Mr Walkern was, and how important they all thought it was to make a fresh start in a new town. Their arguments were powerful, and I was eager to come to an agreement with them, because I didn't want to say goodbye to my new friends. Their liveliness was a tonic to me. Having friends was a new experience. I had been too busy in Boston to cultivate any. These women liked me for myself, which was a good feeling. I wanted that good feeling to go on for ever.

'I will agree to one thing,' I said finally, making sure they were all paying attention, and that they all understood me. 'If Roxanne can steal some, just *some* of the money, say a hundred dollars, and put a promissory note in Bullmouth's pocket saying I'll pay him back in sixty days, I'll agree to it.'

They saw that their arguments had prevailed, and were ready to agree to my conditions with great solemnity. Many oaths were given in the next minute or two. I was too tired and too overwrought to consider that it is not possible to be just a little dishonest. In a haze of grief and insecurity, I made myself party to a plan which required me to abandon all my principles. I was preparing to behave in a way my grandmother would have said was sinful, and my mother would have called stupid.

4

We listened to Roxanne's strategy for stealing the money from Bullmouth. She was very confident, making us believe in her special talents as much as she did. Then we began making a few plans. The important moment was when Roxanne actually took the money. Everything had to be just right: everyone had to play her part, or we would all end in the penitentiary. The risks were so enormous, the consequences of failure so great, that we found it best not to dwell on the subject, except when we were actually practising our parts.

On the morning of our departure, I took the three of them to a daguerre artist, and we had a picture taken.

When we arrived at the studio, there were four Easterners waiting to have pictures taken for their families back home. Self-conscious in their unaccustomed clothing, they spoke of the fortunes they would make with a minimum of effort. Nuggets as big as your fist were sure to be lying around in full view. Panning for gold was a simple skill which could be quickly learned. Not one of them anticipated having to lift his pick. In spite of their convictions, picks were favourite props in the daguerreotypes, as were small bags with *$80,000* printed on the sides. These were supplied by Mr Burns to be held in the pictures, and were greatly appreciated by the greenhorns.

Horace Burns, the daguerre artist, was doing an excellent business. He said he had been making plenty of money ever since gold fever struck the nation in February. He made a nice group of us: Minnie and I were seated, with Roxanne and Tilda standing at the back. There was a small table with a plant on it where I was to lean my arm. Roxanne had a better idea. One of us should hold the bag marked *$80,000*. As a result, when we came back to Mr Burns' studio to collect the tintype, we discovered that we looked exactly like a gang of lady stagecoach robbers.

Forty seconds is a long time to keep from blinking. I managed it by keeping my eyes half-closed. Minnie opened hers as wide as they would go, and looked slightly demented in the picture as a result.

'My goodness,' she said when she saw it. 'That's not bad, is it?'

I had bought her a bright calico dress in Krautzheimer's store. Roxanne and Tilda had arranged her hair in a more becoming style, even twisting a curl or two to fall in front of her ears. A little rouge (which they insisted on buying) had helped. Minnie looked younger in the picture than she did in real life. Tilda thought she looked very much fatter in the picture than in real life, and was not happy at all. While I admit that daguerreotypes are a clever invention, they do look on the bad side of people, making everything seem so dreary and lifeless.

Roxanne took her turn at holding the likeness, and I saw tears spring to her eyes. 'It makes me look just what I am, don't you think, Carlotta? A seventeen year old whore. Only I don't look seventeen. I look as old as Minnie.'

'You look very pretty,' I said. She did, too. Unfortunately, she looked like a very pretty whore.

As for my image, it gave no hint of my recent sorrows. What I saw, to my dismay, were my mother's eyebrows and curve of lip. The way she had always lifted her chin defiantly in bad times was there in my pose, reminding me of my lineage.

Roxanne took the picture from my hands again, and walked away a little to stare at it. 'Going with men done that to me. And it's not as if I ever liked a single one of them. They were all weak or cruel or drunk. And sometimes they was all three.'

48

Minnie was looking over Roxanne's shoulder. 'Here, gimme that!' She snatched the picture from Roxanne's hands. 'Where'd you get that pin? You didn't have it on when we went into Krautzheimer's store, and I *know* Carlotta didn't pay for it. Where'd you get it? Funny thing – I never noticed you wearing it, but it stands out like a sore thumb in the picture.'

Roxanne jerked the photograph away from Minnie. 'Get your fingers offen my picture! You'll spoil it, you old crow. I stole the pin, so there. Carlotta ain't got much money, so we have to do the best we can. Besides, I needed the practice.'

'Do you need the practice in going to jail?' I asked sternly. 'You must not take any more chances.'

Tilda began to whine. 'Now, don't nobody start to fight. We all got to get along. If Roxanne wants to practise, I think we should be grateful. But if Carlotta don't want anything stolen, then Roxanne mustn't do it any more. There, that's fair, ain't it?'

Time passed slowly as we waited for the dangerous hour of four o'clock on Friday afternoon. When we arrived at the *Daisy Lou*, Bullmouth was on the main deck, standing by the gangplank and looking anxious. We had deliberately waited until the very last minute. Our plan could not work otherwise. It was not until the evening before we were due to sail that I heard steamboats were often late in departing, and might be held up for a whole day. If that happened to our packet, we would go to jail for sure.

Roxanne went aboard first, all dressed up, her cheeks rouged, her eyes sparkling. 'How do, Bullmouth!' she said, and came right up to him, looking flirtatious.

We all four crowded round him, looking crestfallen as he told us off for being so late. He had put down a small bag – black leather with a strong clasp – and clamped it between his feet as he talked to us. Roxanne was pressing

49

herself up to him, smiling and saying how excited she was to be going away.

After a minute or so, I stood back a pace or two as Minnie pressed forward, wanting to tell Bullmouth what she thought of him for leading four women into sin.

'Ouch!' yelled Roxanne. 'Minnie, you old crow! You stepped on my foot! Damn near crippled me.' Roxanne bent down to rub her foot. This was unexpected. Bullmouth's money was surely in an inside pocket! I wanted Roxanne to press closer so that she could get her hand into that pocket.

Roxanne stood up; Tilda moved close to her. The plan was for Roxanne to drop the money into Tilda's carpet-bag. But I hadn't seen a movement when Roxanne could have taken the money. Time was running out. When were they going to do it?

Tilda began edging away towards the gangplank. This was our signal to get off. I had to assume that Roxanne's hands were swifter than my eye. Or perhaps something had gone dreadfully wrong! Wiping my sweating palms on my skirt, I backed away beside Tilda.

The steamboat bell clanged. The roustabouts were moving to draw in the gangplank. Bullmouth was still enraged. He was not accustomed to being so roundly insulted, and Minnie had found some choice words to call him.

Now Roxanne and Minnie were fighting, slapping at each other and pulling hair. Minnie's bonnet was comically awry. Tilda and I left the packet, as passengers closed around the two to urge them on and laugh at their vulgar language.

Suddenly, Minnie, apparently getting the worst of the fight, turned and ran off the packet. She quickly caught up with Tilda and me. Roxanne was in hot pursuit. Bullmouth stood at the railing, yelling for us to return to the packet at once, because it was about to sail.

The packet moored next to the *Daisy Lou* was the

Spread Eagle,, already about to draw in its gangplank, and bound for St Jo, a journey of five hundred miles. I stood aside, allowing the other three to board the *Spread Eagle*. Bullmouth had left the *Daisy Lou* and was pushing past the crowd to reach us.

'Where the hell's my bag?' he called. I stopped running. The others were already aboard and waiting for me. 'Where's my bag? Two thousand dollars!'

I looked up at the *Spread Eagle* in dismay. The three women were standing by the gangplank, urging me to run.

'Get yourself on here!' shouted Minnie.

I almost didn't make it. The deckhands were pulling in the gangplank as I stood on it. The jerk of the planks beneath me almost sent me flying back into the shallow water and disaster. I threw my weight forward, however, and landed on all fours, to be lifted up by my friends. Bullmouth stood on the shore as we drew away, shaking his fist at us, his voice inaudible now.

'Minnie, did you know they were going to take it all?' I asked under my breath.

'Well, of course I did.'

'But I said just one hundred dollars! You heard me.'

'Now, how was Roxanne going to count out exactly one hundred dollars? I thought you'd figured that out, and just didn't want to let on you knew what we was up to.'

'Roxanne, did you put my promissory note in Bullmouth's pocket?'

'It's there,' she said, grinning as we moved out into open water. 'He'll find it sooner or later. I don't know what he'll make of it.'

I didn't know what he'd make of it either. It said I promised to pay him one hundred and ten dollars – I had even calculated generous interest on his 'loan'. I had signed it. Now, I had a contract with Mr Walkern saying I was taking his two thousand dollars, and promising to pay back six when our business got going in California. And I had signed another note saying I would pay Bullmouth Boyd one hundred and ten dollars! Minnie was quiet, her face rather pale in spite of her exertions. Roxanne and Tilda were jubilant. They hugged one another and danced around. They had no sense of right and wrong at all. But I was the one the law would be after.

Their dancing came to an abrupt end when Wick Estes suddenly joined us, looking incredibly grim. 'Does this little pantomime – ' he indicated Bullmouth gesticulating on the levee ' – mean that you three have stolen money from him?'

'Well . . .' I stammered, flustered by his sudden appearance from nowhere. 'Well, if you must know, yes. So there.'

The captain joined us, demanding payment and asking what all the fuss was about. In recent weeks I had done a considerable amount of travelling on steamboats, Captain Childs of the *Spread Eagle* looked like the captains of all other packets: bearded, arrogant and gnarled like a piece of driftwood.

'I am Miss Schultz, sir. I booked two cabins to St Joseph for four. I sent my luggage to be loaded this morning. I do hope it arrived safely.'

'Oh, it arrived all right,' said Captain Childs. 'It's just over there, but you didn't give me an address where I could reach you, Miss Schultz. I haven't got a single cabin free. Y'all are going to have to bed down right here on the lower deck.'

I was living in a nightmare. Roxanne's wary look had returned to her eyes as she stared at Wick. He stared back, a sneer on his lips. The captain, I was relieved to see, did not appear to be aware of our run-in with Bullmouth. I wondered how long it would be before Wick told him.

'We must have a cabin to sleep in.'

'I can't go up there on deck and build you one,' said the captain, nastily.

I lifted my chin. 'I am not accustomed to – Mr Estes, can you help us out? The captain says there are no cabins available. We need two desperately, but I suppose we could manage with one.'

'Is that a fact?'

'Do *you* have a cabin, sir?'

'I do.'

'Well, then?' I smiled at him in my most ingratiating manner.

'Well then, ma'am, when I'm lying snug in my cabin, I'll be thinking of you four bedding down here on the open deck. I hope you brought your own food, because you'll find none is provided for ordinary passengers like yourselves.'

'We've brought food, Mr Estes,' said Minnie. 'I guess you can't help smiling at the thought of Carlotta suffering all this aggravation.'

'Over there's a bucket on a rope if you need water,' said the captain. 'Just dip it over the side. The Missouri's a trifle muddy, but you can let it settle a while before you use it.'

Wick frowned. 'I think you should warn the ladies that if they drop the bucket over the side of the boat while she's going at a fair crack, the force of the water into the bucket could easily pull them overboard.'

I looked from one man to the other. I was beginning to shake, now the immediate danger was past. 'You can't expect us to drink muddy water.'

The captain sucked his teeth. 'I don't *expect* anything. I'm telling you the current runs at about ten miles an hour, and I don't stop to pick up those who are foolish enough to fall in. Miss Schultz, this ain't one of those fancy boats that sail between St Louis and New Orleans. We cater for a different trade, and I don't want trouble from your sort. If you want to, you can get off at St

Charles. I'll let you travel that far for nothing, and you won't have to pay me.'

I looked at the others. They all shook their heads. 'We'll go on, Captain. I will give you our fares just as soon as we sort out our parcels.'

Now Wick wore a sardonic smile. 'And when you have sorted out your *parcels*, I suggest you put the rest of the money in the captain's safe.'

I felt myself blush. However, one glance around the lower deck at the faces of the roustabouts and green-horns convinced me that the money would not be safe with us. I nodded. 'Shortly. When . . . after I have paid our fares and . . . whatever.' Wick threw back his head and laughed loudly.

The captain turned to go, and Wick clearly intended to go with him. 'Well done, Carlotta. Your mother could not have managed so daring an escapade. She would have been proud of you. At least, I think she would have.' He lifted his hat a fraction and left us alone.

Minnie chuckled gleefully. 'I swear I don't know how you three are going to manage. Not one of you is used to the hard life, but I've known worse. Where's our things? We've got a skillet, but I don't think they'll let me build a fire on the deck,'

'If the first stop is St Charles, we can buy some food there,' said Tilda.

'I don't believe we will be travelling at night.' I consulted a card giving the scheduled stops and distances from each other and from St Louis. Wisely, the owners had not given the times of expected arrival. 'I think we will stop overnight in Washington. That's where we can buy food. Anyway, we brought bread and cake, didn't we?'

Minnie had found our possessions neatly stacked at the stern, close to the gigantic paddle wheel and its roaring water. 'Come down this way. That engine makes a terrible racket. I think it's going to shake my teeth out.

We got them two feather mattresses we can get out to sleep on. We must make ourselves a bit of room before the others think of bedding down. Them folks look like rough customers. We gotta watch our things night and day or have 'em all took away from us.'

Roxanne unfolded one of the feather mattresses and shook it briefly to plump up its stuffing. I removed the price of our tickets and two ten-dollar gold eagles from the bag which, surprisingly, was not locked. Roxanne ran off with the black bag and the money to pay the captain for our tickets.

Wick returned, leaned against the railing and folded his arms. 'Settling in comfortably, ladies?'

'We'll manage,' said Tilda.

'The devil you will! You'll be molested before morning.' He grinned viciously. 'And that's not precisely what y'all had in mind, is it?'

'We don't have a choice, do we? You wouldn't let us have your cabin.'

'I don't like some woman coming up to me and saying "Well, then" in that uppity tone of voice, Carlotta. That was a bit high-handed of you and very bad manners.'

'Please, Mr Estes . . .'

'I told you before. You can call me Wick.'

'Please, Wick, may we have the use of your cabin for the voyage to St Joseph? How far are you going, by the way?'

'I am going to St Jo on business, and yes, you may have the use of my cabin. Here's the key – it's Cabin Four. You'll still have to provide your own food. *I* intend to eat with the captain.'

Expressing our gratitude, we began moving our possessions. Wick watched for a minute or two, then with a loud sigh, said he had nothing better to do, and began to help us.

The cabin was little more than a cupboard: eight feet wide and ten feet deep with a small window that looked out on to the passenger deck. A nightstand between the two box beds held a bowl and pitcher. The only privy the boat possessed was suspended over the paddle wheel on this deck. I could smell it from our cabin. There was scarcely room for the four of us to stand. We would be packed top to tail when two of us made up a bed on the floor, because for fear of having something stolen, we had crammed all of our luggage, except the newly-purchased tent, into the cabin. When the door was shut, the room felt completely airless.

'I've got some whiskey,' said Roxanne, 'if I can just find it. Will you stay and have a drink with us, Mr Estes?'

'With pleasure, but do you mind if I stand out here on the deck? It's a bit crowded in the cabin.'

Roxanne removed the bung and handed the jug to Wick. 'Better than Missouri mud.'

'But not much,' said Wick, grimacing as he passed the jug to me.

'My husband used to make real good whiskey,' remembered Minnie. 'You take a quart of raw alcohol, a bottle of Jamaican ginger, a pound of black molasses. Then you add river water as much as you like.'

'Where I come from, they call that Missouri skull varnish,' said Wick.

Minnie disagreed. 'That's a different thing altogether. Although I expect if you wanted to get your skull varnished, you could do it on Husband's brew.'

Having had his drink, Wick said the captain had offered to share his own cabin, and left us alone. We decided to leave our room to explore the small packet which would be our home for eight days or more.

A small party of Osage Indians sat morosely on the main deck, staring at the river bank while two stokers fed logs into the huge firebox. Eight red-eyed greenhorns lounged near their dismantled covered wagons. The pleasures of St Louis had taken their toll. One of their

56

number sprawled across the stacked supplies, snoring loudly. The others slumped for support wherever they could find a keg or sack to lean against; all appeared to be suffering from the after-effects of drink. Although several passengers were strolling about on the upper deck, so far there were no women in sight. I hoped there weren't any aboard.

As I had predicted, the packet stopped at St Charles only long enough to unload some cargo and take more cordwood on to the deck. We did not quite reach Washington before dark, but the captain decided that the short distance left could be safely negotiated if the first mate went ahead in the yawl to light the channel by setting burning candles on floating debris.

Coming into the little town was a pretty sight. We watched with pleasure as the packet 'ate up the lights' and safely reached shore. We were ravenous and the first to cross the gangplank, eager to go in search of food. The public sitting-cum-dining room was next to our cabin and for the previous half an hour we had been tormented by the smell of hot food being delivered from the kitchen below.

Wick joined us just before we reached the first of a huddle of houses set well back from the river, and offered to take us to a small inn he knew where he promised to buy us a hearty supper.

'No point in spending Bullmouth's money,' he said.

Minnie had already appointed herself as my defender. 'It's really Carlotta's money. That there Mr Otis Walkern gave it to her to take us to California. Bullmouth's a mean man. He was going to travel all the way to New Orleans with us and see us on to the clipper. *And* he was thinking about not giving us all the money Mr Walkern meant us to have.'

'That was Walkern's money?' asked Wick in surprise. 'I do hope old Walkern sees your removal of the money in the same light as you do. Or else, I hope he never catches up with you.'

The inn was small, but the landlord did a regular business with passengers on the steamboats, so he was able to supply the party with a generous beef stew that didn't have too much fat floating on the surface. Conversation lagged while everyone ate the stew, and didn't revive until we were waiting for our apple pie and second cup of coffee.

'Mr Estes,' said Minnie, 'are you going to tell on us? I mean, now that you know we stole that money.'

Wick leaned back in his chair. 'I have had a few ups and downs in my life recently. I've been busy as a bee for six years and I've ended up almost back where I started from. I've had a good look at the human race and I don't like what I see. I'm getting out of it. I'm not going to interfere in anybody's activities ever again. If you want to steal some money, that's your business. I don't like Bullmouth. I know some terrible things about him. But you say the money belongs to Walkern. Well, I don't like him either. I'm just surprised, that's all. I heard you were a schoolteacher back East, Carlotta. I heard you were ashamed of your ma and what she did. Now here you are stealing money. I thought you'd be too shocked to do anything so wicked.'

'Let's get a few things straight, *Mr* Estes,' I said belligerently. 'I was brought up in a brothel, and knew how the business was run and what was the product on offer before my grandmother ever came to take me to Boston when I was ten. It was my good fortune to spend six years with her learning right from wrong, learning God-fearing ways. Nothing, I promise you, *shocks* me. I've just learned to choose a better way.'

'I see.' Wick's lips curled in a mocking smile. 'And this better way is to steal some money that you say Mr Walkern had already given you, is that it? You've got me all confused, Carlotta. Just exactly what are you going to do out West?'

Under the circumstances, it was foolish to have said

58

that I had learned a better way. No wonder the man was sneering at me. I felt an overwhelming urge to shock him, let him know I was no longer the little girl who had been willing to do her mother a favour.

'Well, it's like this, Wick,' I drawled, sounding just like Missouri Belle. 'We're going out to the gold fields to set up a brothel. We'll be making money for ourselves *and* for Mr Walkern. So what do you think of that?'

His face turned a deep red. 'Not a whole hell of a lot, Carlotta. But I shouldn't have expected more.'

5

Sleeping in the small cabin was every bit as unpleasant as I had imagined it would be. There was much turning and tossing at first, much giggling and gossiping, until the people in the next cabin hammered on the adjoining wall and a woman's voice, laced with disgust, asked: 'Must your sort carouse all night?'

I was almost getting used to being despised as a whore. All the clichés of distaste were familiar to me from the days of my childhood, when the good ladies used to turn up their noses at my mother. My grand-mother, on the other hand, was a highly respected woman. She always went out of her way to be rude to the ladies of the demi-monde if she happened to encounter them.

'It's bad enough that we know your mother,' she used to say. 'We don't have to tolerate other fallen women.'

There were just three female passengers on the packet, good women with husbands and two pairs of gloves and hats that gave them very little protection from the sun. Minnie said that in their place she supposed she'd look down on the four of us. 'Because, what *are* we, when all's said and done?' I was unable to give her a satisfactory answer.

I turned over now, and composed myself for sleep, resigned to the insults and snubs that were bound to be our lot over the next few days.

I thought I had forgotten the hurt of Carlton's rejection. But he visited me in my dreams to tell me that he would never have married the daughter of Missouri Belle. The pain was intense and woke me at dawn, gnawing at my brain.

After a second or two, I realized it was the noise of the engine starting up again that had really awakened me, but I couldn't sleep any more. I had gone to bed in my underwear and now managed to find my calico dress and put it on without too much trouble. Shoes were another matter.

Easing the door open, I stepped out on to the passenger deck in my bare feet. The grey dawn light had set the birds twittering. The river mist still hung over the surface, and would soon dissipate in the heat. It was a heart-stopping sight; the town of Washington, up the hill apiece, was still asleep. There were trees in full leaf on both sides of the old muddy river as far as the eye could see. It was chilly, cool enough to make the goose pimples stand up on my arms, with a breeze that ruffled my hair, while the throb of the engine rose up through the soles of my feet.

I hadn't stopped to watch the dawn for years. I was always so busy that there was never any time to *think*. Now, I squeezed my eyes tightly shut to hold back the tears and marvelled that the view could make me cry. The very feel of the air reminded me of my youth when I used to crawl out of bed and go downstairs to sit on the back porch, dressed only in my cotton shift. Those were the good times, before the house began to stir. Later, Minerva would come into the kitchen to light the stove. Cassius would arrive with his broom to sweep the porch and the brickwork, and I would be told I was in the way. But my mother and her girls would not be awake for hours.

My grandmother's house had not enjoyed a porch. You could sit out on the front steps and watch the world go by, if you wished, but you couldn't be alone. I laid a hand on the cool railing, damp with dew, and walked to the bow of the packet. Memories are hell. I had kept them at bay all these years and hadn't intended to dredge them up now.

61

It turned out that I wasn't the only person awake so early. There was a man on the deck, but I didn't know it when I first came to the front of the boat to look at the way ahead as we edged out from the shore. The man crept up on me, said: 'Good morning, ma'am,' and laughed when I jumped.

He must have been about thirty. I thought of him as a sandy fellow, fairer than I. His type was common enough. Not as tall as Wick, but built solidly. His face was sly, holding secrets behind those smooth cheeks, that neatly trimmed sandy moustache, those light brown mocking eyes. A dandified man with beautiful hands, he had never done a proper day's work. At this hour of the morning he was wearing a frockcoat, cravat and beaver hat. He held leather gloves in one hand as if wearing gloves was nothing special to him at all.

My mother was accustomed to sizing up men in a split second, sorting the fools from the vicious brutes, and behaving accordingly. She used to say you could always tell if a man was a professional gambler. If he was sober, clean, properly dressed and polite, then he was after your money. No one was a better authority on gamblers than Belle Schultz. Perhaps the reason why she lost so much money to them was because they spoke to her politely. I was beginning to agree that it was a service well worth paying for.

'Good morning,' I replied pleasantly. 'You are up very early, I must say. I would have expected you to be sound asleep in your bed after a late night at the card table.'

He lifted his eyebrows in surprise. 'I did play cards until a late hour, I must admit.'

'And you lost – it being the first night on board. You'll win tonight, I daresay.'

He was grinning now, giving me a conspiratorial wink. 'Only a small win tonight. It really is too soon to win in a big way. I've got till he gets off at Independence

62

to reel in the biggest fish on board. Shall I make a guess about your occupation?'

'Don't waste your energy. I'm Carlotta Schultz. If you spent any time in St Louis, you'll have heard of Belle Schultz. I'm her daughter.'

'The one they call Missouri Belle? There was some talk about the four of you at dinner last night. There are three married ladies of a certain age on this packet and I'm sorry to say they are keeping to their cabins for fear of being forced to acknowledge you. I do believe they would have been prepared to starve to death, except that they were promised you wouldn't be dining with the other cabin passengers.'

I saw Wick open the captain's door and head our way. 'Another early riser,' I said. 'I don't know your name, sir, but this is Mr Wickcliffe Estes,' I looked up at Wick. 'This gentleman and I were just passing the time of day.'

'Jenkins,' said the man, extending his hand to Wick. 'Albert Jenkins, ma'am. The Prince Consort and I share a Christian name.'

'Are you an Englishman?' asked Wick, shaking hands. 'What are you doing in these parts, Albert Jenkins?'

'I'm travelling to St Joseph, sir,' said Mr Jenkins. 'Thought I might spy out the lie of the land, see if I fancy making the long journey to California territory. If not, I shall return to St Louis.'

'Is that a fact?' asked Wick. 'And how many times have you already travelled to St Jo to spy out the lie of the land?'

Jenkins' eyes narrowed and he went a trifle pale around the mouth. 'Never before, sir, I promise you. I have never worked the Missouri. And what, may I ask, draws you to the state's western border? Gold mining? Or perhaps you don't plan to go so far.'

'I'm going all the way to St Jo, Albert Jenkins. I'll be right here on the packet with you till you disembark. Business interests, you know. I've been to California, as a matter of fact – don't intend to go again. I shall be returning to St Louis in due course. We may be travelling companions on the return journey.'

'It would be an honour, sir.'

The two men stared at one another. I thought they might take to growling and circling like a pair of fighting dogs, but just then my cabin door opened and Roxanne came to join us. Her hair was a mass of tangles tumbling round her shoulders. Like me, she was barefooted. With some difficulty, I had persuaded her to wash her face the previous night. As a result, her clear skin was free of rouge, and she looked ten times prettier than she usually did. It was immediately obvious that Albert Jenkins was very taken with her and Roxanne brightened considerably.

'Ah, Miss Carlotta's companion!' said Jenkins, looking Roxanne up and down. 'Miss Roxanne – am I right?'

'You are, sir. And you're the gambling man. Am *I* right?'

Roxanne blossomed in the sunshine of Albert Jenkins' admiration. With her hands well back on her hips, she was inviting him to admire her bosom. Her chin was lifted, her lips parted, her eyes half-closed. Mr Jenkins couldn't help raising a hand to smooth his moustache into place as he stared at her.

'Miss Roxanne, I feel the need of a little walk. May I offer you my arm for a turn round the deck?'

'I don't mind, gambling man, but I ain't got no shoes on.'

'That won't bother me if it doesn't bother you.' He offered her his arm with great ceremony, and the two of them walked away as if Wick and I had not been present.

'She's just given you a lesson,' said Wick.

'In what, for heaven's sake? She behaved like a little hussy.'

'But isn't that your line of business now? Do you want a girl who won't earn her keep? You'll have to learn how to sashay like that. On the other hand, why bother? You were a schoolteacher. Missouri needs schoolteachers. You could probably get a position very easily.'

'Yes, for twenty-one dollars a month. I can't pay back Mr Walkern on that kind of money.'

'You damned fool! You won't have to pay back the money if you don't spend it.'

'And let the others starve? I'm going to use Mr Walkern's money to get some of the good things in life that I've been missing out on. I'm tired of living hand to mouth. I want to be comfortable, and you can't stop me.'

'Stop you? Why, Miss Carlotta Schultz, I've no intention of trying. I told you, I don't interfere in the ways of my fellow creatures. If you don't mind, I'll just watch. And maybe laugh a little. Good day to you, ma'am.'

I am a seasoned steamboat traveller. The journey I had already made from Boston to Chicago was much longer than the five hundred mile cruise from St Louis to St Jo. I have slept in crowded conditions, shared a dinner table with fifty rough, silent men who hardly knew what a fork was for. I have weathered strong winds and endured the sea-sickness that often troubles passengers on the Great Lakes.

But this journey was proving to be the most irksome one of all, primarily because the *Spread Eagle* was by far the smallest packet I had ever travelled on. Thirty greenhorns and Indians lived and slept on the lower deck in company with the boat's crew, exposed to all weathers. In the main cabin, another thirty men paid for the privilege of sleeping on the floor. Their kit was cleared away each day and they all ate in the same room, together with the fifteen cabin passengers.

Captain Childs told me that the *Spread Eagle* drew only two and half feet of water unloaded and could 'tippy-toe right cross the sandbars'. Loaded, she sat much lower in the water, in constant danger from hidden shallow-water hazards.

The Missouri river snakes its treacherous way right across the state, past Independence, where it makes a rather sharp turn northwards and travels upwards for many miles, marking the state border for some of its long length. It is shallower than the Mississippi, sometimes wider, twice as muddy and fraught with danger.

Whole trees floated past us every day of our journey. We could see their roots rising above the water line. Sometimes branches would interlock and collect debris so that we seemed to be passing floating islands. All these snags and logs could rip the bottom out of the packet in seconds. As if that were not bad enough, the river could change course from day to day, making life exceedingly difficult for the pilot. Creating steam to turn the stern wheel required prodigious amounts of wood and Missouri river water. Several times a day, the boat would pull into the bank, and the crew and passengers from the lower deck would swarm ashore to cut wood. Each night, the firebox was raked out, and the stoker went inside the boilers to remove the mud that had collected there during the day.

All day long and far into the night, the men on the lower deck would carouse, drink, gamble and fight at the top of their voices. Sometimes, one of them would get out a fiddle and scrape a tune. *Old Dan Tucker* was a favourite, played several times each night. When there was a sudden outbreak of acute homesickness *The Old Oaken Bucket* was requested, and the party would be relatively silent for a while.

On the Sunday morning, the captain let it be known that the main cabin would be turned over to those who wished to hold an informal religious service. Women were not normally allowed into the main cabin during the day except for meals, but Sunday was an exception. At eleven o'clock, Minnie and I took up our Bibles and entered. Wick was already there, as well as eight or nine men, mostly cabin passengers. The good wives were seated together right at the front. The husband of one of them was standing, facing the row of chairs, apparently about to lead the service.

We were just moving to the back to take our seats when the oldest woman looked up at the temporary minister and said sharply: 'Jesse! Are you going to allow this?'

'Now then, my dear, we mustn't . . .' he mumbled. I saw his leathery cheeks redden as I sat down.

'Ladies, I think this is not the place for us,' said his wife loudly to her companions. 'It seems a shame on a Sunday morning to be driven away, but we must remember we are in the Wild West now, and trust in the Lord to deliver us.'

Wick got to his feet slowly. 'You know,' he said, 'I feel an absence of the Christian spirit in here. I think I'll be going. Do say a prayer for this sinner, Mrs Morgan, before the devil takes over my soul and makes me say something I'll be sorry for.'

Minnie and I stood up at Wick's signal, and walked out of the cabin with him. Mr Jesse Morgan stammered some sort of apology, but I pretended not to hear.

'What have I ever done to deserve such treatment?' I asked when we were once more in the open air.

'Nothing yet, except steal a little money. But those ladies don't know that.'

'That's unfair.' Irritably, I removed Wick's hand from my elbow. 'Even if Minnie and I were the fallen women they imagine us to be, we still had a right to take part in the service.'

Wick scratched the back of his head as if to remove an uncomfortable thought. 'I guess that's true. I was counting on a quiet Sunday, but if you want to go back in there and fight it out, I'll come with you.'

'There'll be no fighting,' said Minnie. 'I was once a respectable married woman and mother. I guess I would have behaved every bit as heartless, though I'm ashamed to say so now. Let's just forget it, shall we?'

The packet reached Jefferson City on Monday morning. I stood at the railing of the passenger deck with Wick in order to admire the state capital building with its fine white dome. The town was awfully small and rough-hewn by Boston standards, and yet this was the seat of Missouri's government. I felt as if I had left civilization behind.

Without considering my words, I burst out: 'Oh, Wick, what am I thinking of, going to St Jo? I miss Boston and the people I used to know. Minnie is a good woman, but she's never read a book in her life! She smokes a corncob pipe and talks about things like preserving apples and concocting remedies for the rheumatics. As for Roxanne and Tilda, I have nothing whatsoever of importance to say to them, nor they to me.'

'You are an ill-assorted party, I must admit. What you want is a better class of whore, Carlotta. Women you feel are your intellectual equals, without embarrassing you with higher morals. But if you're pining for a learned conversation, maybe I can help you out. I've read a few books in my time.'

Wick had a way of insulting me and then moving on before I could think of anything to say in my defence. But I thought I saw a way of bringing him down a peg, so I swallowed the remark about whores and asked him sweetly if he was familiar with a book called *Pride and Prejudice*.

'I'm familiar with it, but I didn't like it at all. A lot of nonsense, I thought. I don't like books written by women, and especially not those written by English women.'

I tried to conceal my surprise. Why had this Missouri businessman read Miss Jane Austen's book? Silently, I calculated the risk of asking him which writer he did like. I might, after all, be further embarrassed by not having heard of the novelist he preferred. 'Perhaps you don't like fiction at all. Some men don't, I believe.'

'Oh, James Fenimore Cooper is all right, but I can't think of anyone else I like. You're right, I prefer factual books. That reminds me. Have you read Fremont's book about travelling on the Oregon Trail?'

'I've never heard of it.'

'Just as well. Better to be ignorant than ill-informed. You know, you will be in good company on the Oregon Trail. It's full of greedy, ignorant people trekking West to get something for nothing. Like you, they don't like work, preferring dreams. They drag their wives and brats on a journey that's not suitable for respectable city folks, then wonder why so many get sick and die.'

'Oh, you're such a cynical man, Wick! Don't you have a good word for anybody?'

'No, I don't. I believe in human frailty and man's inhumanity to man. I'll give you an example of what I mean. Take those Indians sitting down there on the lower deck like a bunch of wooden dummies. Everybody's afraid of them. We all assume they're stupid and have no decent feelings. They'll kill you as soon as look at you, everybody says. Well, that's maybe true enough. I'd advise you to keep your party well away from them. But they've got good reason to hate us.

'Let me tell you what happened to the Indians in these parts about twelve years ago. A steamboat, the *St Peters*, was on its way from St Louis to Fort Union. At Fort Clark, a chief of the Mandans came on board and stole a blanket from one of the crew who had smallpox. Three days later, the Indians began falling sick, which you *could* say served the chief right for stealing, because he was one of those who died. But his tribe paid heavily for his small crime. There had been seventeen hundred Mandans, but within a few weeks there were only three hundred left. The Pawnees and Minnatarees began to get it.

'The captain of the *St Peters* didn't care. He steamed on up the river, carrying the disease right along with him. Then some damned fool doctor gave bad inoculations to a bunch of Assiniboin squaws, and they all died. During all the time that the *St Peters* was steaming back to St Louis, having made a damn good profit, the Indians kept on dying. Crow and Blackfoot, too. I was told by an Indian agent that about *fifteen thousand* Indians died altogether. And I've yet to meet a white man who didn't think it was a blessing.'

'Smallpox kills people wherever it strikes.'

'We brought it to them! This was their land. We're getting too arrogant about what some call our "manifest destiny" to own the whole of the continent from shore to shore. Last year in the war we killed a lot of Mexicans unnecessarily to get their land in Texas. We've already enslaved the black people and run the Mormons out of the state. And I can tell you when you get to California, you'll find we don't treat the Chinese out there all that well.'

'If your eyes see only injustice everywhere you look, why don't you try to do something worthwhile to improve matters?'

'Not me. Not Wick Estes. I'm through with the human race. You never can tell how your interference is going to turn out. You could be doing more harm than good. I intend to look after myself in future. Why, if I was in the mood to interfere every time I saw a wrong being done, I might have felt it my duty to turn you over to the authorities when I saw Bullmouth looking for his money.'

'You're a hard selfish man, and I'm ashamed for you. Besides, I keep telling you, that money did not belong to Bullmouth.'

'So *you* say. The world is full of greedy lazy people and you're right along there with them, Carlotta. You've got that much in common with Tilda and Roxanne. I'm ashamed for *you*.'

'I'll have you know – '

'Why, that's my father on the landing!' cried Wick,

70

and left my side to descend the staircase to the main deck.

I saw a tall distinguished-looking man talking to Captain Childs on the landing. They shook hands, and the captain turned to board the *Spread Eagle* as Wick leapt ashore. Father and son stared solemnly at each other for several seconds. Mr Estes was wearing a very fine coat and beaver hat. His shoes gleamed and his linen was blindingly white.

By contrast, Wick was dressed more casually, as befitted a traveller on a steamboat – pants tucked into his boots, a waistcoat and a red shirt open at the throat. The two men had in common a proud upright stance and keen eyes, but the father lacked that mischievous look that suffused Wick's features even in repose. The older man would be a bad one to cross. After a couple of dozen heartbeats, the elder Estes extended his hand, and Wick took it readily. Now, for the first time they smiled, both men talking at once. I couldn't hear what they were saying. Their expressions and gestures were slightly guarded, but definitely affectionate.

A handsome woman in an expensive blue costume and fetching off-the-face bonnet hurried to join the pair of them: unmistakably Wick's mother. They embraced without a word. Her intelligent face was long, enlivened by expressive features, showing anxiety and grief at this moment as her eyes devoured her son. She was the one who would have set him to reading Miss Austen and other great writers, would have introduced him to all that is beautiful in the world, would have been devastated as he rejected them in favour of unrelieved cynicism.

A girl of about sixteen approached, her hair a perfect match with Wick's. With her was a boy a year or two younger, lanky, freckled, obviously adoring his older brother. A family to make your heart swell: well-dressed, courteous and respectable.

71

The steamboat rang out its intention of departing. The Estes family began saying their farewells, their attitudes heavy with strong emotion as this brief reunion came to an end. I wondered if all families displayed such obvious signs of intense love mingled with sorrow on parting.

I turned away and went to my cabin. Men frightened me, made me uneasy, and none more so than Wick Estes. I had grown up in two households without men, had seen those exotic creatures only from a distance. I knew how to be flirtatious with them, having seen how my mother did it. I knew how to let them know they were inferior, having watched my grandmother put a man in his place on many an occasion. But I didn't know how to talk to one just naturally, as if we were both simply ordinary human beings under the same sky. My mother had thought all men were fools, my grandmother that all men were sinners.

And what did I think? I thought men were whatever they chose to be, depending on whom they were talking to. In the company of respectable women, they behaved with great circumspection, saving all their humour and liveliness for male companions. In the company of whores, they paraded their vices, boasting of evil deeds, laughing about wickedness, their own and other men's. And when I was a maid in a well-to-do home, the men of the family had spoken to me as if I were barely human.

In my company, Wick was relaxed, didn't hesitate to swear and to speak of whores or any other topic that interested him. I had seen another Wick just now. The loving, respectful son, ready to protect his mother from the slightest word that might cause her distress.

Needless to say, Carlton had always made me nervous. When I agreed to marry him, he had leaned forward and kissed me squarely on the lips. It had given me no joy, just a problem. I thought of it as a papery kiss – dry, accompanied by the slight rustle of starched linen.

But how to respond? With the sensuousness that came so naturally to my mother? Or perhaps, with the tight-lipped disdain that would have been my grandmother's response? In fact, I had sat as if turned to stone. Carlton had said bitterly: 'Never mind, Carlotta, you may get used to it.'

Later that day, I heard that Wick's father was a Representative in the state legislature, but by that time I had my envy more or less under control and didn't dwell on this new information for long. I couldn't help wondering, however, what it must be like to have a parent of whom you could be proud.

6

Two days later, Captain Childs joined us as we sunned ourselves on the upper deck. We four women were all seated on chairs taken from the main cabin. It was close to noon, the hot sun high in the sky. We sat near the paddle wheel and sweated in the heat. At the front, in the shade, the good wives enjoyed the view in comfort with their men.

Albert Jenkins had joined us briefly earlier in the day, but we hadn't seen him for several hours. Wick was our only companion now, seated between Minnie and me with his long legs stretched out so that he could rest his feet on the guard rail.

'I think we got ourselves a little problem, Wick,' said the captain. 'That Englishman is mighty lucky at cards, they say. Have you played in a game with him?'

'No, I'm staying away from card games for a while. I have watched him play, though, on several occasions. I think he's pretty good at what he does. Are you planning to throw him overboard?'

'I will if I have to. On the other hand, throwing people overboard kind of gives a boat a bad name. I'll let him stay if there's no trouble. He's due to play with Mr Butcher in about half an hour. Fixed it up last night. They've got some sort of challenge going. Don't know whether it's true or not, but Butcher says Englishmen can't play poker. Says they're only good at blackjack. Thinks he'll win, you see.'

Wick folded his arms. 'Butcher was somewhere else when they gave out brains.'

Captain Childs nodded his head seriously. 'I'm sure Jenkins will win. I'm not against gamblers as such. Folks

74

on boats get bored. They like to gamble. If he was to win a few dollars off that preachy fellow, the one who's got a wife with a face like a mud fence, that'd make me chuckle. And the greenhorns can look after themselves. If our professional gambler doesn't wipe them out, somebody else will. But Butcher is not a man to trifle with. As you know, he lives out West. Got some land and a Mex wife out there in California territory, and a reputation for shooting men who get in his way.'

'I'm not much impressed by reputations,' said Wick, 'but maybe this one is justified. If he kills Jenkins, then you won't have to bother about throwing him over the side.'

'Aw, be serious, Wick. I don't want stories going round about my boat. It's bad for business. Women are terrible gossips, and the females on this trip are already raising Cain, because of these four girls, here. I want you to sit in on the game and keep order.'

'Oh, no,' laughed Wick, removing his feet from the railing. 'I don't know why you think I could do anything useful, and I'm not about to try.'

'Men listen to you. They mind you. Couldn't you just go to the cabin and watch? It's not much to ask.'

I could keep silent no longer. 'Why do you refuse to do this for the captain? You have nothing better to do, heaven knows. We don't want a riot on the boat, do we?'

'Don't we?' asked Wick. 'I'm bored half to death. There's not a lot to do on the *Spread Eagle*. A fight might liven things up a bit. But if you want peace, I guess I'll try to see you get it.'

Captain Childs expressed his gratitude and went below, as Wick got up slowly and stretched.

'Let's go watch,' said Roxanne, jumping to her feet.

Tilda was not interested. 'It'll be hot in there, and smelly with all them men smoking.'

Minnie said she had no intention of being anywhere near when the gambling started. She thought she'd just go up forward and torment the good wives by her presence. See if she could drive them into their cabins.

'I'll go with you,' I said to Roxanne. 'I too, am bored half to death.'

Wick looked disapproving, but said nothing. He headed for the main cabin, and Roxanne and I followed.

Albert Jenkins was already there wearing a white shirt, cravat and heavy black frockcoat on this hot day as he arranged the chairs around the dining table.

Wick closed the door behind us and leaned against it, plunging his hands deep into his trouser pockets. 'You're dressed very formally for a friendly game of cards, aren't you Jenkins. I do hope you're not planting a few extra cards in handy places.'

'You are offensive, Estes. I advise you not to make such remarks in company. I won't permit slurs on my honour in the presence of other men. I've no need to cheat; I can win by fair means.'

'Is that so? Then what have you been doing in here?'

'Shortening the odds. Neither you nor any other man or woman,' he nodded at Roxanne and me, 'is going to stand behind me when I play. Does that satisfy you?'

'I'll let that pass. Butcher may be quite good at poker. I've heard he's lucky at cards.'

Jenkins smiled wryly. 'Luck plays a smaller part in poker than in other card games. To succeed you need a clear head, a knowledge of the odds, a good memory for the cards already played and the ability to keep your thoughts to yourself. I'm relying on the fact that I can read Butcher's every thought. He's relying on the fact that I'm a stupid Englishman. Will you be joining us?'

Wick shook his head. 'I'll be sitting at the table only to see fair play. If the play is fair, I promise you I won't mind if you take every cent Butcher has.'

Jenkins never stopped smiling. His teeth gleamed and his lips were drawn back tautly, but his knuckles, I noticed, were whitening as he gripped a chairback. 'You

76

know, Estes, I don't like you very much. You're nothing but a bloody nib sprig, an upper customer with a weakness for rubbing shoulders with the Johnny Raws.'

'*What?*'

Jenkins didn't have a chance to explain. Someone was trying to open the door. Roxanne and I walked to the far end of the room, close to Albert. Wick stood aside to allow Mr Butcher and just about every male passenger except the Indians to crowd into the room. Caleb Butcher, a mountain man and one time fur-trapper, wore a leather coat and leggings and gave off a slightly musky smell. His straggly brown hair was streaked with white. His moustache grew rampantly over his upper lip and down into his mouth, a regular soup-strainer. The thick black beard which covered almost all the lower half of his face must have caused him constant discomfort, because he continually scratched it. One calloused hand held a shotgun which he leaned handily against the chair next to the one he planned to occupy.

Before he could seat himself, Wick picked up the fowling piece and handed it to a bystander. 'Take this back to Mr Butcher's cabin.'

'Touch that gun and I'll blow your head off,' said Butcher.

The bystander, deciding he could enjoy himself better without such a close view of proceedings, returned the gun to Wick and melted to the back of the crowd.

Wick headed for the door. 'I guess I'll have to put this in your cabin myself. I don't mind you shooting Jenkins here, but you've had more than your fair share of cider. I don't think your aim can be all that good, and I don't intend to be shot alongside the gambler.'

'You leave go of that gun, Estes!'

Butcher grabbed the gun but Wick held on. They tussled for a few seconds. The gun went off with a deafening noise and blew a hole in the ceiling of the main cabin. For a moment or two everyone was silent, then a

77

great shout of laughter went up. This was more entertainment than the passengers had enjoyed since board-
ing the boat in St Louis. There was a loud cheer as Wick
left the cabin with the shotgun.

Butcher, swearing imaginatively, sat down at last to
play cards. Already the smell of dirty clothing and
unwashed bodies was fouling the air. Now, sixty men
decided that they really could not watch a game of cards
without a pipe, cigar or cigaritto. Those who did not
light up chewed tobacco, and very soon began to spit on
the filthy red carpet.

Tilda and Minnie later told us about what happened
next. The main cabin was almost directly beneath the
wheelhouse. The blast from Butcher's shotgun nicked a
corner of the pilot's domain and broke the glass on the
starboard side. The pilot took his eyes from the shallow
river to examine the damage.

Fatally, he left the wheelhouse shouting, 'What the
hell's going on down there?'

Captain Childs had been below on the main deck. The
two men – captain and pilot – met on the passenger deck
and went into the big cabin together to see what was
going on. Minnie had left the bow of the boat and had
already reached Tilda when there was a scream from the
good wives. The *Spread Eagle* nudged a sandbar and
came to a juddering halt alongside the bank, its paddle
spinning fruitlessly. The stoker stopped the engine and
banked the fires. Every member of the crew then went
upstairs to squeeze into the main cabin.

Minnie was worried about Roxanne and me, but the
room was so crowded, she couldn't get inside the door.
Meanwhile, we were pushed to the far side and had no
chance to get out. It was a disgraceful thing for the pilot
to leave the wheelhouse, but not, I've been told,
unknown. Pilots are very much a law unto themselves.
The noise was so great, I couldn't hear what the captain
said when we ran aground. He looked extremely

78

annoyed, as well he might. No one else paid the smallest attention. Wick was smiling broadly, no longer bored, and certainly not attempting to keep the peace.

Before the poker game could get under way, the rules had to be agreed. Butcher wanted to play draw poker and Albert wanted to play five card stud. They agreed to let the dealer choose. No one else wanted to join the game at all.

I could see their point. This was not going to be a friendly game of cards. Mr Butcher was a violent, erratic man who had been drinking for several hours. No man of sense would want to win against him. On the other hand, Albert was known to be extremely skilled. No man of sense imagined he *could* win against a good professional gambler.

Albert, probably thinking of the size of pots he might win, refused to play a two-handed game, so Wick, having returned from putting Mr Butcher's gun away, reluctantly agreed to sit in. They decided on a two cent limit, and agreed that the game should last for no more than three hours. All three men then anted up their two cents for the pot.

The room was hot and smoky, and I was already bored. I leaned close to Roxanne and suggested that we leave. She pointed out that it would be difficult to push our way to the door on the far side of the room. Besides, she insisted, it was going to get interesting any minute now. I very much doubted it.

A funny thing seems to happen to men when they sit down to play cards. They start looking very important; they sprawl in their seats; they give each other hard, suspicious looks and talk out of the sides of their mouths. On the other hand, I had seen my mother playing poker on many occasions and had never known her to lose her natural good humour.

Albert picked up the new pack of cards, showed it to Wick and Mr Butcher, then slit the seal with a thumbnail. With the backs of his fingers, he slid the pack across to Mr Butcher on his left, who cut the cards and turned up a six of clubs. Wick's cut showed us a ten of diamonds. Albert cut what was left of the pack and turned up an ace. Mr Butcher mopped his forehead and accused Albert of cheating. There was a collective groan of impatience from the crowd.

Albert was to deal, and since it was dealer's choice, the men would be playing a hand of five card stud. Wick shuffled once and returned the pack. Butcher cut then Albert picked up the cards and dealt a card face-down to each man. With a great show of secrecy Albert, Mr Butcher and Wick then lifted a corner of their cards to take a peek. For once, Mr Butcher made no complaint. In fact, such an idiotic grin spread across his ignorant face that everyone knew he was play-acting to impress Albert. The man was a prize fool. After all, what could one card tell him?

The next card each man received was dealt face-up. When an ace of spades came to rest on top of Mr Butcher's face-down card, he was practically hysterical. Wick got a two and Albert a ten. They bet on the round and continued in this way until there were four cards face-up in front of each man, and one face-down. Both Wick and Albert had a collection of odd cards before them. No wonder they folded, refusing to bet any more. Mr Butcher was furious. He won the pot but it wasn't worth much.

When it was Wick's turn to deal, he also chose stud, and won the hand for a modest pot. The game continued with modest or small pots being won by both Wick and Mr Butcher. Albert always folded as soon as he saw, or thought he could tell, that he had no chance of winning. This tactic made Wick smile wryly. Mr Butcher swore a lot.

It was once more Mr Butcher's turn to deal, and once again he chose to deal a hand of draw poker. In this version of the game all the cards are held in the hand, but a player may ask for up to four new cards, while discarding the same number. Albert asked for two cards. Wick gave him a speculative glance, asked for three cards, looked at them briefly and folded. Mr Butcher took three, then tried to look as if he didn't care two cents what cards he held. He might try to hide his elation behind his bushy beard, but it was no use. Everybody knew he expected to win.

The bidding continued between the two men until – I suspect – Albert thought Mr Butcher's nerve would fail him. But the mountain man kept on betting until he ran out of friends to borrow from. Then he called.

'Three of a kind,' said Albert quietly as he laid his cards face-up on the table.

'Two pairs!' cried Mr Butcher. He reached out to scoop the money towards him. 'Two pairs beats three of a kind, gambling man.'

Wick half-stood to reach across the table and grab Mr Butcher by the wrist. 'Three of a kind beats two pairs, Butcher. You know that. You've been living out in the wilds too long, I guess. You mustn't have had anybody to play poker with, except maybe grizzly bears, and I'm not too sure you could beat them! Three of a kind *always* beats two pairs. You lose.'

A comical look of disappointment passed across Mr Butcher's face as he realized his mistake. 'He cheated. You can tell he did. I seen his hand go inside his coat. Anybody else notice that? He was quick but I seen it. Why else is he wearing a coat in this heat? Tell me that.'

'Just shut your mouth and play poker, Butcher,' said Wick. 'You stink up the room every time you speak. You've got very nearly three hours to get your money back.'

'That's a hunnert dollar pot!' yelled Mr Butcher.

I thought Wick said something at that point, but whatever it was, it was drowned out. The crowd roared

81

with delight as Butcher, having had enough of reasoned argument, stood up to take a round-armed swing at Albert across the table.

Several of Mr Butcher's friends had loaned him twenty dollars or more. They were quite prepared to cry 'Cheat!' What had they to lose by discrediting Albert, after all? I thought Albert was in deep trouble.

The gambler was prepared for whatever might come. I supposed sore losers were a well-known hazard in his line of work. With both hands on the table edge, he pushed his chair back against the wall and out of his way. Butcher's fist missed him by at least a foot. In one fluid movement, the gambler rose to his feet, seemed about to remove his coat, thought better of it, and braced himself for battle.

In the seconds it took Butcher to move around the table, I glanced at Wick. Captain Childs was screaming in his ear. Wick remained seated, leaning on the back two legs of his chair, smiling unconcernedly.

'You chicken-pluckin' coward!' yelled Butcher, giving Jenkins a shove on the chest that sent the slighter man staggering back against the wall. 'Puny damned thief! You can't cheat Americans that-a-way. We don't give our money away to foreigners.'

Jenkins recovered and began some shoving and name-calling of his own. Unfortunately, his aggressive words lost him what little sympathy he had among the crowd. Everyone was now calling him a cheat, except Wick who was quietly gathering up the money on the table.

Albert and Mr Butcher continued name-calling for almost a minute. I wondered if I was the only person present to notice that the years had fallen away from them and they were boys again, puffing out their chests and issuing wild challenges. I had seen all this so often among the boys I taught. Why didn't everyone just laugh and tell them to stop being so childish?

Alternatively threatening and bragging, the two men were working themselves up to fighting pitch where caution would desert them, and they would be prepared to risk a blow by throwing one. Amazingly, the male spectators clearly thought it was all so noble and manly! In spite of the bad feeling and name-calling, the quarrel might have ended without a blow being struck, if someone – anyone – had acted sensibly.

Two greenhorns who had most unwisely loaned money to Mr Butcher began shouldering their way forward, pushing Roxanne and me out of the way so hard that we crashed against the wall. They grabbed Albert and held his arms behind him, inviting Mr Butcher to take a swing. A look of intense fear, quickly suppressed, disfigured Albert's face. I felt bile rise in my throat, and at the same time, sensed Roxanne's fear.

The other passengers seemed to be elated by this unfair tactic. They pressed even closer. Roxanne and I took a buffeting. Out of the corner of my eye, I saw Wick return his chair to its proper position and begin to stand up. Butcher's blow just below the ribs drove the wind from Albert's lungs. The next one – to the nose this time – drew a fountain of blood, the sight of which sent the roaring crowd into a frenzy. For the first time, I began to fear for my own safety, and Roxanne's.

Jenkins' legs gave under him as fresh blows rained down. I was sickened, but couldn't look away. The men were at boiling point. Wick was battling his way towards Albert against a sea of jostling elbows, flying fists and trampling feet. My own feet were beneath several stomping boots. I thought I would be lucky if no bones were broken. The roar of sixty voices calling for the death of one man was deafening, an ugly animal sound, vicious enough to chill the blood of any sane woman. I don't think they knew or cared why Albert should be picked on. It was just that the lust for violence had them in its grip.

There was no room to keep out of the way of the fighting men and seemingly no way of escape. Wick reached Albert, began to prise clutching fingers from his arms, began dragging the gambler by one arm through a hail of blows towards the door. He incurred the wrath of the crowd in doing so, of course.

He turned to me. Although he was but two feet away, I couldn't hear his voice. I read his lips, however. 'Come on!' He held out his hand to me.

I grasped the outstretched hand, reached for Roxanne with my free hand and we trailed through the crowd. The door was opened for us by the captain who was vainly pleading for order.

Albert stumbled to the guard rail and vomited over the side. Wick released my hand, only to grab me by the forearm, the better to deliver a stinging lecture.

'Can't you ever behave like a lady? Must you go where you're not wanted? Even you must have been able to guess that there was going to be trouble.'

'Of course I couldn't guess. You were there to keep order.' My feet were beginning to throb, my arm hurt where he was holding it. Minnie and Tilda joined us. Directly behind us, the uproar continued in the main cabin.

Robbed of their foreign victim, the men were turning on one another, complaining of imagined insults, pushing and shoving and roaring expletives, fighting for the fun of it.

'We've run aground,' said Wick close to my face. 'We'll be here for hours. Get yourselves off this boat and stay away until you can see and hear that everything is back to normal. They're fighting now. Next they'll turn to you four for a bit of fun. Do you think you've got the sense to stay out of trouble for a while? I've got to see this man to his cabin and guard him. I think they'll be coming for him if they don't tire themselves out fighting one another.'

'We'll get away,' said Minnie. Her plain face was red with anger. 'Just don't go talking to Carlotta that way. You ought to be ashamed of yourself.'

Wick snorted, heaved Albert back from the rail and started with him towards the cabin. We four quickly made plans to go ashore in search of peace and quiet.

7

Before leaving the *Spread Eagle*, Minnie returned briefly to our cabin. As a result, we had a change of clothing and four canteens with us. We could find a stream for sure, she told us, have a bath and put on fresh clothes. We could fill the canteens and have fresh water to drink tonight and tomorrow morning. All we had to do was find the stream.

'You know,' said Minnie, 'I'm really enjoying walking through the woods here. I was born on a farm in Kentucky and spent many a day walking in the hills. Husband came through Kentucky about twelve year ago and carried me off to St Louis. I thought I'd never stop crying after saying goodbye to my pa and four brothers, but I've never heard from them from that day to this, and I've got used to it now. Wouldn't have been the same if my ma had been living when I left home.

'We rented a few acres about twenty miles from St Louis and tried to grow vegetables and fruit for the big city market. Husband was a bad farmer. Lazy, and later on drunk, too. Many's the time I had to make do with what I could find in the woods to help out.'

Minnie didn't think they had ever been as desperate on the farm as the four of us had been these last days on the *Spread Eagle*. Our cabin was loaded to the roof with flour, bacon, sugar, coffee and tea. But without a fire, we were unable to use our supplies. Captain Childs didn't want us aboard and showed it by refusing to let us cook our food in his kitchen. On the other hand, he let the greenhorns boil water for coffee. The greenhorns bought bread and strong drink on shore or ate in taverns that we four would have been afraid to enter. The rest of the time they gnawed on beef jerky whenever they were hungry. We didn't have any jerky. Minnie lamented the lack of it, blaming herself for the omission.

She cooked as best she could on the landings after dark when the boat was moored for the night. We liked bacon and eggs when we could get eggs. They were expensive, eight cents a dozen, and we could eat a dozen at a time. We couldn't butter the bread we bought, because Minnie had decided that it was best to wait and purchase butter in St Jo. It didn't matter, though, because bacon dripping tasted wonderful on fresh bread. We always ate as much as we could at night. During the day we listened to our stomachs playing tunes on our backbones.

We found our stream after about a fifteen minute walk. It wasn't very large, but it would do. It was rather picturesque, and at one place fell into a small pool from a ledge three feet above. Minnie filled the canteens, then we took turns stripping down and sitting in the icy water for a two minute bath. I went first and ducked my head in the water, giving my hair a good scrub with bar soap, so that I could later arrange it the way I liked it. The others followed suit. We all looked better in fresh clothes and neatly combed hair. It makes a woman feel good to know that she's clean and looking as fine as she can.

We crept back to our cabin and got some supplies, then returned to the shore. Minnie could get a good fire burning in no time at all. We three gathered firewood to keep it going while she fried up some bacon and johnny cakes. Wick had given us a jug of cider and four small potatoes, which Minnie put around the fire. We sat around the blaze and ate with our fingers like squaws, and passed the cider until there was nothing left to eat and very little liquid sloshing in the bottom of the jug. Then we found ourselves a shady spot in full view of the packet and went to sleep.

Captain Childs was in a temper. The excitement of the

fight was over and he was beginning to calculate the damage. The main cabin was in a poor state, apparently. The cabin passengers were forced to eat their midday meal on deck.

The important thing was to get the packet moving as soon as possible. The captain had already called for a wad of steam and instructed the paddle to be reversed. He ordered the steam capstans – two long spars at the bow of the boat – to be lowered on to the sandbar at an angle of forty-five degrees. With the poles giving some purchase, the cables could then haul the boat backwards a few feet. The spars could, if necessary, be lowered again and the process repeated. Grasshoppering, as it was called, was slow and tedious but remarkably effective. It was also preferable to unloading the boat until it was light enough to float over or off the sandbar. Using this method, the roustabouts took five hours to get the boat off the sandbar.

'I've got the devil's own luck,' the captain said to Wick. 'We'll have to stay tied up here overnight. I'm sending the men ashore to cut some wood – it took a powerful lot of steam to get her off that bar. I couldn't get up enough steam now to reach Lexington. I'd like to give that pilot of mine a good hiding, but I can't say a word to him, because you know what he's like. If I so much as look cross-eyed at him, he'll be off. And then what would we do? He hasn't even apologized to me, nor is he likely to. And me paying him one hundred and twenty-five dollars a month.'

The sun was low in the sky when the *Billy Jo,* an old sidewheeler, steamed past the moored *Spread Eagle.* Wick was in the wheelhouse. We four were on the shore side of the passenger cabins.

'Estes!' shouted a man from the *Billy Jo* and the four of us stood up and cowered in the shadow of the cabins. 'Where's them women?' Bullmouth's voice shattered the peace of the early evening.

'Got off at Hermann!' replied Wick without hesitation.

'Why'd they do that?'

'They like rich Germans!' called Wick cheerfully. The *Billy Jo* was making good time. Bullmouth's next remark was inaudible.

Very soon Wick joined us on the cabin deck, smiling broadly. The captain came up the iron steps from the main deck and met him as he reached my side. 'I grant you,' said the captain. 'The town of Hermann is full of Germans, many of them rich. And I'm quite sure these girls would like to get their hands on some vine grower's money. But why did you bother to tell any lie at all? That was Bullmouth Boyd calling to you, wasn't it? What are you up to?'

'I'm merely trying to save you some aggravation. Bullmouth is a trouble-maker and a thief, as you well know.'

Captain Childs gave me a suspicious look. 'Is there anything going on I don't know about?'

Wick smiled pleasantly. 'There are lots of things going on that you don't know about, but nothing that need concern you. Don't worry. Everything is under control.'

The captain shrugged, then turned away to go below. It had been a very bad day for him. He would be glad, he said, when it was over.

'A word with you, Carlotta.' Wick's smile had slipped away as soon as the captain turned his back. He led me to the stern, leaned on the rail and studied the stationary paddle wheel. The sun had long since dried the paddles that were above the water. The wood was grey and dull. The twisting river was headed due north at this point, which meant that the stern was exposed to the setting sun whose red glow cast long shadows. River smells, forest smells and the hot damp air clutched at my throat, making me feel as if I might not be able to draw one more breath.

'Keep yourselves out of sight when we get to Lexington,' he murmured in a low voice. 'With any luck, Bullmouth will head back towards Hermann tomorrow morning in search of you.'

'Thank you for your kindness, Wick. Bullmouth has an evil look about him. Mr Walkern wanted us to travel to New Orleans with him. We couldn't do that.'

'You are the biggest damned fool I ever met. I have to admit you had me fooled. I thought you were different. Maybe you aren't so dumb, after all. Maybe I'm the one who's a fool.'

'You don't understand.'

'I'd be happy to hear your explanation.'

Male voices rose up from the deck below. Profanities filled the evening air. The men were gambling and would carry on noisily until the small hours of the morning.

'Everybody, men and women, have been mean to us, although we have not harmed anyone except possibly Bullmouth Boyd and Mr Walkern. We have been snubbed, denied drinking water and cooking facilities, and turned away when we wanted to pray.'

Wick sighed as he turned round and leaned his back against the railing. The dying sun fell full on his face, rinsing the blue from his eyes, making them a ghostly grey. 'Far be it from me to defend bad behaviour. I know you have been dealt with harshly by these people, but try to see it from their point of view. We're going to a frontier where life is hard and dangerous. Some will die. All these people are just looking after their own. They haven't got energy enough to care about strangers. The Good Wives think you are going to woo their husbands away from them, maybe give them a disease. The captain thinks you are going to be a source of trouble, perhaps cause a few fights.'

I banged my fist on the railing. 'In future, I shall be looking after *my* own. We have been forced to stick together. Minnie, Roxanne and Tilda are the only family I have. Back in Boston, I never realized how some people are picked on unjustly. My mother protected me from unpleasantness when I was a child and, of course, she was so strong – but no one, I now see, thinks we are even human. *"If you prick us, do we not bleed?"* '

Smiling broadly, Wick leaned close to me. ' *"If you tickle us, do we not laugh? If you poison us, do we not die? And if you wrong us, shall we not revenge?"* What will be your revenge, Carlotta?'

Amazement took my breath away. 'You know *The Merchant of Venice!* But I thought you disliked English writers,' was all I could think of to say.

'I don't like English writers, and that includes Shakespeare. But I had a good schooling, and my mother insisted I read everything the man wrote. I have to admit he said some real good things.'

I felt incapable of defending myself against the criticisms of a man who had read Shakespeare and thought he had written some 'real good things'! What would Carlton have said about that literary pronouncement?

It was all so unfair. The little learning I had managed to snatch for myself had been purchased with hours of domestic labour. Wick's education seemed to have been effortlessly gained. He didn't appreciate what his mother had done for him.

'It's getting dark,' I said. 'I'll have to see what Minnie wants to do about cooking this evening.'

'Don't go ashore tonight. We're in pretty wild territory here. Anyway, the cook is making an apple pie for me. I'll bring it to you after I've had my dinner.'

'Why are you being so kind to us?' I asked sarcastically. 'Are you looking after *your* own?'

I was already walking away as I spoke, and therefore almost didn't hear him say: 'I reckon I am.'

A funny thing happened to me just then. I

remembered a girl of my mother's describing the first time she had fallen in love. It made her, she said, sick to her stomach. Hearing Wick's deep voice saying, 'I reckon I am,' made me feel just the same. The feeling took the starch out of my legs, a glorious sensation, followed almost immediately by intense pain. It was hopeless, of course. I could never win this beautiful man's respect.

I thought about turning around and telling him that I intended to pay back all of Mr Walkern's money that was left. Tell him I was a good girl, and would leave the others to look out for themselves. But I *couldn't* leave them. Not Minnie, because I loved her. Not the other two because my mother had ruined them. And, anyway, what if I told Wick I would? Would he love me then? More likely, he would cast me aside just as Carlton had done. I couldn't bear that. I would never again give a man the chance to hurt me as Carlton had.

So I clutched my stomach where the pain was and walked up to Minnie at the bow, talking brightly about I don't know what. After a few minutes, Wick left the stern railing and went to his cabin.

When the pie was delivered to us, hot and smelling of cinnamon, we divided it into four and ate it all, washing it down with cup after cup of coffee so strong even Minnie thought it was worth drinking. The evening was cool and pleasant on deck, under a full moon. We sat and swapped stories about our early days. Roxanne said I was not a bad sort of person, considering what a soft life I had led. That surprised me and I said so. I never thought of my early life as *soft*. I was told by all three of them that living in a fine house with servants was very much softer than anything they had known. They said I was spoiled, but that I hadn't let it ruin me.

'If you want to know what hard is,' said Roxanne. 'you ought to of been in my home. My ma wouldn't stir herself to cook or clean or pay any attention to her kids.

There were three of us and I was the youngest. My pa was a roustabout on the levee, and my oh my, could he drink! Pa used to love to beat up on me. Not the others so much, but just me. I don't ever remember him saying one kind word to me. And I don't remember my ma ever telling him not to treat me so bad.'

'I'm sorry to hear it,' I said. 'You are right about my soft life in one respect. Neither my mother nor my grandmother ever beat me.'

'Maybe you never did anything wrong, Carlotta,' mused Minnie. 'Is that why you left home, Roxanne? Because of your pa? What happened?'

'About four years ago, my pa said he was tired of working on the levee. I think he was tired of all of us, too. With some friends of his, he built a raft to take cargo to New Orleans. They used to float all the way down the Mississippi with the current. Then they'd sell the cargo, break up the raft and sell the timber. They had to walk back, which took them three months, because it's about a thousand miles. He made more money than he done on the levee, so we always had food in our bellies. But the best part was he would be gone for four months at a time. Two years ago, while he was away, my ma and the boys all got yellow fever. I couldn't nurse them properly, and they died. Funny thing, I never got sick at all. Well, I got them buried, then I just packed up my things – I only had one other dress – and left the old shack. I wasn't about to wait around until that mean old man came home. Thing is, I don't think he ever *did* come back. I was fifteen and I was glad that Belle took me in, I can tell you.'

Tilda said she would be twenty in October, but didn't say anything about her family. Minnie told us about the hardships of her life in Kentucky, but stressed that she had been very happy until her mother died. She never would have married her husband if her mother had still been alive. Being tired of cooking and washing for five

93

men, she had accepted the first man who asked her to marry him.

'I thought things would be better,' said Minnie, 'but they was worse. My father and brothers was all hard-working sober men, and we always had meat on the table. Husband was *weak*.'

'And Tilda here,' said Roxanne spitefully. 'Her ma was a common old street whore, and she don't know who her father was any more than you do, Carlotta. You was working on the streets with your ma until she died, wasn't you, Tilda? I bet you was as glad as I was when Belle took you in.'

'These mosquitoes are aggravating me to death,' said Tilda. 'I'm going to the cabin. Anybody else coming?'

Roxanne said she would go with Tilda. Minnie and I sat in silence for a minute or two.

'Well,' said Minnie finally. 'I'm tuckered out. I think I'll sleep tonight, and if I do, it will be the first time on board this old rattletrap. You see, you was wrong about Tilda, at least. She's a whore from way back. Born to a whore.'

'So was I.'

'I know, but I reckon your daddy must of been a mighty fine man.'

'He went with whores, didn't he?'

'Aw, don't be so hard on him. All men do that.'

'Neither of those girls have had a chance in life, Minnie. I've got to keep trying.'

Minnie stood up and stretched. 'Sometimes I get so aggravated with you, Carlotta, I could spit blood. When we get to St Jo, *they* won't help get started in some good business. You won't see them washing clothes.'

'You won't see me washing clothes, either. There must be something better we can do.'

I was reluctant to go indoors on such a night, so I stayed on deck alone. It amused me that my friends thought I was grand, because I had always slept in clean linen and eaten well. My mother had been a rather casual woman, but she had shown her love in little ways. I had been the recipient of many hugs and kisses, and was frequently given small presents.

My grandmother had been an altogether sterner person, but she devoted her life to me. I couldn't doubt her love. Even my few years in service had enabled me to live in a fine home and eat properly. Perhaps I had been spoiled, after all.

I felt very sad for the others. Their stories made me more determined than ever to create some sort of decent life for them in St Jo. But as we came nearer to that town, I had stopped dreaming about miracles and started worrying about realities. What could we possibly do? Especially considering that Minnie's idea of heaven was to have her own clothes-line so she could take in washing. And the other two? Ignorant, untrained and lazy. What future did they have? Then, too, I worried because the more of Mr Walkern's money I spent, the more I would have to pay back one day. Before I could pay it back, the man might well come for us and accuse us of stealing. Whenever I thought about going to the penitentiary, my hands went sweaty. I had committed a serious crime. Nobody would want to know why I had done it. Really, this short journey on the packet was a little holiday, a time of rest and safety before the bad times. I was finding it increasingly difficult to sleep at night, and when I did sleep, I had terrible nightmares.

Wick left the main cabin and silently sat down in the chair next to me., Together, we stared out at the dark woodland, listening for the night noises of animals and birds, but hearing instead the carousing greenhorns on the deck below.

'Nice night,' he said. 'I'll bet it beats any night you ever saw in Massachusetts.'

'I had very little time to study the Massachusetts nights, and never went near a river. But I agree, it is a beautiful night. Missouri is a pretty state. I never said it wasn't, but it gets too hot in the summertime.'

Wick chuckled. 'That's true. Sometimes it's a hundred and fifteen in the shade, and so humid you think you're not going to be able to draw your next breath, and then it only cools down to ninety after dark. Those are the times when I think of the desert. Out there it's hot and dry, but at night it can get real cold. Sort of sets you up for the hot days.'

'I don't really know much about Missouri. My mother liked towns. She used to say St Louis had everything anybody could want. We only once took a trip out into the country. I got stung by poison ivy. My arm came up in blisters and I felt terrible. My mother said that was the last time she'd go out into the wilds.'

'How far out into the country did you go?'

'Eighteenth Street.' Wick laughed loudly. 'All those years ago, it *was* countrified on Eighteenth Street,' I insisted.

'And back in Boston, there's nothing but sidewalks and streetlights turning night into day. I'm surprised you're not scared to be out on deck at this hour.'

'I'm being brave,' I said.

The door of the main cabin opened. A man stuck his head out and demanded that Wick came back inside to finish the game. Wick said goodnight and was gone. I decided I had had enough of the outdoors and went to our cabin.

The room was a terrible change from the sweet night air, smelling as it did of smoked bacon slowly going rancid in the heat. Tilda and Minnie were undressed and in bed. Roxanne was still fully clothed.

'I'm not staying in here,' she said sulkily. 'I'm not sleepy. I don't even feel like having a real good fight with Minnie.'

Tilda clapped her hands like a child. 'Oh, goody! Where are we going, Roxanne? There's not a lot to do at this time of night, and the mosquitoes were mighty fierce out there on the deck.'

Roxanne patted her hair into place. 'I don't care what you do. I'm going to Albert Jenkins' cabin to see how he is. I understand he was beat up pretty bad.'

Tilda sat up on her bed as Roxanne left the cabin. 'Spiteful cow. Why'd she leave me behind?'

'Maybe because she's tired of dragging you around,' said Minnie. 'You are the most useless woman I ever did see. Why, it's a wonder you ain't too lazy to eat! Although anyone can see you got plenty of energy to reach for second helpings.'

Tilda looked around for something to throw. Finding nothing she turned her face towards the wall and began wailing loudly.

'Minnie,' I said, 'why don't you take my turn in the bed?'

'I'll sleep on the floor. I know I'm older than you, Carlotta, but I'm not decreipt! Besides, I do believe it's more comfortable on the floor.'

The Morgans had the next cabin to ours. Mrs Morgan banged on the party wall. 'Can't you people ever act like decent folks? Keep quiet.'

'Can't you ever mind your own business, you old buzzard?' called Tilda.

I reached her in one stride and put a hand over her mouth. 'Shut up before you get us thrown off the boat. For God's sake, go to sleep. I'm so tired I can hardly stand.'

Twenty minutes later, I was happy to be woken so that I could hear Roxanne's account of her time with Albert Jenkins.

'You know what? He's been lying there all that time alone. Wick Estes sort of washed the blood off his face, but you know what men are. I cleaned Albert up properly, although he kept cussing me out, saying he didn't want to be fussed about, and why didn't I go

97

away. I said I'd come back tomorrow and shave him, but he said he'll be able to look after hisself tomorrow. His lower lip is swole right up so that he can hardly talk, and I think his nose is broke. He's not going to be so pretty from now on.'

'Did anybody think to feed him?' I asked.

'Wick offered to bring him something, but he's not hungry. He's been hurt real bad. Say, Carlotta, you remember when he said all them funny things to Wick Estes? "Nib sprig" and things like that? Well, what he meant is, Wick is a rich man's son who likes to keep company with low types like us. He don't fancy his own sort. That's what Albert meant. I think it's true, too, don't you?'

I supposed it was. That would explain why Wick sought out our company. Minnie had said it was because he was sweet on me, but I had always known that wasn't true.

Roxanne held up three well-used playing cards. 'Albert gave me these. Look at what he taught me. Now see here, a nine, a ten and a jack of hearts.' She placed them face-down on Tilda's bed, showed us that the jack was in the middle, then began to slide them around, changing their order. 'Now then, find the jack.'

I picked up the jack. 'This is a card trick that's lost money for a lot of people. Is that how he earns his living?'

Roxanne was sliding the cards around again. 'Different things. This is the quickest way, he said. That's why I asked him to show me how to do it. If I get good at it, we can make money for ourselves, can't we? Find the jack.'

Minnie lifted a card and held it out for us to see. It was the jack. 'I hope you didn't pay him anything for teaching you this trick, because he sure didn't teach you very good.'

Roxanne tossed the cards across the room. 'I guess I got to practise.'

'As I understand it,' I said, 'these men practise for years before they're good enough to fool others. Don't expect to be able to do it yourself. It could be very expensive and rather dangerous to find out you are no good at it.'

'Aw, it was just an idea. I'll see what else I can find out from Albert. One thing is certain. He's got plenty of money, and anybody can see he don't work for it.'

8

Most of the cabin passengers and all the greenhorns left the boat at Independence, a favourite starting point for the trek West. It was a pleasant town of about two thousand people, with rows of two-storey houses, an imposing county courthourse and roads choked with wagons, oxen and mules. I was thankful that we had not decided to disembark at this popular town. The citizens of Independence might bless themselves that so much business was coming their way, but the travellers were to be pitied.

I was sure St Jo wouldn't be nearly so crowded. The town was very small and hadn't been a town at all for too many years. Wick said it was built on a hill and had a nice landing. I expected the residents to be reasonably civilized, but not in too much of a hurry. Not like this madhouse of Independence. My only fear had been that most of the passengers would decide to travel all the way to St Jo by river, to shorten the overland trip by a few days.

Fortunately, we four were the only passengers left aboard, except for Albert Jenkins, Wick and the Indians. Captain Childs' mood improved mightily when the Good Wives left the packet. He gave us an extra cabin and actually invited us to take our meals with him in future. Fresh water became available to us, and we were able to wash out a few items of clothing for the first time since we had left St Louis.

It was a pleasure to sit down in convivial company to a well-cooked hot meal. Albert Jenkins had almost recovered from his injuries, and he and Wick managed to pass an evening in each other's company without quarrelling. Everybody enjoyed a good night's sleep, undisturbed by the noise on the landing.

We awoke to grey skies and the promise of rain. From that morning until Saturday afternoon when we arrived at St Jo, the rain varied from slight to torrential, but it never let up for so much as an hour.

We rounded a huge bend in the capricious river, and saw before us the town occupying hilly ground for a good half-mile inland from the landing. There was a smattering of brick buildings, but most of the houses were made of wood, some of them no more than shanties that would blow down in a strong wind. To my great disappointment, I saw that the houses were far out-numbered by tents on the hillside – large ones that a man could stand up in, and small, single-pole ones that were exactly like the one we had brought with us. Whatever their size, tents are a pathetic sight in the rain. They reminded me of the woebegone dogs which trotted about on the landing, tails tucked in, noses poking into anything that might be edible. Dogs and tents were both sagging, and no match for hostile elements.

Moored next to the *Spread Eagle* was a fat ferryboat with a wide main deck and narrow superstructure. The sturdy gangplank bent under the weight as covered wagons rolled aboard, some of them pulled by as many as four yoke of oxen. A second ferry was just on its way back from the Kansas territory side. This one on the St Jo side was quickly taking on board its full complement of wagons and owners. I didn't think there was room for more than six rigs at a time.

On shore, men hung their heads beneath shapeless felt hats, lifted their boots with effort out of the ankle-deep mud every step they took and huddled as much as they could under their India-rubber capes to keep off the worst of the weather. We hadn't bought any India-rubber capes. We hadn't even thought of it.

I saw women and children peeping out from beneath

101

the canvas covers of their wagons where it must have been very crowded. The wagons were no more than ten feet long and half as wide. How could a family possibly carry enough supplies in such a small space to last them for five months over two thousand miles? In one wagon the top of a grandfather clock was just visible above the head of a desperate-looking woman who was seated on the box. The rain spattered the wooden case every time the wind gusted. Before long this precious family treasure would begin to warp.

'Look at the long-case clock,' said Wick beside me. 'They'll never get to California with that.'

'It will be warped if they do.'

'I said they'll never get to California with it. You can't eat it, mend the wagon with it or put it to work in the place of a lame ox. It's just unnecessary weight. Three weeks out, when the going is heavy and the beasts are tired, they'll throw it out, and the missus will cry a little. By the time they get to California or Oregon territory, there will be nothing left in that wagon but necessities, a few sick children and a woman worn to the bone – *if* none of them die on the trail.'

There were not too many hours of daylight left, but I could count at least a hundred equipages lined up in pairs right up the main street. The mules and oxen seemed resigned to a long wait. There were restless sheep, small herds of shorthorn cattle, cows, and hundreds of chickens setting up a terrible row in cages hung from the outside of the wagons. Everyone looked bored, angry and anxious, all at the same time.

'They won't all get away tonight,' said Wick. 'But they won't dare move out of line for fear of losing their turn. So they'll stay right where they are all night long.'

I was beginning to feel a little queasy. St Jo was the end of the line for us. This was the place where we had planned to start a new life and make a lot of money very quickly. But what could we possibly do here? Desperate alternatives to disembarking from the *Spread Eagle* flitted through my mind. I could slip away from the others, return to St Louis and throw myself on the mercy of Otis Walkern. I could give him back what was left of his money. We hadn't spent much of it. But to do that, I would have to get the money out of the captain's safe without the others knowing.

When we left the packet, Albert Jenkins lifted his beaver hat and said goodbye. Wick lifted his soft felt hat and said, 'Be good, ladies,' which made Albert laugh.

We had already retrieved our money from the captain. I took a few gold coins from the purse, and we deposited the rest in a small bank. The clerk counted out the money very carefully and told us how much there was. We made him count it again. On the second counting, it still came to just under twelve hundred dollars. Not two thousand at all. We had no doubt that Bullmouth had stolen some, but how could I prove that to Mr Walkern? He would claim he had loaned me two thousand and that I owed him six! What a fool I had been to sign that contract! I deserved to go to the penitentiary for being stupid, if not for stealing.

We huddled together for comfort and told each other what an evil man Bullmouth was. I wished I could just give up, but there were the others to think of. Minnie had been desperate once. She had sat by the waters of the Mississippi and waited to die. In the face of this new blow, she was stronger, saying stoutly that it didn't matter. We'd manage somehow. I took a deep breath and told the women we had better get ourselves settled for the night; I was pleased to see that Roxanne and Tilda were reassured by our outward calm. Our moment of despair and panic was over.

Livermore's general store was so crowded, we had to wait outside in the rain for our turn to go in and buy a few things. We had already tried to rent a room at St Jo's only hotel, but there were none to spare. Renting ten to a room, the proprietor told us. Now there wasn't even room to sleep on the floor.

So it would have to be the tent on the hill, after all. We bought an India-rubber sheet to put on the ground and capes which we put on over our wet clothes. It was cold now, with no hint of the fine weather we had enjoyed on the packet. We finally found a boy willing to load our supplies into a handcart. He demanded two dollars to take them up the hill!

It was fortunate for us that Minnie knew how to erect the tent. The work was quickly done, so we soon knew that four women could not sleep stretched out in it. It wasn't even big enough to hold our supplies.

There were several places in town which served food, but long lines of miserble men stood outside every one of them. Minnie said that was just fine with her. We couldn't afford to eat in hotels and saloons, anyway. She would cook for us if we would collect firewood.

There were so many people looking for firewood in the nearby woodland, I was surprised there were any trees left. Certainly, the hillside had been churned to mud. Every blade of grass had been trampled on or eaten by the animals. There were no eggs to be bought anywhere, so we had bacon, hot biscuits and coffee. Our spirits were low, but we managed to get through the first night somehow.

The next day the rain stopped. The sun came out and warmed us all. Best of all, I found a way of making ten dollars.

A spelling bee was to take place that night. An area in front of the new courthouse had been roped off, and a platform erected. You paid five cents to get inside the roped off area. If you wanted to enter the bee and try for the ten dollar prize, you paid another five cents. Twenty-five cents would get the four of us inside the rope, and me into the competition. I was a good speller.

Hundreds of people turned up, and there was a lot of

104

confusion that night. The weather had been miserable for days, and people had been cooped up with nothing to do. Now that the night looked like being fine and dry, almost the whole of St Jo had turned out for the entertainment. The competition was supposed to start at eight o'clock.

The organizers – three gambling men in their late twenties with grease on their hair and knowing looks in the eyes – had made rather haphazard arrangements. We contestants, all thirty of us, were left standing around for almost an hour. Half the contestants were women, and we all had to step up on the platform so that the crowd could look us over in good time.

The gamblers were not arranging an evening's fun out of the goodness of their hearts. The crowd were invited to bet on us, and the gamblers not only set the odds but took the bets. I felt like a cow at an auction, or a slave on the block.

Albert Jenkins was there. He pushed his way to the platform and signalled for me to bend down so that we could talk.

'How good a speller are you, Carlotta?'

'Better than some people might expect. I was a schoolteacher.'

'So I heard from Estes. I'm glad you didn't tell anybody else. They're offering very good odds on you. You're the youngest contestant.'

'They haven't looked at my teeth yet,' I said, but he didn't answer. In a hurry to place his bet, I supposed.

The preliminary rounds took an hour. To my surprise, there were a great many good spellers in St Jo that night, and even more people who didn't stand a chance but wanted to win ten dollars. When there were just ten of us left, four women and six men, the questioner declared a recess so that people could place more bets.

I had seen Wick in the crowd before the contest started, but he hadn't shown any sign of recognition when our eyes met. Now, he brought me a glass of cider. I was grateful because I was very thirsty, but I drank sparingly, not wanting to dull my senses. I asked him if he had bet on me. He smiled, shook his head and took away the half-empty glass.

The words became difficult after the intermission. You had just one chance. You had to be sure before you opened your mouth. The man next to me went out on 'Mississippi', which he probably could have spelled in his sleep. Unfortuately for him, he was nervous, stumbled over a letter, started again and was counted out. The word was given to me and I didn't hesitate.

In the next round there were eight of us left. I was asked to spell 'prestidigitator', which was easy. I've used the word myself when organizing spelling bees for my pupils.

At the end of that round we were down to five, and I was the only woman left. Two of the three men before me fell by the wayside over 'antidisestablishmentarianism', but my neighbour got it right. He was a tall gaunt man of about sixty, who spoke oddly because he had lost so many teeth. They called him 'Preacher', and he seemed determined to win.

Now it was my turn for a word, but the questioner wasn't ready to end it all so quickly. He said the contest was getting close. There were just two of us. There was no doubt that I was the prettier contestant, but the question was, could I spell better than the preacher? And would anybody like to place a bet? The crowd roared, so they stopped the contest to give the dumbest members of the audience a chance to bet on a contest that was a bit like betting on the toss of a coin. The preacher stood calmly to attention despite the clamour, with his hands clasped behind his back and his eyes closed.

I, on the other hand, was beginning to feel very nervous. I wanted to win so much that it made me feel faint. We should never have been made to wait at this crucial stage in the contest. For the first time, I had a chance to consider what I must look like. My brown costume was badly crushed, and I would like to have been able to polish my shoes. I used to say you could tell what sort of person you were dealing with if you looked at the shine on his shoes. Now, I hoped nobody was judging me by the state of mine.

I could pick out a few faces in the crowd; Minnie smiling broadly and talking to the woman next to her; Roxanne holding on to Albert Jenkins' arm and looking up into his face. Even from this distance, I could see that Tilda was bored. Wick was over by the side of the platform, talking seriously to two men: one of the organizers and the man who was giving us the words to spell. They looked like brothers, same plump face and waddling way of walking, although neither of them was fat.

Only a few drunken fools chose to bet at this time. The questioner tried to whip up a bit of excitement, but the crowd was growing restless, wanting to know the outcome.

I was given my word. 'A-C-C-O-M-O-D-A-T-I-O-N!' I said quickly. The crowd roared. Minnie waved her hands in the air as she turned to say something to the woman next to her.

'Wrong!' bellowed the questioner, and I thought there might be a riot right there in front of the courthouse. Nine-tenths of the audience couldn't have spelt the word if their lives depended on it. But they had all placed their bets. Those who had backed me to win were not prepared to admit that I had made a mistake, and neither was I.

I turned to the questioner to protest, but the preacher stepped forward, and the people suddenly went quiet. 'A-C-C-O-M-M-O-D-A-T-I-O-N.' The preacher rapped out the letters like a drum roll.

107

'The winner!' croaked the questioner, his voice cracking in the excitement.

In a red-hot rage, I dashed forward to complain, taking first the questioner and then the preacher by the arm, forcing them to look me in the eye. They couldn't hear what I was saying, because of the noise. I didn't notice at the time, but there were more than a dozen fist-fights going on. I did hear several men discharge their shotguns into the air.

Wick came up on the platform. I turned to him, telling him to get a dictionary; these ignorant people didn't know what they were talking about. He took no notice, just tried to drag me off the platform. When I resisted, he put his arms around my waist, lifted me off my feet and carried me away.

'Calm down, Carlotta!' he shouted in my ear. 'You know as well as I do there are two m's in accommodation.'

And, of course, I did know it. It was a tricky word and a favourite in spelling bees. I felt like the damn fool Wick was sure to call me. So much tension had built up inside me that now I just wanted to let go and cry. All I could think about was that I had not only misspelt an easy word, I had also been a poor sport and made a spectacle of myself before a huge crowd.

The organizer waved the crowd to something approaching silence. 'Ladies and gentlemen, we've had a real good time here tonight. It was a close competition – ain't that right?' Shouts, hoots, and a smattering of applause. 'So we're going to change the rules and award the little lady a *second* prize of five dollars!'

Roars from the crowd. I looked suspiciously at Wick. He didn't seem surprised at all, just pushed me back on to the platform so that I could receive the five-dollar gold piece. The organizer then handed the preacher his money, before taking us both by the arm and leading us forward to take a bow.

'Come on, folks, you've had fun tonight. I want y'all to show your appreciation.'

He was expecting applause, and so were the preacher and I as we both bowed deeply. But the crowd had other ideas. A coin landed on the platform. Another and then another, big old pennies and some gold pieces sailed through the air and hurt like the devil when they hit us. Within seconds, the air was thick with them. The prudent thing would have been to move off the platform, but the feeling of exhilaration that came over me as all these people clapped and threw money in appreciation, quite inured me to the stings of coins landing on my face and arms. I bowed again. So did the preacher. We loved it. The ovation lasted for several minutes, accompanied by war whoops and gunfire. I didn't mind about losing the contest. I liked being up there on a makeshift stage, feeling the goodwill of the crowd.

Four young boys picked up the money, supervised by the organizers and Wick. The preacher thought he ought to have two-thirds. Wick said it had probably all been intended for me out of sympathy, and because they thought I was pretty. In the end, we split it equally, and I got a further ten dollars.

Minnie, Roxanne, Tilda and Albert were waiting for us as Wick and I came away with the money. The women didn't seem to be sharing my euphoria.

'Fifteen dollars, Minnie!' I cried, and gave her a quick hug.

'These two no account girls bet five dollars on you and lost, so it's only ten dollars.'

I looked at Roxanne and Tilda in anger, but Albert, the peacemaker, intervened. 'Come on, everybody, let's go get drunk. You, too, Estes.'

I took Albert by the arm. 'You seem very cheerful. Didn't you lose money on me?'

Albert smiled like the cat that ate the cream. 'I bet on you to reach the final five. Got good odds and won ten dollars. I also bet on the preacher to win. Won another five dollars. I'm very grateful to you, Carlotta. I owe you a drink, I think.'

There was a large saloon down on the waterfront, next door to a house of ill-repute that had set up business in a temporary way in a tent. There were three of the girls from the house sitting in the saloon when we arrived, but they soon left. After that, we were the only women present. I wondered what my grandmother would have said if she could have seen me.

'You know your trouble,' said Wick to me as the others talked to one another in loud voices, and all at once.

'I'm sure you're going to tell me.'

'You haven't got a cool head. Now, your ma wouldn't have been able to spell "whore", let alone "accommodation", but if she had been able to spell, she wouldn't have rushed at it the way you did tonight. Cocksure, that's what you were.'

'You don't know what it's like to be standing up in front of a crowd like that. And I can't imagine my mother entering a spelling contest.'

'She entered her own sort of contest. The ladies of St Louis did their damnedest for years to get rid of her. In the early days, I've heard that several men tried to nose their way into her business and take the profits. They got pretty mean. She just hired a few roughnecks and got even tougher.'

'Nothing I do is right as far as you're concerned.'

'It's not as if you can't spell "accommodation". It's just that when the going gets hard, you flap around like a chicken with its head cut off.'

'Thank you. I always like to hear how stupid you think I am.'

'When you get out to the gold fields, if you start getting in a tizzy the first thing that goes wrong, you could find yourself dead.' He had another thought. 'Or on the trail!

110

Big old grizzly bear comes at you, you wouldn't know what to do, and if you did, you probably wouldn't have the sense to do it.'

There was a whiskey bottle sitting on the table. I had refused a drink from it, preferring cider. Now, in a blind fury, I picked up the bottle and took a hefty gulp. As it hit my stomach, I gasped for breath and tears sprang to my eyes.

'See what I mean?' murmured Wick coolly. 'You get mad and don't even know what you're doing.'

About two hours later, Wick and Albert walked with us back to our tent. In the meantime, cider and cautious sips from the whiskey bottle had eased my anger a little. But when we got to the tent, we saw at once that someone had stolen all our bacon. Tilda burst into tears. I wanted to find the culprit and thrash him.

'Never mind, girls,' said Wick, clapping Albert on the back. 'Albert here will buy you some more. He's done very well out of Carlotta tonight. I think he owes it to y'all to buy some more bacon.'

When the men had left, we pulled all our remaining supplies inside the tent for safekeeping. Then we slept as best we could, hunched against them or draped over them. I cuddled up to a bag of cornmeal with my feet stuck outside the tent.

9

The next morning, Albert arrived early with the bacon, two loaves of warm bread which he said were a present from Wick, and an offer of work from the women we had seen in the saloon the night before.

Bacon was seven cents a pound, and we had lost twenty pounds of it. Albert Jenkins' gift was of a better quality than we had lost, and there was more of it.

I put the slab inside the tent. 'The sort of work those girls are offering isn't at all what we had in mind. We've finished with that kind of thing.' I addressed my remarks to Albert, but all the time I was looking at Roxanne and Tilda to gauge their reaction.

Tilda was unimpressed by Albert's offer. 'Looked a dirty old place. Even worse than that shack on the levee what Belle had.'

Roxanne's attitude didn't surprise me. 'Why work, so long as we've got money in the bank?'

'Where are you staying, Albert?' I asked. 'And where's Wick?'

'I'm staying at the hurdy-gurdy house. That's how I happened to know they've got enough business for a few more. I take my meals in the saloon, but the women said that they will see to my linen. In my profession, you have to look smart.'

'One look at your fancy clothes,' laughed Roxanne, 'and people know to watch out, so that they don't lose everything they've got. You ought to dress scruffy like, so's people won't know what you're up to.'

He smiled at her, unoffended, and turned to me. 'Wick has a plot of building land right on the waterfront. He's sleeping there under the stars. Hardly my idea of comfort. He's already arranged for a loan from the bank. I believe he hopes to lay the foundations of a two-storey hotel there in the next day or two. Six rooms and a large dining-room, I think he said.'

'You've looked after yourself right nicely,' said Roxanne, giving him a sassy look.

'There's room for two in my bed if you want to come with me. We could be quite comfortable.'

'Naw, I'm going to please myself for a little while longer.'

'She's staying right here,' said Minnie. 'Tell Wick we're grateful for the bread, and would appreciate it if he'd save us a room in his hotel as soon as it's built. Is there a bath-house in town?'

Albert picked up a leaf and attempted to scrape the mud off his shoes. 'Yes, but you might have to wait for several hours to get in.' He told us he had better be on his way. Card playing began early in St Jo, and he wanted to get back to the saloon before some other gambler took all the greenhorns' money.

It was the last day of May. Summer had arrived; the sky was cloudless, the temperature already climbing rapidly. Soon the ground would be bone hard and much easier to walk on, but we were almost as uncomfortable in the dry heat as we had been in the cold rain. All day we trudged around the town, seeing what it had to offer, arguing about what enterprise we might go in for to make some money. We counted nineteen general stores, a couple of flour mills, sawmills, no less than nine blacksmiths and a great many saddlers and harness-makers. What could we make of that? Washerwomen, said Minnie. Good hot food and clean clothes were what the people of St Jo needed.

St Jo had a permanent population of about a thousand, as well as hundreds of travellers, but it was still a small town. There wasn't all that much to see. We wasted most of the day waiting in line for supplies, for a hot dinner, for a tepid bath, and climbed the hill at dusk with four large canteens of fresh water. Minnie said tonight we could make do with flapjacks. Tomorrow, maybe she would make a rich stew now that she had some bones with a bit of meat on them.

The woman she had been talking to at the spelling bee lived just a few tents away. There were not more than half a dozen women in the whole of this tent city, apart from ourselves, and we soon learned that none of them were going to the gold fields. They were all headed for Oregon territory where the land was rich, and their husbands thought they would make their fortunes by farming.

Roxanne and Tilda said they were dead tired. When they had crawled inside the tent for a gossip, Minnie suggested that we two go over to visit with Mrs Joel Huggens.

She was about Minnie's age, scarecrow-thin, with the pallor common to those who are seriously ill. She moved slowly, and then only if it was absolutely necessary. She had been sitting on a three-legged stool, and ordered one of her sons to bring out the other two stools when she saw that we were coming to sit with her.

There were three children: boys of eight and ten, and a girl of two. The children were filthy, and didn't appear to have had their hair combed for years. All were bare-footed and listless. Mrs Huggens apologized for their appearance, explaining that she just didn't feel she had the strength to clean them up in this place. She reckoned it would do them no harm, and didn't we all have to eat a peck of dirt before we died? That's what she had been told.

The boys stared at us solemnly or played mumbly-peg with clasp knives. The little girl sat on her mother's lap and turned her face away when I spoke to her.

'Remember I told you last night we was going to Oregon territory, Mrs Taylor?' said Mrs Huggens in a weak voice. 'Well, you'll never believe it, but Mr Huggens has gone and changed his mind. We're going to the gold fields. I don't know what to make of it.'

'You ain't got the strength to travel anywhere, Mrs Huggens. You're looking pale as a ghost. Won't you let me fix you something to eat? Broth, that's what you need.' Minnie stood up, ready to return to our tent for food.

'I don't feel hungry, to tell you the truth. And the children, well, they've et. Mr Huggens thinks we're all going to get rich in California. He says if I'm still tired when we get there, I can get me some help around the house. I don't know who'll build the house, though. We had a nice place in Kentucky, but we lost it all. We've come all them miles from Louisville. Now I'm too tuckered out to lift my head.'

Minnie snorted. 'Is he dumb or something?'

'Not when he's sober,' sighed Mrs Huggens. After a while, we stood up to leave. Mrs Huggens said she thought she would just go inside and lie down. Mr Huggens was down in the town, because his mouth was a little dry. He'd be back directly. Minnie and I were not to worry about her.

That night I made the flapjacks, and Minnie made the coffee. The flapjacks stuck to the pan. The coffee, however, was strong the way Minnie liked it. Made your teeth squeak, was the way she put it. She drank four cups.

When we had eaten our fill and finished off the coffee, Tilda stood up and stretched, rubbing her back a little. 'What are we going to do tonight, Carlotta? We can't just sit here on the ground all the time.'

Minnie was tired and made no attempt to hide her irritation with the girls. 'We got a lamp now. We can sit around and talk. What's wrong with that? I would invite Mrs Huggens over to sit a spell, but she looked too sick, and besides we haven't any stools. We'll have to buy ourselves some, Carlotta.'

I thought there might be a storm brewing between Minnie and the girls, so I told them to go down the hill to the saloon. Minnie and I would stay here, because we needed the rest.

'Buy yourselves one glass of cider or one shot of whiskey,' I said sternly. 'If I hear you've been going with men, I'll kick you out. Do you hear?'

Roxanne stepped up to me, hands on hips, chin out-thrust. 'Listen here, Carlotta. We don't like being spoke to like that. I'm just too nervous to sit here by the tent all evening, and that's a fact. Tilda and me, we're used to talking to folks and laughing and everything. But we ain't never going to go with men again. I can promise you that.'

I looked hard at Tilda, but she refused to meet my eye.

'Don't spend too much of what little money we got,' said Minnie. 'Y'all ought to think of our responsibilities.'

I thought we might be on the verge of another quarrel, so I quickly sent the two girls on their way. When they had gone, Minnie and I settled ourselves by the small fire, our eyes drawn to the comforting glow of the embers.

'Sometimes I think I'm no better than them two,' said Minnie quietly. 'I knew they was going to steal all Bullmouth's money. I don't know why I had a part in it. I been a decent woman all my life. But them two's a bad influence. I just thought . . . well, I don't rightly remember what I thought.'

'I know. We must have been crazy. Four women afraid for the future, het up because of the fire. I blame myself. I don't know what made me say it would be all right to steal a hundred dollars, if it wasn't all right to steal two thousand. I fooled myself by calling it a loan. I won't ever judge others harshly again. Maybe a lot of bad things are done when people are het up. But that's not important. What is important is, we've got to find a way to pay it all back.'

116

'Can't you get the bank to send back what we've got left? They do that sort of thing, don't they? And tomorrow I'll start taking in washing. We'll manage.'

I sighed. She meant well, and I hated to upset her but it was important that Minnie should understand what sort of trouble we were in. 'Remember, we've only got twelve hundred dollars to send back. If I send it, Mr Walkern will know it came from St Jo. He'll know where we are. And I signed a contract with him saying I'd borrowed two thousand dollars, not twelve hundred. I daresay that bag did hold two thousand when Mr Walkern gave it to Bullmouth. But how do you think we'd manage to convince Mr Walkern that Bullmouth stole the rest?'

'Oh, Lordy! Can't we just say we warn't thinking straight? Because we warn't, Carlotta. We was all mixed up.'

'I don't think the law takes that sort of thing into account. We got ourselves into trouble. Now we've got to get ourselves out of it.'

I didn't remind Minnie of the promissory note that Roxanne had so carefully put into Bullmouth's pocket. She seemed so totally worn down by our troubles with Mr Walkern, she didn't need anything more to worry about.

We sat in silence for several minutes, but when I saw her wipe away a few tears, I scoured my mind for a subject that would turn her thoughts away from the theft. Very soon we were discussing apple pies, of all things.

Minnie chuckled at remembrance of times past. 'We used to dry apple rings over sulphur. They'd come out as crisp as autumn leaves, but juicier. We used to eat them like they was going out of style.'

Somebody further down the hill had a banjo, but he couldn't hit a right note no matter how hard he tried. A dog began to howl in sympathy, then another. Male voices were raised in anger. The banjo stopped.

117

'Do you know what I fancy right now?' asked Minnie. 'Frog's legs. A couple of pair of frogs' legs dipped in flour and fried till they got a nice crisp skin on them.'

'Where would we get frog's legs?'

Minnie waved her hand. 'Up there in the woods by the big watering hole. The boys all go swimming up there in the daytime, but it'll be full of frogs now it's dark. They'll be sitting there croaking away at each other and waiting for us to come up there and catch them. I expect they'd die with pleasure, just to know we was going to feast off them.'

'It can't be that easy.'

'I tell you, it's almost that easy. Why don't I go over to Mrs Huggens and ask her two boys to come here and keep an eye on the tent? Then we'll take the lamp and a gunny sack and walk up there so I can show you.'

Five minutes later we were on our way. The boys had been promised a penny each. Mrs Huggens said she didn't mind, and no she didn't believe she could be bothered to fix frogs' legs even if we brought some back for her.

Without the lamp it would have been hard going finding our way through the camp, but with it we could see that the camp site was thinning out a little. Wagons had left on the ferries all day. There were not all that many more to go, surely. Soon, the old hands said, it would be too late in the year to make the journey. The time had to be exactly right. You couldn't go too early, because the grass might not have grown enough to feed the cattle. On the other hand, you daren't set out too late, because previous wagon trains would have trampled the earth and their beasts would have eaten all the grass.

At this time of the evening most of the men were down in the town drinking and gambling, but we passed an old man sitting all alone. He had a fiddle resting on his chest, and was stroking a melancholy tune from it with surprising skill. The melody followed us into the woods for some time. I asked Minnie if she really thought this little adventure was safe.

She was confident. 'What man would come up here now? They'd rather be down in the town. Nobody will know it's two women on their own even if they do see our lamps. Come on, I don't think it's much farther.'

It took us well over twenty minutes to reach our destination. If it had been up to me, we would never have found it, because I have no sense of direction. Minnie was as sure-footed as a hunting dog. We didn't have to backtrack once. A minute or two before our lamp glowed on the water, we heard the frogs singing to one another.

Minnie handed me the sack and told me it must be kept open. 'There's nothing to it. I'll just shine the light on them and walk right over and pick them up. We'll get us eight or ten, and then head back to the tent.'

The lamp's glow showed us two straight away. They were sitting on a ledge, their necks bulging. Minnie picked them up and put them in the sack. They made no attempt to save themselves at all. I said maybe they were willing to die to please us, after all. She moved the lamp until it fell on four of them crouching not too far apart. Knowing she couldn't carry all of them at once, I put the sack down and went to help her. We turned around with a frog in each hand and walked back to the sack. But it wasn't there.

'Somebody's taken it,' I whispered, feeling the hairs lifting on the back of my neck. 'We're not alone!'

'Naw. Here. Hold all four, will you? Take them by the legs.'

I struggled with four frogs who objected very much to being held upside down, while Minnie picked up the lantern and moved it in a wide arc. There was the sack, about ten yards from where I had left it. As we watched, the sack leaped up and moved another foot or two away. I was so surprised, I squealed like a schoolgirl. Minnie took out after it, stopping only to pick up a big stick. When she reached the sack, she began pounding on the moving lumps and kept on even after both frogs were obviously dead.

We put the four frogs we had just caught inside. Minnie killed them with the stick before we hunted for more. Eventually, we had ten squashed frogs in the sack. Minnie decided to separate them from their legs right there by the pond.

'This old sack is full of frogs' innards now, and in a day or two it's going to stink something awful. We can't never put nothing in it, so we might as well leave it here. We can take the legs home in my apron. You know, we're going to be mighty uncomfortable if we can't do some washing soon. I ain't got a clean apron left.'

Minnie had a claspknife with which she did everything. If, as on this occasion, there was water nearby, the knife received a quick washing. Otherwise, it was wiped on her apron and folded away until it was needed to pick her teeth, gut a fish or cut a potato. At first, I had found this all rather sickening. But recently the sight of Minnie's trusty claspknife going to work had produced a soothing effect on me.

We returned to the tent city and soon had the frogs' legs sizzling in the pan. The Huggens boys looked so hungry that we prepared two pairs for them, and even let them have a bit of our cider. Minnie said it would make them sleep soundly for a change. We sent them home happy, each one clutching his penny. I don't remember that either one of them spoke at all.

I sat back on my heels and poked the fire with a stick, smiling at my memories. 'Did you ever see a gunny sack hop away on its own before? I thought it was a ghost.'

'It was fun, wasn't it?' Minnie tucked two more pieces of firewood in among the red embers. 'This has been a good night, Carlotta. And do you know why? Because them two girls ain't here. If we could just get rid of them, we could settle in this town. I tell you, St Jo needs a good washerwoman like me. Folks always need clean clothes. Especially men, because they won't ever wash out anything if they can help it.' She gave a melodramatic sigh. 'Yes, I know the money's on your mind. But we don't have to return it right away. You know, Carlotta, I feel as if you was my sister. I never had a sister. Having four older brothers ain't the same at all. They always went off to play together, and never would take me. I was always left at home when they went hunting with my pa. I learned to cook and sew and grow a few things for the pot. And what was it all for? Why, to look after the men, that's what.'

Minnie was my friend, perhaps my first friend. She was the rock upon which I would build a new life if I could just hit upon a scheme for making some money. I certainly had no intention of spending the rest of my days washing other people's dirty clothes. It paid well, but not as well as I needed. We would have to be a bit more ambitious.

Roxanne and Tilda were a problem. They showed no signs of wishing to return to their old life, so they must be given a chance to improve themselves. I must do what I could to save them, to show them there were better ways of living.

I was about to say so to Minnie, but a little snuffle told me she was asleep, slumped against a fifty-pound bag of flour. I banked up the fire and sat staring into it until the girls returned from the town. They were drunk, which made me wonder out loud why I should bother about them. Minnie woke up, and the three of them began to bicker. The golden time was over, but I could still plan and dream a little, huddled against the night chill in my feather bed.

The next morning, Minnie went over to Mrs Huggens' tent, but she soon returned, looking worried.

'Mrs Huggens is real bad. Her husband's there

wringing his hands, and those poor children ain't had a bite to eat. I must get back to her. Will you cook up some bacon and eggs for the children, Carlotta?'

I said I would. Roxanne stood up and began to tug on Tilda's arm. 'Come on, Tilda. I ain't hanging around here to look after a bunch of brats. Let's go down in the town. Carlotta, I've taken five dollars. We got to get ourselves some clothes.'

'Clothes?' screamed Minnie. 'You two got more than anybody. Get out, go on. Take off and never come back. We don't want you. Couple of lazy whores. Carlotta, you'll stay, won't you? Mrs Huggens ain't got cholera or nothing like that.'

Minnie's mistake was in turning her back after speaking so sharply to Roxanne. The girl leapt at her, hands clawed. I stepped between them, but it was all I could do to prevent Roxanne from drawing blood. Minnie was caught by surprise, but she soon recovered and gave as good as she got. I was thrust aside. The fight lasted only a few seconds, but the name-calling carried on until I could persuade Roxanne and Tilda to go away.

Minnie went back to the Huggens' tent, and in a few minutes three tearful children came silently to our fireside and watched as I made their breakfast. They ate well, stuffing the food into their mouths without a sign that they had ever been taught their manners. I thought it had probably been some time since they had eaten properly, and persuaded them to have second helpings.

As soon as they had finished eating, the lads who were called Caleb and Amos, went back to their tent. They couldn't bear to stay away, knowing their mother was struggling for her life. Little Martha was prepared to stay with me provided I held her close all the time. I sang to her and told her stories until she fell asleep. She didn't even wake when I laid her inside our tent on the feather bed.

I had cleared away the breakfast things and had

another pot of coffee keeping hot when Mr Huggens came over to talk to me. Normally a clean-shaven man, he had a day's growth of beard, and his eyes were red-rimmed. He would not have been a bad-looking man if he were cleaned up, despite his round shoulders and hollow chest.

'Miss Carlotta, my wife's real bad. Mrs Taylor says will you go into town and find a doctor? She says she don't know what else to do for Mrs Huggens. I'd go but . . .' His voice broke. 'I dassn't leave for fear she'll slip away while I'm gone.'

I told him Martha was asleep in my tent, invited him to help himself to coffee and to take some to Minnie. Fifteen minutes later I was down by the landing, having been told by a passerby that a doctor lived somewhere close. I had just realized that I was walking in the wrong direction, when I saw Wick standing forty yards ahead.

Apparently, his building plot was on the corner of Water Street. Two men were busy laying a stone foundation and seemed to be getting along quite quickly. But in the middle of the site was a stack of lumber, some of it already ashes, some still smouldering, or hauled out of the way with just a singeing. Wick was rummaging among the remains of what looked like ten or fifteen window frames and sash windows.

'Did you have a fire?' I asked unnecessarily.

'I had some carpenters working by the light of lamps, and then I left the lamps burning so that no one would steal the windows while I slept. And a fire, of course. I had a fire. I went to bed late, and I was so tired I must have slept very heavily. I woke up when it got hot. I'll never know now whether it was an accident or arson. Anyway, I've got to have another set of windows and frames built, and I don't know how the bank will feel about that. I paid a hundred and fifty dollars for this plot and had just enough money left after the fire in St Louis to build a small hotel here and get started again.'

123

I looked at the foundations of Wick's hotel, at the fire damage, and wondered how soon it would be earning money.

'I could lend you some money, Wick. Maybe in exchange for a share of the business.'

He straightened up and gave me a mean look. 'You may choose to wallow in the gutter, but I've still got my standards. I don't mind borrowing from a bank if I can but I'm damned if I'm going to dirty my hands with stolen money.'

He was so angry, I backed away and turned to go in search of the doctor. After walking for a minute or two, I couldn't resist looking over my shoulder. Wick was squatting beside the burnt-up window frames. Even his back expressed anger and bitterness.

Dr Keedy came readily enough, but he said there was nothing he could do. Mrs Huggens was dying, and was unlikely to last out the day. The grief of Mr Huggens and his children was more than I could bear at that moment. My own grief was too raw; I had no sympathy to give. Minnie was tenderly wiping Mrs Huggens' face with vinegar, cooing to her and holding her hand, trying to ease the woman's departure from this world.

I picked up Martha to take her back to my tent once again and we spent the rest of the day together. At five o'clock Minnie, Mr Huggens and the boys came to our tent. He said his wife was dead. He took his daughter in his arms, and they all cried. When he could control himself a little, Mr Huggens spoke softly about what had to be done. He asked us to keep the children by us while he went down into the town to make the necessary arrangements.

Minnie did her best to comfort the children. She prayed with them and talked to them about how Mrs Huggens had gone to heaven and might meet her own boy, Toby, who had died two years ago.

Martha crept from my arms to Minnie's loving

embrace. I went into the tent and wondered what reserves of strength Minnie had found which enabled her to give so much of herself to the motherless children. Especially after she had suffered so much in the last few years herself. Perhaps, I thought, that made it easier. She knew the right things to say to give comfort.

It was ten o'clock when Mr Huggens returned to us. We hadn't seen hide nor hair of Roxanne and Tilda all day, which we considered a blessing under the circumstances. Mr Huggens said the funeral would be tomorrow, and the body had already been taken away. He thanked us for looking after his children and said they would go back to their tent now and try to get some sleep.

'But who is going to look after my motherless children?' he cried out suddenly in despair. 'How am I going to manage? I can't just leave them to run wild.'

Minnie seemed to have prepared herself for the question. 'I'm willing to marry you, Mr Huggens. Then I can look after your children. And you, too, come to that.'

'No!' wailed Caleb. 'You can't! Don't you never marry again, Pa! I don't want another ma!'

'Course not,' said Minnie gently. 'Nobody else can ever be your ma. But I can look after you and cook for you and see that you and your pa have clean clothes and all. But it wouldn't be fitting to live with you, unless your pa and me married. That's all it is.'

I stood beside her, too astounded to speak, while Mr Huggens chewed his lower lip and scratched his head.

'I don't know. It's a bit soon . . .' He looked Minnie up and down appraisingly. 'But you're right about it not being fitting . . .'

The boys were both crying loudly now, clinging to him, begging him not to give them a new mother.

I guessed Joel Huggens was about the same age as Minnie, certainly no more than forty. He looked much older at this moment, a grieving man with harsh lines running down from nose to chin. He ran his fingers through his greasy brown hair and shook his head, a man too crushed by grief to be able to think clearly.

'Let me sleep on it, Mrs Taylor. I appreciate your offer, I surely do. Hush now, boys. I got to do what's best for us all. I got to think real careful. But it's got to be my decision. Y'all will do whatever I decide.' He wiped a hand across his mouth. 'I thank you both for what you done for my wife. Like I said, funeral's tomorrow. Will y'all be coming?'

'Of course!' exclaimed Minnie. 'Mrs Huggens was a fine brave woman, and I'm sure she was a good wife and mother. I know she would of wanted her family to be properly looked after.'

The bereaved family went away. Minnie sat down in front of the fire and began poking it fiercely with a stick, avoiding my eyes as she prodded.

'I got to explain, Carlotta.'

'Explain! You heard Mrs Huggens say he's going to the gold fields, planning to drag his family with him. You heard her say he's not always sober. What in God's name are you thinking of?'

'I'm thinking of three kids needing a mother. I'm thinking of a son I lost and how I never got over it. I want children to love, and I want that man tied up legal! It's what a woman is made for. When I rock little Martha in my arms and squeeze her plump little legs, it feels so good my heart's about to bust. And Caleb! He's the age my Toby was when he died. It's like I got a second chance at being a mother, with Amos and Martha as extras. Try to understand, Carlotta. I want them kids so bad I can taste it.'

'You'll have to take the father along with them. You don't know anything about him, except that he drinks. Oh, and I almost forgot. He's so dumb he couldn't even see how sick his wife was. He was going to take her on the Oregon Trail. *Healthy* people die out there.'

126

Minnie turned to me, and I saw her teeth gleam in the light of the fire. 'He's not going to take anybody anywhere. I'll see he never leaves St Jo. He's a mild man and I can handle him. We'll stay right here. I'll get a comb through those kids' hair if it kills me. And Mr Huggens is going to find something useful to do. You just wait and see. Mr Huggens will help us get out of trouble.'

I had run out of arguments. Our close, special friendship had lasted just one whole day. So much for my day-dreams. I also knew all about what women were for. I wanted a home and children, too. But unlike Minnie, I wasn't prepared to settle for second best, for any man who came along. The man I would marry would have to be clever, well-educated and able to look after himself. He would also have to believe I was a decent woman who would not willingly steal twelve hundred dollars. If no such man ever came along, I'd just stay a spinster all my life.

'I think,' I said, 'that I'll walk down to the saloon and tell Roxanne and Tilda about Mrs Huggens dying, and your plans.'

'I'll come, too. I want to explain why I got to do this thing so quick.'

'No, you had better stay here. Mr Huggens might need you in the night.'

I left her as quickly as possible, pausing just long enough to pick up a shawl. Desperate to be alone for a while, I stumbled down the hill, half-blinded by my tears. It seemed every time I gave my heart to someone, they went off and left me.

10

I soon regretted having come into the town. There were men everywhere. I didn't see any women, either alone or in company. The families that were heading for Oregon territory seemed to have departed. More greenhorns were arriving in town by the hour, reckless greedy men who had thrown off their responsibilities in order to have a great adventure in the gold fields. They stood about on the rutted streets, because there was no room in the saloons, but they had a ready supply of liquor just the same. They staggered around, they roared and hollered like Indians, fought, fired their rifles and laughed uproariously at every coarse remark. Nobody was sober that night. In my dark clothing, I passed them like a wraith, praying that I might go unnoticed.

I approached the single-storey tavern where Albert Jenkins presided over a gambling table like a spider in a satin waistcoat, waiting for some juicy greenhorn to land in his web. Seconds before I reached the open doorway, a man was ejected from the house. He tiptoed out involuntarily, with a brawny hand on the seat of his pants and another on his collar, then rolled in horse dung when he was abruptly dropped into the road.

Observing the spectacle with loud laughter were men with bottles in their hands who leaned against the buildings as if trying to hold them up. Actually the other way around, I thought. Buildings supporting men.

I moved into the middle of the dusty road which had its own hazards. There was too much congestion for any fool, no matter how drunk, to ride hell for leather down it, but it was a custom in St Jo to toss the slops and food scraps out on the road for the browsing pigs to devour.

The pigs did not always cooperate as they should, and sometimes made more mess than they cleared.

I came to a part of the road where there was nothing but trees for twenty yards on either side. I hurried along afraid that some lout would pounce on me. In spite of my vigilance, an arm suddenly snaked out and grabbed me around the waist while another arm behind my knees swept me off my feet. I was lifted up and carried ten yards into the trees. The man carrying me stumbled over tree roots and stones in the dark.

'Well, well, Carlotta. Going to work at last, are you?'

'Wick! Damn you! Put me down!'

'The daughter of Missouri Belle has finally gone into the family business. What's your price, wildcat lady? I don't mind telling you, I've dreamed about this night. What are you? A nickel whore? A dollar one? You'd be worth it, I'm sure, honey. But let's not haggle about the price right now. Give me a kiss.'

I put the palm of one hand under his chin and pushed. 'Stop making a damned fool of yourself and put me down. I've come looking for Roxanne and Tilda. That woman in our tent city who was sick has died, and Minnie's got her heart set on marrying the widower.'

Wick grunted in surprise, set me on my feet and stood back a pace, keeping his hands to himself. 'Is that a fact? Y'all are full of surprises, I'll say that for you.'

Somebody fired a shotgun not too far away, and I jumped. Wick put a hand on my shoulder and sort of caressed my neck with his thumb. 'I've made a fool of myself and I'm properly ashamed.' He didn't sound ashamed in the least. 'I do apologize, although I only took for granted what every other man in town is thinking. I was . . .' he searched for the appropriate word '. . . feeling lonesome, I guess. And if that's the way I feel, you can bet your bottom dollar a few hundred hard drinking men in this town are feeling the same way. It might not be safe for you to walk alone on the waterfront.'

'I was so upset, I knew I had to get away from Minnie to sort out my thoughts. I don't suppose I need to tell Roxanne and Tilda about it tonight. They probably wouldn't be interested, anyway. I was going to look for them in Rowley's saloon. That seems to be their favourite place. But on second thoughts, I would rather not know what they get up to in the evenings.'

'Teasing the men is what they're up to. Letting any man who's got five cents buy them a drink, then refusing to do business when he begins to feel romantic. Some greenhorn is going to decide he has been cheated one of these nights. Then there will be trouble, because those girls have *not* gone back into the business. It's a fact – you can't be half-respectable.'

'I'll have a word with them. In the meantime, I'd be grateful if you would walk back up the hill with me. I made a mistake coming down here alone. The trouble is, I can't think what has got into Minnie. The widower, Mr Huggens, has three children. They are the reason she wants him, but that's not a good enough basis for a marriage. She believes she's stronger than he is. She says she will make him stay in St Jo, settle down and do something useful.'

'I can't do anything about Minnie's mad ideas, but I'll take you home. I owe you that much for giving you a fright. You know, a proper lady would have had a heart attack right here in my arms. But you gave me a pretty good punch on the jaw.'

'It was just a push. I didn't hit you.'

He laughed. 'That's your story. Come on. You may be able to go three rounds with me, but you would be no match for that bunch of roaring boys in the street.'

He put his arm around my waist, and we started back along Water Street. He wouldn't have been so bold as to put his arm around me if he thought I was respectable. And if I was respectable, I wouldn't have allowed it. I had to admit that my actions might confuse Wick a little.

130

As we came upon groups of drinking men, they made bawdy comments of the most basic nature. I wasn't shocked, hurt or embarrassed. There's no point in pretending I was. But the menace in their voices was a different thing. I had the sense to be afraid.

Only Wick's cruel remarks could hurt me, yet I put up with them. What Minnie called not thinking well enough of myself to be offended. I knew he did it to goad me. If only, I thought, I could make him as mad at me as I was at him . . . One day I would discover his vulnerable places.

Meanwhile, the warmth and strength of his steadying arm felt good. It was comforting to know that I was being protected by a man who could, if necessary, send half a dozen drunkards about their business. Even so, we pretended not to hear the shouted insults. It seldom paid to *start* a fight in St Jo.

Neither of us spoke until we were up the hill, and I could see the banked fire in front of our tent and Minnie's stockinged toes sticking out of the flap. That old man was playing the fiddle again, a sweet tune this time that sent goose pimples up my spine. We stood under the branches of a tall hickory tree. Wick picked idly at the vine clinging to its trunk.

'I've got a few things to say to you, Carlotta, and this is as good a place as any. The way you're going, the company you're keeping, sooner or later you're going to have to take up the whore's life. I just want you to tell *me* when you've decided to do it. I think I have the right to be the first. You know why – because of that night at your ma's. So just send me word, and I'll come get you.'

'You think I'm just no good, don't you?'

He took me by the shoulders and shook me a little. 'Tell me I'm wrong. You're going to the gold fields, aren't you? With those two whores and now without even Minnie for decent company. That is what you plan to do, isn't it? Tell me it's not true.'

'I don't have to tell you anything. But just because I'm tired of hearing you cuss me out, I'm going to say a few things myself. We're all staying right here in St Jo. My ma brought Roxanne into the life. It's different for Tilda, her mother was a whore. But then so was mine. The difference is I was saved by my grandmother. Tilda and Roxanne didn't have anyone to save them from my mother's clutches, so I'm going to do it. I'm going to save them.'

'The difference is they don't want to be saved.'

'They do! You don't understand them. You look at what's on the outside – '

'The paint, the bold looks, the drinking.'

' – and don't see that they're just two high-spirited young girls who haven't seen the Light. If it hadn't been for my grandmother, I would have ended up the same way.'

'It wasn't your grandmother who saved you from me the first time we met. It was your ma.'

'A weak moment. She regretted her act of kindness.'

'So did I. So you're not going to California.'

'I have other plans.'

'A hurdy-gurdy house right here in St Jo?'

I tried to slap him, but he was too fast for me, catching my wrist and forcing my hand behind my back.

'Dammit, Carlotta, that's twice in one night! You're not going to beat up on me.'

He pulled me to him, took my face in one big hand and laid his lips gently on mine. That first touch felt like being struck by lightning, which I suppose is why I didn't draw away. When the kiss became more insistent, he put his arms around me and held me so close I couldn't move. Not that I tried. His mouth felt so sweet against mine, gentle but strong.

Could this be lust and nothing else? I didn't want to believe it. He loved me, after all. I was sure of it. Ever since Carlton had run off, I had been feeling that I was of

132

no account. I had to believe someone thought well of me. And I had to think well of myself, or else there was no point in living.

At last he released me. We were both breathing heavily. He smoothed the hair from my face, kissed my forehead. I almost purred. 'You're one hell of a woman, Carlotta. That kiss was to let you know what's in store for you if you ever decide to set up in business.'

There was no point in trying to hit him yet again. I stepped away and wiped the back of my hand across my mouth. 'I have to hand it to you, Wick. You've got a way with words. All that education you had, I suppose. I just want to know one thing. What have I ever done to you that you *always* want to hurt me?'

I heard him draw in his breath sharply. 'I don't know. I guess it's because . . . Damned if I know why I do it.'

'Goodnight, Wick. I must thank you for walking home with me and protecting me from the unwanted attentions of *other* men.'

'You sound just like a schoolteacher,' he mocked. 'But you kiss like a . . . like Belle's daughter. Come on, Carlotta. We understand each other.'

He took a step towards me. I took a step back. He hesitated, then gave a little salute, adjusted his soft felt hat and began walking very fast down the hill.

I tarried by the tree awhile, leaning against it, imprinting the pattern of the bark on my cheek. Gradually, the strength came back into my legs, and I thought I could walk over to our tent. 'Damn you,' I said to myself. 'Damn and blast you, Wick Estes. I'll make you sorry. You see if I don't.'

When I crawled into the tent, Minnie awoke and asked drowsily: 'Did you tell them?'

'I'll tell them tomorrow. I couldn't find them among all those hard-drinking men. I met Wick. He walked me home, because it wasn't safe to be on my own. I told him what you're planning to do.'

133

'What did he say about it?'

'I can't remember exactly what he said.' Only certain parts of our time together stood out in my mind. Everything else was blurred by longing and the pain of his contempt.

Minnie broke in on my thoughts. 'Why don't you tell him the truth about yourself? Tell him you want to stay in St Jo and pay back the money we owe to Mr Walkern.'

'Do you think he'd believe me? I don't. I don't want to speak to him again until he shows me some respect. He talks to me the way he would have talked to my mother. I won't forgive him for that.'

'He won't show you any respect until you tell him the truth. What's the matter with you, girl? Uh-oh. I think I know. You want him to see that you're pure as the driven snow in spite of what it looks like. That's it, ain't it? He's got to be a mind reader to show he loves you.'

She rolled over on her back, and began daydreaming aloud about how wonderful it would be if Wick and I were to get married and live in St Jo. I could start a school and teach the Huggens children. Eventually, there would be two houses full of kids, and we could all have a wonderful time. She didn't realize how painful that sort of talk was to me. I finally shut her up by telling her I probably *would* be going to the gold fields, after all.

As I feared, she eventually fell asleep on her back and snored continuously until Roxanne and Tilda came home. They had been drinking, as usual. For the rest of the night, or so it seemed, they all three snored. I lay awake thinking about Wick and the way his kiss had felt, so different from Carlton's papery lips. I hadn't spent so much as a split second wondering what was the proper thing to do. I had known what I wanted to do, and I had known what I *had* to do to keep from getting my heart broken.

The funeral service for Mrs Huggens was conducted by

the Reverend Reeves at the First Presbyterian Church on the corner of Fourth and Jules Street. The church was full, as it was for Minnie's wedding in the afternoon. Wick and I stood up for the couple. Roxanne and Tilda tried, without much success, to keep the boys from crying too loudly during both services.

After the wedding there was a combined wake and wedding breakfast at Josiah Beattie's tavern. Neither Minnie nor Mr Huggens knew anybody in town, but I soon found it impossible to keep complete strangers from joining the festivities. At twenty-five cents a gallon, I was able to send a goodly portion of the transient population out into the night dead drunk. And all for ten dollars.

Minnie took no part in the celebrations. She sat in a corner with Martha on her lap, smiling with quiet satisfaction, looking at least ten years younger than when I had first seen her in St Louis. From time to time, she would reach out and smooth the dark hair from Caleb's forehead or put her arm around Amos and give him a bit of a squeeze. Caleb was infuriated by her attentions. Amos was quietly long-suffering. Martha, on the other hand, seemed to have taken to Minnie. The child had been cleaned up and looked quite pretty. The Huggens children were all very dark like their mother. Minnie was also dark. I thought they were already beginning to look like her.

Joel Huggens didn't seem to know what he was doing. At first, Wick tried to keep him from drinking too much. Mr Huggens was determined, however. He kept returning to the jug on the bar, and within an hour was too drunk to stand. He sat at one of Mr Beattie's tables and let the tears roll down his face. He never once looked in Minnie's direction.

Wick came up to me, holding his elbows up playfully, as if to ward off any blows. 'You willing to speak to me, ma'am?'

'Don't play the fool, it doesn't suit you. Can't you keep that man from drinking himself unconscious?'

'He's grieving in his own way. He's going to wake up in the morning with a terrible headache and wonder why he's taken a new wife so soon.'

'He strikes me as a pretty useless man. More than most,' I added, giving Wick a sidelong glance. 'One of these days he's going to be quite glad to have Minnie to look after him. I just hope she doesn't live to regret this day's work. She deserves some happiness.'

A six-foot tall greenhorn with long greasy hair and the worst pockmarks I'd ever seen got Roxanne upon his back for a piggy-back ride. All the men formed a circle round them. There was a call for somebody to take up Tilda so that the two couples could try to knock each other over. The game quickly got out of hand. Roxanne fell off. Men began to fight over who was going to have her next. Tilda began swearing and demanding to be put down. Her mount paid no attention, so some of the men began trying to pull her off. The noise was terrible.

'You know,' said Wick, 'my father has a saying: "If you lie down with dogs, you get up with fleas." You're associating with dogs, Carlotta, and you're going to get fleas. You don't owe those girls anything.'

'I suppose you think my mother was a dog, too. I can't get away from having been related to Missouri Belle. I tried in Boston, but it didn't work. So I guess I'll just have to scratch when I get fleas. I suppose you think your father is a clever man, but – '

'No,' said Wick, with a sudden bitter laugh. 'Sometimes my father is a fool. But he was right about dogs and fleas. When I first saw you in St Louis a few weeks ago, you had a funny way of talking, like they do in Boston. Now you talk differently. To begin with, I thought that was a good thing. Not putting on airs, I thought. But lately I've changed my mind. Now you talk like Minnie and the other two, except when you get mad at me. And do you know why? Because you've let yourself go. You've dropped your standards, and it's showing in your speech. I don't like you to get mad at me, but I preferred you when you talked Boston.'

'I haven't thought about the way I talk, but now that you mention it, I don't suppose I do sound too Boston these days. That's being realistic, knowing what I am and knowing that I can't change it.'

He shook his head sadly. 'You're mixed up, you don't know night from day. And you certainly don't know who you are!'

Minnie slept in our tent that night, but she was up at dawn and cooking breakfast for the children before the rest of us realized what was going on. Roxanne did her untrained best to help me make the fire so that I could cook our breakfast, but Tilda refused to get out of the tent. She was tired, she said. She had a headache. Roxanne kicked her on the backside, and they screamed at one another for a few minutes. Then Tilda went back to sleep and didn't get up until noon.

On her wedding day, Minnie had managed to persuade Wick to take Mr Huggens on as a carpenter, although he had been a hemp farmer before his farm was repossessed. She had rather more trouble persuading Mr Huggens to do the work. He was still determined to transport his family to California as soon as possible. Fortunately for Minnie, the night Mrs Huggens had taken sick, he had gambled away half of his stake money, and now had no alternative but to wait until next year.

I had no respect for Mr Huggens. On the other hand, it's a fact that women need the help of men if they are to keep themselves decent. Or so my grandmother used to say. She had been fond of telling me how well off she was, because of my grandfather's hard work as a butcher, and his saving ways. Men were inferior to women, as everybody knew. You kept a man the way you might keep a pig, feeding him well, because he would give a good return on your investment of time and effort.

My mother, so my grandmother said almost every day of her life, would never be secure, because she didn't have a man to look after her. It had seemed to me at the time that my mother was doing quite well. She had the big house on Second and Walnut, after all. But Grandmother had proved to be right in the end.

So Mr Huggens had to be our saviour, drunkard though he was. I went into town on my own and entered the office of the *St Joseph Gazette*. The smell of the ink and noise of the press made me suddenly feel homesick for the old *Boston Eye*. But Mr Ridenbaugh's newspaper was much more successful than Carlton's had been. The *Gazette* seemed to be making money hand over fist.

The editor, Mr Archer, was a lawyer who wore a handsome waistcoat and a high starched collar. I couldn't see his feet behind the counter, but I knew his shoes would have a shine on them, just as I knew he laid down his head each night in a high, cherrywood bed, and always had meat on the table. Being a newspaper editor was a respectable profession, and being the owner of one was even better. The *St Joseph Gazette* was a weekly paper that charged six cents for its single folded sheet! I couldn't begin to calculate how much money that paper made each week.

I bought a copy and soon found what I was looking for: a smallholding that was not going to be auctioned, but sold outright for one hundred and fifty dollars. I reasoned that if I bought the property, Mr Huggens could work it with his boys. That way we would all have a roof over our heads. It would be no more than fair if Mr Huggens then gave me the money necessary to pay Mr Walkern two thousand dollars as soon as he sold his crops.

But in the meantime, I had no intention of being idle. For a dollar, I placed an advertisement in the next edition of the *Gazette* offering my services as a teacher. A dollar a month for each pupil. Now if I could just get Tilda and Roxanne in gainful employment . . .

Mr Archer was happy to give me instructions for reaching the property advertised. Within half an hour, I was knocking on the door.

The house had looked very attractive from a distance; a two-storey block with a central door and four windows. Close inspection showed it to have been thrown together with any old lumber that came to hand. The tiled roof seemed to be sound, however, and at the back there was a single-storey block attached to the main building. The kitchen range was there, just ten or fifteen paces from the pump. The property consisted of the house, a large henhouse and run, an empty pigsty and five acres planted to hemp. The owner, a wiry bachelor in his fifties, said he wanted to sell up and hunt for gold.

There were four small rooms upstairs, and one of them held a bed with a rope-lace base. Downstairs, the main room was about twenty-five feet long and half as wide. A fireplace with a shoulder-high mantel took up most of one end, with rudimentary cupboards on either side. A long, rough-hewn table, two benches and three or four chairs completed the furnishings that the owner, Horace Brace, was prepared to leave with the house. I admired the wallpaper, which made him smile. The walls were papered with old sheets of the *St Joseph Gazette*. I made sure that the flock of two dozen hens and a rooster were included in the price, and agreed to buy.

Horace Brace and I then walked downtown in search of a lawyer. Mr Brace preferred to do business with Benjamin Hays. Since I had no objection, we soon managed the transfer. Only then did Mr Brace inform me that he had paid just one and a quarter cents an acre for the land six years previously, and had built the entire house for fifty dollars. I still thought I had a bargain, and went in search of Minnie.

139

Minnie was so pleased she almost wept when I told her about the property. 'I'll get Mr Huggens to pay off the debt just as soon as he can. You just see if I don't. Only he don't have but twenty-three dollas and fifty cents right now. I know because I asked him.'

'Minnie!'

'I know. I thought it was more. Now, don't get down-hearted. You done the right thing. Why, we can keep those chickens and sell the eggs. If you don't mind spending just a little bit more of Mr Walkern's money, we can buy us a hog and slaughter it in October. I always fancied having one of them Berkshire hogs. That'll keep us in bacon and sausagemeat all winter if we're careful. And we can grow corn and vegetables. At least enough for the table. And in the fall when Mr Huggens sells the crops, we can maybe – '

'In the fall? But – '

'But you're just a city girl and don't think things through, Carlotta. There won't be no money except egg money coming in for months. Mr Huggens will have to go on working for Wick, I reckon. But there's washing. We can all do that.'

I saw then what I had done. I had taken on responsibility for Mr Huggens and his three children, as well as Minnie, Roxanne and Tilda. I hoped Mr Walkern would one day appreciate how he was keeping half of Missouri from going hungry. And still there would be no income sufficient to pay off the debt, before Mr Walkern found out we were all hiding in St Jo.

Minnie soon had everybody, including Tilda, working to get all of us moved to Brace's farm that day. She said she would share a room with Martha. The boys were to be given a room to themselves. Mr Huggens must have the only bed in the house. That meant Roxanne and Tilda and I once more found ourselves thrown together. At least we now could sleep under a sound roof with rough-sawed planks beneath our feather beds, instead of mud.

140

The boys guided their father to his new home from his first day's work, by which time the few Huggens possessions had been distributed. Minnie had cooked a generous meal, all ready to be brought to the table.

Tilda didn't like the fact that 'our' money had been spent on providing a home for the Huggens family, but Roxanne said anything was better than a tent. Mr Huggens accepted everything that was shown to him, nodding professional approval when he had inspected the hemp in the fields. He did not utter one word of gratitude, which prompted Minnie to tell him he was a hog.

'Don't you give me no sass, woman!' snarled Mr Huggens, giving us all a new insight into his personality. 'I'm not going to be pecked at by some woman I took in offen the streets. Peck, peck, peck. Just like them chickens. Did you ever see how they act? They all get down on one hen and peck her to death. Well, you're not going to do that to me, you hear?'

Minnie was spluttering with rage. 'What street? You're the one's been taken in offen the street. By Carlotta here! We've got a roof over our heads and a place for the children to sleep and eat their meals at a table, instead of crouching round a fire like savages. And I can keep them clean, too. Mrs Huggens, poor soul, must not have had the strength to wash anything for months! I've spent the whole afternoon boiling up clothes so's you can look decent when we go to church on Sunday. You *are* going to church, ain't you?'

Mr Huggens, no match for Minnie, mumbled that he was. He sat down at the table and helped himself to a rich beef stew, hot biscuits and greens, piling his plate high. He did not speak again, except to say 'More biscuits,' and 'Stop tormenting your brother, Caleb, lessen you want to get a licking.'

Minnie maintained a falsetto monologue for the benefit of Martha. The child seemed to appreciate this, and smilingly ate everything she was offered.

'She's said a few words, you know,' Minnie said to me in her normal voice. 'She's just a might shy.' Then, falsetto again: 'Ain't you baby?'

Roxanne groaned comically and the boys giggled.

'One time,' said Minnie, good-naturedly addressing herself to the boys. 'I knew a pair of twins about two and half years old. One of them said: "Pass the dravy," and the other one said: "If you can't say dravy, say drease." ' Minnie chuckled loudly at her own story.

'That's not funny,' said Caleb.

'What's funny about that?' asked Amos.

Minnie was patient. 'They couldn't say gravy or grease. "If you can't say dravy, say drease." '

'Baby talk,' explained Mr Huggens with his mouth full.

'That's not funny,' said Caleb. 'Baby talk's not funny.'

'Shut your mouth, boy, before I shut it for you!' growled Mr Huggens.

'No need to get riled,' said Minnie mildly in the sudden silence.

I decided that as soon as Wick's hotel was finished, I would move in. I just hoped my nerves lasted that long.

11

There seemed to be no end to the new, hopeful arrivals in town, although it was getting late in the season for travelling West. All the stores were busy. When I went into Livermore's to make a few purchases for Minnie, Mr Livermore was complaining bitterly to a customer about his hired help having decided to hunt gold, leaving only himself and his wife to wait on the trade.

I didn't know if Mr Livermore would take on a woman, but marched right up to him and asked for a job. He seemed doubtful, so I assured him that my arithmetic was very good. I could calculate faster than lightning. I started to add that I was honest, but at the last minute, thought better of it.

Mr Livermore, a tall stoop-shouldered man in his forties, looked around his store at the barrels of nails and sugar, crackers and gunpowder, and decided to take me on then and there. What with so many people in the store, all milling around and poking their noses into things, Mr Livermore said he was worried he would lose a lot of stock to light-fingered folks. He handed me an apron, and said to start right in.

He agreed to send his eight year old son up to Minnie's to tell her I had a job and wouldn't be home until late. There were so many customers I didn't have time to collect my thoughts before starting in, and was surprised how much there was to learn about weighing and measuring the stock, and the price of different things. The day passed swiftly because the work was interesting, but I was glad to take off my apron and say goodnight to my employer at nine o'clock that night.

To my surprise, Roxanne and Albert were waiting for

me. Roxanne gave a little twirl so that I could appreciate the new gown Albert had bought for her. It bared her shoulders, reflected the green of her eyes, and showed off the smallness of her waist. When I had admired the dress, we walked over to Beattie's tavern where I made short work of a catfish supper.

'Albert's ever so smart,' said Roxanne, meeting his eyes and giving him a warm look. 'He's been telling me about all the hoaxes he got up to over in England.'

Albert smiled at her. I never saw a man so silly with lust. Even when he was speaking to me, he looked hungrily at Roxanne. He found occasions to touch her arm or squeeze her hand. Once he bent over to place a playful kiss on her cheek. She would laugh or pout, slap his arm in mock annoyance, or toss her head so that her curls swayed provocatively.

I had high hopes for the two of them. Albert might take Roxanne off my hands and give her a better life than she could possibly manage on her own. There would be no trickery involved. He knew what she was and it didn't seem to bother him. I could tell his feelings for her ran deep. He genuinely loved the girl.

Roxanne's emotions were harder to fathom. Although she could read and write no better than many a six year old I had taught in the past, I soon discovered that she was quite intelligent.

Her past life was against her, of course. She had never been taught good manners or self-discipline or how to put the needs of others before her own desires. She would probably make Albert a demanding companion. Yet there was much goodness in the girl. Her moods might swing from hysterical happiness to blackness in the space of a few seconds, but I could usually calm her down by appealing to her sense of humour. It was unfortunate that she had been so well-trained in the art of deceiving men. In the future, that might be a problem for Albert. But at least I wouldn't have to worry about what she was getting up to!

'Tell Carlotta,' she said. 'Tell her about the tricks you played on folks.'

Albert leaned back in his chair and hooked one thumb in a waistcoat pocket. 'I must begin by telling you that I know horseflesh. My father was a dealer in a small way, and I grew up with the beasts. Raising horses and dealing honestly can be a good business, but you won't get rich at it. My father made enough to rent a decent house and keep a couple of servant girls – '

'Did you hear that?' asked Roxanne, her eyes sparkling. 'Two servants.'

'I had a fair schooling, but I didn't take to books, I'm sorry to say. I thought I was Jack the lad, but I had two younger sisters who brought me down to earth every chance they got. My father thought they were perfect. He was not so sure about me, so I ran away from home when I was fifteen. I was all for adventure and soon found it. I joined a gang whose trade it was to sell screws to the flats.'

Roxanne giggled. 'He always talks like that. He means he sold no-good horses to gentlemen what didn't know any better.'

'We were up to other shams as well. You always had to have partners. Five or six sometimes. But when I was about twenty, I left the gang and teamed up with Jem Smallbone.'

'Tell Carlotta about the salt trick. We could maybe do this one, Carlotta. It's a good 'un.' Roxanne rubbed her hands together.

'I don't advise you to try it,' laughed Albert. 'It worked like this. Jem and I would go into a public house, each pretending not to know the other. We'd strike up a conversation and order a pint of heavy wet. I'd have a little bag of salt, and I'd be rubbing the bag against my jaw like this. Back and forth.

145

'Jem would ask what I was doing, and I would say I was rubbing this bag of salt against my jaw, because I had a toothache and a dentist told me this would cure it. Then after a while I'd get up and go out to the privy, leaving the bag on the table. Now here's the clever part. Jem was very good at it. He would try to get some others interested, and they would all decide, with Jem's help, to play a trick on me. They would empty the salt out of the bag and fill it up with some of the sawdust from the floor.

'Then I would come back, pick up the bag and start in to rubbing my jaw and saying how good it felt and how much it was helping me. One of them – the mark, we called him – would say there must be something else besides salt in the bag, else it wouldn't work. I would say no, there wasn't anything but salt. Somebody, usually Jem, would say something like: "You wouldn't care to bet on that, would you?"

'Since this was the point of the whole business, I'd say I would be glad to make a small wager. By this time, usually everybody in the public house would be watching and ready to laugh at me. As soon as the money was on the table, I would open the bag. Naturally, there was never anything in it but salt. I had switched bags, you see. Sleight of hand. Takes a lot of practice. I was, and am, the best there is at sleight of hand.'

I was frankly sceptical. 'No one would be so foolish as to fall for so crude a prank, surely. When the bag was opened and salt was found, everyone would know you had switched the bags, and that it was a trick. Didn't they refuse to pay?'

Albert shook his head. 'It never worked that way. Everyone else in the house would laugh at the joke, and the fellow who had been bamboozled just had to put a smile on his face and pay up. No man would endure being tricked by a woman, of course, which is why I said you two ought never to try it. We got away with it, because there was never much money involved.

146

'In the more important dodges, the ones that made good money, like selling a bog spavined six-guinea horse for eighty guineas, why then you had to nip off smartly or risk being nabbed by the law. It was an exciting life. One spring day, Jem and I went up to Shrewsbury to a fair, hoping to sell a couple of flashy screws to some chaw bacon. We hadn't been there more than fifteen minutes when we saw a man give a coin to a boy for him to keep an eye on the man's flock of sheep. Jem and I went into action. Jem chatted to the boy a few minutes and led him off to see a show. I was to look after the flock – about twenty sheep, as I recall.

'There's so many fools wandering about at fairs, if you turn round you're apt to step on one. It wasn't but five minutes before somebody came up and believed me when I said I had to sell the flock right away, because I'd just got word that my wife was dying. It's greed, you see. This chap thought he would be getting a bargain. Well, I'm sure he did get a bargain, providing the owner didn't come back before my customer got the sheep safely away.

'Anyway, as soon as I had the money, I dashed round to the show where I knew Jem would be. We left the boy there and scampered off back to London.'

I was horrified. 'That was a cruel thing to do to the boy, to say nothing of the cost to the owner and the confusion it must have caused.'

Albert shrugged. 'It was just a way of earning a living, Carlotta, and no worse than the sly gentry in the city selling shares that aren't worth the paper they're printed on. You've got to do whatever you can to put bread on the table. You ought to know that, my dear. Life hasn't treated you that well.'

'They deserved what they got,' said Roxanne. 'Go on, Bertie.'

Albert was amused by my disapproval which he no doubt considered hypocritical. 'All I was going to say is, two days later in London I saw the chap I'd sold the sheep to. He didn't see me, but I wasn't about to wait around there until he did. Besides, it was time I said goodbye to Jem. We had been partners for ten years, but I was getting bored with the business. Would you believe it? We hardly saved anything during the whole time we were together. We dressed like toffs. We ate well, and never bought anything but the best gin. But, somehow, the rest of the money, the folding kind, just slipped through our fingers.

'England was getting a little small for me, so I decided on a bit of travel and came to America. Arrived in New York. Didn't like it. Thought I might as well see what this country's all about. I've been here for four years and seen a few sights, but I've never found the exact place I'm looking for to put down roots. I suppose I must carry on travelling.'

'You could do worse than stay right here,' I said. 'Did you know, the state of Missouri is over sixty-nine thousand square miles? I looked up England's area in one of my textbooks last night. England is only fifty thousand square miles. And I believe the city of London has more people than there are in the whole of this state! There are just six hundred thousand people in Missouri. There's plenty of land for everybody. I don't know why people want to travel out to Oregon territory when they could have all the good farm land they want right here.'

Albert looked so intently at Roxanne that she eventually turned her head away, unable, I supposed, to respond to the warmth in his eyes.

'I've thought about staying in St Jo,' he said slowly. 'The United States are certainly empty. Seems strange to a man like me who is used to the hustle and bustle of a big city like London. A man could certainly make his fortune here. A man like me, that is, who knows horseflesh. I suppose I'd have to deal in Missouri mules, as well. Damnedest animals I ever did see. But excellent for some jobs, of course.'

The tavern door opened, and Tilda hesitated in the doorway. When she saw us, she came directly to our table, threading her way past grinning men, wearing her customary mulish expression. 'There you are, Roxanne. I been looking all over for you. That's a mighty pretty dress you're wearing. Where'd you get it?'

'Bertie bought it for me. I like green taffeta, but it's a mite hot to wear in this weather. I'd let you borrow it sometimes, but you're too fat.'

'Tilda, would you like something to drink?' asked Albert. 'Are you hungry? I could get you some catfish. Carlotta says it's very good.'

'I've already et. Minnie made some old rabbit stew that didn't hardly have no meat in it. All the time we was eating, those kids of Mr Huggens didn't do nothing but fight each other and sass Minnie. And Mr Huggens can get tight faster'n any man I ever did see. It's been a terrible day, what with Carlotta working when she don't have to, and you taking off with Albert. I was stuck at the house with Minnie. Why, she even had me hanging out clothes on the line!'

Roxanne made an unsympathetic reply, and the two young women were soon trading insults and whining about which of them had suffered the most ill-luck during the day. I would have thought Roxanne's day had been a most fortunate one, but she regretted a very expensive gown which Albert had refused to buy for her.

'Albert,' I said above the rising voices. 'How is Wick's hotel coming along?'

'Not as fast as he would like. He's got a stone foundation, but the rest will be constructed of timber. He hasn't the necessary funds for a brick building. He's having trouble getting hired hands. Everybody who can work and is willing to bend his back is already employed in this town. They say seventy buildings have been put up since March and as many again will be built before

149

the winter sets in. If you ask me, St Jo is growing too quickly for its own good.'

Since I had to get up early the next morning, I urged Roxanne and Tilda to come along to Minnie's so that we could go to bed. I shouldn't have been surprised when they refused. It was only ten o'clock, the hour when these two began to wake up and look for mischief. Albert gallantly offered to walk up the hill with me, and told the girls he would rejoin them in about half an hour.

Trudging up the hill again, I couldn't help remembering my previous walk on a dark night with a male escort. Wick had not been very pleasant to me that night, but at least he hadn't had another woman's name continually on his lips. Albert could talk of nothing but Roxanne – what a hard life she had led, how he knew he could make her happy and give her some security. I had guessed correctly, he said. He planned to settle down in St Jo and deal in horses and mules, if Roxanne would have him.

I said I hoped she appreciated her good fortune, and realized with a stab of envy that this girl had all that I desired – a man so deeply in love that he was willing to change his whole way of life for her.

The next day Minnie made sure I had a good breakfast before I left for my new job at Livermore's. She and I were the only ones to sit down at the table that morning. Mr Huggens had resisted her efforts to get him up for work. His head ached, he said, and besides it was raining cats and dogs. There wouldn't be any work done on the hotel on a day like this, so why should he take himself down there just to stand around with his hands in his pockets looking like a wet hen?

Minnie didn't press him too hard, nor did she wake the children. 'Grief wears a body out,' she told me. 'I know how they feel better'n they do themselves.'

Since Roxanne and Tilda never left their room before ten o'clock, the house was very quiet. Minnie and I sat across the table from each other with steaming mugs of her lethal brew, while rain lashed the shutters and seeped in beneath the door. She had lit a small fire in the fireplace. It didn't give off much heat, but the air seemed less damp because of it. The small glow lit our corner of the table. We cradled the mugs in our hands, smiling at each other as we drank in silence.

'Minnie,' I whispered, 'I haven't had a chance to talk to you alone. Do you regret what you've done? Getting married, I mean. Mr Huggens and the boys don't seem to appreciate you as they should.'

Minnie chuckled as she forked the last piece of bacon on to my plate. 'Mr Huggens don't speak civil to me from the time he wakes up in the morning until he goes to bed at night, and the boys is so sassy I think if I started in to boxing their ears, I wouldn't know when to stop. But in answer to your question, I don't regret what I done at all.'

She sawed a thick slice of bread from the loaf and dipped it in hot bacon fat. 'You see, honey, you're young and you got fancy dreams about what you want in the future.'

'You may be right,' I laughed.

'I was like that once, but I got all that sort of thing knocked out of me a long time ago. Mr Taylor warn't nearly so good a husband as what Mr Huggens is. That'll give you an idea what sort of man he was. And another thing, he warn't nearly so good a father. Mr Huggens, when he's not feeling too bad on account of grieving for his wife, he'll take one of the kids up on his knee and talk to 'em real sweet, or he'll maybe play some fool game with all three. I can tell he's a decent man deep down by the way the kids love him so. And what sort of children would they be if they could forget their ma at the snap of somebody's fingers?'

She sat back in her chair and heaved a mighty sigh. 'Yes, ma'am! The Lord has smiled on me. I put my trust in Him. You picked me up offen the levee at a time when

I was thinking about doing away with myself. I believe you were sent to me. You've been a good friend which I ain't never had before, and now you've gone and bought this house where we can all live. I got me a family. I don't care if the five of us scratch and fight and kick until I'm in my grave. It's still better'n being alone.'

Much moved, I stood up and reached for an India-rubber cape. 'In that case, my dear friend, I'm very happy for you.'

'You could be happy too, but you're just a bit twisted up inside.'

'Oh, yes?' I asked sharply, and sat down again to hear what she had to say. 'In what way am I twisted up?'

'Why, on account of your ma! It's not natural a girl should feel angry with her ma. Ain't you got any good memories of her?'

'Not a one,' I said, fighting down images of presents, cuddles and sweet, companionable silences. 'I can see her prancing around, making eyes at the customers. My mother was very fat, but she remembered what it was like to be pretty. She used to act – I can't explain it properly – she used to act as if she thought she was still pretty. It's a way of walking, a way of holding your head. I remember her bawling at some man who annoyed her, or telling off one of the girls. Those are the memories I don't want to have. They cancel out all others.'

'She must of loved you, Carlotta.'

It was a reasonable statement, but I found, to my surprise, that I was suddenly having trouble breathing. There was heat in my face and a ringing in my ears.

'She gave me away!'

'No, Carlotta, honey, she couldn't of – '

'She did! I was happy enough as a child. I didn't ask for any other life. One day my grandmother arrived, and my mother said I was going to live in Boston. She hadn't bothered to warn me it was going to happen. I hadn't known that I even had a grandmother.'

'Maybe your ma hadn't knowed your grannie was coming. Maybe it was only your grannie's idea to take you away.'

I winced at the word 'grannie'. How Grandma would have hated it! 'No, my mother would have said something to her in my presence. Or I would have heard of her being surprised about Grandma coming from one of the servants.'

'You was only ten years old, for heaven's sakes. A child don't always understand what it's hearing.'

'No, I tell you!' But as I said the words, dim images began to form in my mind. A quarrel. Grandma saying: 'You're no good, Belle. Let me have the child.' I put my elbows on the table and buried my head in my hands.

'Seems to me,' said Minnie, her voice faint as if coming from a long way off. 'Seems to me your grannie didn't know about loyalty. I do think highly of loyalty. She shouldn't never have said nothing nasty about your ma to you. Why, do you know? I bet your grannie did everything she could to poison your mind against your ma.'

I looked up at Minnie. I think I almost hated her at that moment. 'You're trying to destroy my good memories of my grandmother, aren't you? I only ever had two relatives. I can't be proud of my mother. Now, you want me to be ashamed of my grandmother, as well. She was a good woman. I won't hear anything against her.'

'Don't get mad, Carlotta. I wouldn't hurt your memory of your grannie for anything. But you got to face facts. Sometimes a woman can be powerful jealous of her own daughter. Maybe those two lonely women was fighting for your love. There warn't any other love around, now was there?'

I stood up and went to the door. 'That's a hateful thing to say. I don't want to hear it.'

'Belle was your mother, Carlotta, whether you like it

or not. You only had one ma, and I don't see that she did so bad by you.'

'She was a whore, a drunken, fat, dirty whore. I'm ashamed. Oh, God, I'm so ashamed. I wish she'd never been born. But since she was, why did she have to die before I could see her one more time?'

'Calm yourself, honey. You're all mixed up. Don't be angry like that. Here. Wipe your tears. I didn't mean to upset you. Forgive me. Only, if there's no truth in what I said, how come you're so riled? Carlotta, please!'

I pushed her aside and ran out of the house. I didn't know why I was so upset, didn't know what was happening to me. I felt as if I had lost control of my life, as well as my emotions. Images, fragments of memories began jostling in my head, loosened from some dark hiding place by Minnie's words. I remembered Grandma telling me how evil my mother was. I remembered her asking me whom I loved best. Her or Belle. 'Do you love me, liebchen?' she used to say. 'More than your mother?'

But if my mother had truly loved me, why hadn't she fought to keep me with her? Why had she sent me so far away?

The walk to Livermore's was not pleasant. It didn't take much rain to turn any of St Jo's streets into swamps. Those leading downhill quickly became fast-flowing streams. I fully expected that the store would be without customers because of the weather, and prayed for a quiet day. I needed a little peace so that I could recover my composure, but I should have known better than to expect what I needed.

A trickle of emigrants and St Jo citizens came in until about eleven o'clock when the rain became torrential. Five customers were waiting to be served. Every one of them said there was no hurry, because you couldn't go out in this downpour.

Suddenly, the door opened and seven men crowded

noisily into the store, swearing and stamping their feet and slapping their soft felt hats against their legs to drive off the loose raindrops. Most of them had been working nearby in the open air until the rain got too heavy. They were now happy to sit awhile with Mr Livermore until they could get back to work. Creatures of habit, they took their places on stools and chairs ranged round the black stove, although there was no fire in it.

The oldest man was the preacher who had won the spelling bee. He greeted me with kindness as he stretched out his legs and crossed them at the ankle. Seated next to him was Wick, who didn't notice me at all until the preacher spoke. His look of surprise and approval embarrassed me. With a quick nod, I turned away. I hadn't taken this job to impress the likes of Wick Estes.

A boy of sixteen was my next customer. His mother had made a poor job of cutting his blond hair, and he was too tall for his weight, all elbows and bony wrists popping out of his homespun shirt.

'Got to get some supplies for my pa,' he announced, and produced a scrap of paper from which he read with difficulty. 'First off, a barrel of flour.'

I rolled a barrel over towards the door and made a note of the price: $4.50.

'Sack of salt, ma'am.'

I could have guessed he would ask for salt next. All the emigrants had to stock up on this most necessary supply. I balanced the sack on the flour barrel and added $2.50 to my reckoning.

'Keg of gunpowder.'

'It's too heavy for me,' I said. 'Just there. Can you bring one over?'

The boy went over to the keg and lifted it up without too much effort.

The preacher shuffled his feet and settled his backside more comfortably on his chair. 'I hear, Estes, that you used to be a wagon-master.'

155

'That's true. Led a train from Independence in forty-six. Headed for Sacramento. Made it in good time, and only six dead of natural causes on the way.'

'Seems to me your services are sorely needed at this time. All these men going West, and not enough experienced wagon-masters ready to lead them.'

Wick lit a cigarrito and leaned back in his chair, drawing deeply before expelling the smoke from his lungs. The store was quiet. My customer set down the gunpowder and laid his list upon the counter as he gazed at the man who had actually been a wagon-master.

'Five gallons of molasses,' I read quietly. 'It's forty cents a gallon.' The boy didn't answer, still looking at Wick with awe.

Wick smiled wryly at his memories. 'I was inexperienced when I started out. Fifty wagons, thirty women and children, and at least five men better qualified to lead the train than I was.'

'I doubt that,' said Mr Livermore.

I put the jug of molasses beside the boy's other supplies and took up my pencil to calculate the cost.

'We started out in good time, and Jesse Forbes was to be the wagon-master for ten days, as usual, until we could all vote in a democratic way to say who we wanted to lead us to Sacramento. Jesse was a hard man who had explored all over the West for twenty years. I'd never been more than a mile out from the river on the western side. As some of you may remember, Jesse liked his liquor. On the fourth night out, we drew up into a nice tight circle, tethered the cattle and posted the lookouts. People were still feeling pretty chipper so short a way from Independence. Tiredness gets you after a month or two. Somebody got out a squeeze box and began to play. In no time, we had ten or fifteen couples dancing round the fire.

'Jesse helped himself more than once from the whiskey jug and got to feeling romantic towards the daughter of one of the emigrants, a flirtatious little brunette twenty years younger than Jesse. She had a strong look of the Jezebel about her, and it wouldn't surprise me if she hasn't got herself into trouble out there in California.'

'I knew Jesse Forbes,' said Mr Livermore. 'Never liked a bath, said nature hadn't intended us to take off all our clothes and get into hot water. They used to say he'd been born in the saddle.'

Wick nodded. 'He could have ridden standing on his head, led a wagon train and fought off an Indian war party without even having to spit out his tobacco. But he made a bad mistake that night. I was the one who pulled him off the girl just as her pa was reaching for his rifle. Both of them were hugging and kissing and enjoying themselves in the good old-fashioned style. The girl's father didn't see it that way. He blamed Jesse for trying to force himself on the girl. A few days later, when it was time to vote for wagon-master, old Jesse didn't stand a chance of getting elected.'

'Things like that can get folks riled,' said one of the men.

'I didn't know much more than which way was West, and then only if the sun was shining,' continued Wick, 'but I was ambitious, and I wanted to be wagon-master. I got more votes than all the other candidates put together. Jesse didn't even get voted to one of the other offices. He stood lookout more nights than any other man, had to take his wagon to the back of the train more often, eating our dust, and never made one word of complaint, just smiling now and then in a sad way. I tell you, I couldn't meet his eyes.'

'Well, if the election was fair – ' began the preacher.

'Fair!' cried Wick. 'Don't you men know yet that there's no such thing as a fair election?'

I heard the boy gasp at this heresy, and lowered my head to study the figures. For the life of me, I couldn't calculate how much five gallons of molasses cost at forty cents the gallon. But then, I wasn't concentrating.

'Estes,' said the preacher sternly. 'This great land was founded on the principles of democracy, all of the people expressing their views at the ballot box, and the majority having it their way.'

Wick was getting worked up now. He bent forward and rested his forearms on his knees, looking at the men one by one, making sure they were paying attention. 'To win an election, all you have to do is pretend to be a real good boy, mind your own business and find a way to help some poor devil in trouble, so that everybody will see how kind you are. Then when the time comes, you make a real good speech full of fine-sounding sentiments. Lawyers are good at that. No, siree, there's nothing much to getting elected. But getting elected has nothing to do with being fit for the job.'

'Aw, Wick,' said one of the men, grinning a little, waiting to be told it was all a joke, and that Wick didn't really hold such radical opinions.

'That's all fine and dandy,' said the preacher, getting madder by the minute. 'How *would* you choose the President and Congress and all?'

Wick smiled, a wolfish pulling back of the lips that had nothing to do with mirth. 'Oh, voting is good enough for *them*. What difference does it make which fast-talking man gets the most votes? But a wagon-master, now he's *important*. On his knowledge rests the fate of a hundred or more people. He should be chosen on merit, like in the army, and people should have to obey. What I'm saying is, sometimes too much democratic process means too little justice.

'Take me when I was out on the trail. When things got really bad, I'd have led those people to their deaths. It was Jesse who took me aside each night where no one could overhear us, to tell me what to do the next day. Each morning I'd issue my orders, and everyone would think what a big man I was, and how smart they'd been to elect me.'

158

The boy recollected why he had come into the store, and looked down at the account I was writing, frowning at it upside down. 'I believe that's just two dollars for the molasses, ma'am.'

I mumbled an apology and scratched out my mistake with a hand that wasn't too steady. Wick had a dark view of this world, which perhaps explained his attitude to elections. But I thought there must be more to it than that. His father, I remembered, had been elected to the Missouri state legislature.

'Well, you must have learned something on the way West,' said the preacher. 'Didn't you help rescue the Donner party?'

'No, sir, I did not,' said Wick emphatically. 'But I was in the Sacramento Valley in January of forty-seven when William Eddy staggered into the settlement there with hardly anything left of his boots and frozen feet bleeding so bad, we could find our way to the others that had been with him just by following his blood in the snow. I was with the rescue party that went to find *them*, the ones who had got over the pass to raise the alarm. Only Foster and Eddy and five women were still alive out of the seventeen that had started out a month earlier to get help for the Donner party.'

The preacher shook his head. 'Terrible business.'

'An understatement,' said Wick. 'If we had known at that time what Foster had been up to, we would have strung him up there and then. He was the one who started it, I believe.'

'I heard of the Donner party,' said one of the men. 'But I never did get it straight. What happened, exactly?'

'First off,' began Wick, 'they had a fool for a wagon-master. George Donner was sixty-two years old, and his brother was sixty-five! They were rich men and should have stayed in Illinois where they belonged. I don't

159

know why they thought they wanted to go to California anyway. They did all the stupid things emigrants do.'

My young customer abandoned all attempts to make his purchases and stood to attention, his fists clenched by his sides.

'They started late in the season,' continued Wick. 'They packed up every damned thing they owned, and they took all their women and kids. That was just the beginning. Donner's big mistake came after Fort Bridger. He decided to take a new route that was supposed to cut off four hundred miles. Nobody takes it now, thank God.'

'They got caught in the snow and had to camp out over the winter, didn't they?' asked Livermore.

'Early in October, James Reed killed one of the other men in the party. They didn't hang him, but they did make him leave his wife and kids and go off on his own. He rode ahead, caught up with the Harlan party and was saved. It was this fool Harlan's idea that the Truckee Pass was a good way to go, but Harlan was three hundred miles ahead of the Donner party, and passed through there in good time. The Donners were too late. They couldn't make it over the pass, although they tried hard enough.'

'Must of been a lot died,' said the boy, his cheeks pale.

Wick nodded his head. 'Of the eighty-one travellers who made camp for the winter just below the pass, only forty-seven were saved.'

Although Wick turned his head this way and that, speaking first to one man and then to another, I knew all of the time he was intending his story to be a terrible warning to me. He still seemed to think I planned to go to the gold fields on the Oregon Trail. I would have the last laugh, however. I already knew what hell it could be travelling overland.

I said: 'It must have been difficult finding food during

the long winter up there in the mountains. It's a wonder they didn't all die.'

'That's true,' said Wick quietly.

'Dreadful thing,' murmured the preacher. 'Doesn't bear thinking about.' A very solemn Mr Livermore nodded his head as he studied the dusty floor.

Wick lit another cigarrito, taking his time. 'But some lived, because they had enough to eat. You see, they ate each other. Mostly they ate the women and children, but some men, too. Cut them up and lived off one body for several days. When rescuers finally got through to the camp in April, somebody was boiling away in the pot.'

My young customer gagged, put a hand to his mouth and ran out of the store. I watched the men in disbelief, looking for a wicked smile, a snicker to indicate that this was all a joke to frighten the boy. No one smiled.

'It's true,' confirmed the preacher. 'They mostly ate those who died natural deaths, but I heard they killed a couple of Indian guides and ate them.'

'You see,' said Wick, smiling viciously at me. 'I told you we don't always treat the Indians very well.'

'Well, as far as that goes, they'd do the same to us, I reckon,' said one of the men.

Wick ground out his cigarrito with his heel, screwing it down as if he wanted to push it right through the floor. 'Dog eat dog, you mean. When it comes down to it, we're all just animals, like I've always said.'

I could imagine an innocent child being hacked up by crazed men, its poor little limbs being put in a pot.

The room was beginning to disintegrate, to wobble and spin. I clutched the counter and looked directly at Wick, hating him for telling me something I never needed to know.

'Mr Donner was certainly a no-good wagon-master,' I said as loudly as I could. 'Tell me, was *he* elected?'

There was a burst of laughter, a welcome release from

161

intense emotions. Everybody looked at Wick, delighted that he had been challenged by a woman.

'You know, you've got a sharp mind,' said Wick quietly. 'I'd hate to see *you* end up in somebody's stewpot. No, Mr Donner sort of elected himself. He paid for the whole kit and caboodle. Most of the others were either his family or his hired hands.'

Soon afterwards, the sun came out. The men all left to carry on with their work. My young customer and those who followed him were eventually served. I managed to get my sums right, and charged them the correct amount for everything.

Mr and Mrs Livermore and I were having a quiet afternoon when a lady walked in carrying a parasol and wearing a pretty little hat on her grey curls. I hadn't expected to see her in St Jo. Mrs Morgan recognized me at almost the same time as I recognized her.

'Good afternoon, ma'am,' I said politely. 'May I serve you?'

'*You work here?*' she gasped. 'I do believe Mrs Livermore can take care of all my needs, thank you very much.'

Mrs Morgan went over to Mrs Livemore. The two women spent some time together, although I didn't see many purchases collecting on the counter. After a while, Mr Livermore was summoned. Mrs Morgan finally left. A few minutes later, I was told by a very embarrassed Mr Livermore that my services would no longer be required, as the business didn't warrant taking on a hired hand. He paid me what I was owed, and I left.

For a moment or two, standing out on the street, I felt as if I had fallen into a black hole. Then I said: 'To hell with them all.' I went down the road and bought myself a pale blue cotton costume with a snug bodice that came to a point in the front. It had sleeves that were set so tight, I'd never be able to do anything in it except hold my Bible on Sundays. Some poor woman had parted

162

with this dress before taking to the trail. It was in good
condition. I didn't suppose that she had worn it more
than once or twice. It cost me me every penny I had
earned, and then some. But it was worth it, as I found
out on Sunday.

12

Minnie was settling in to her new house, becoming comfortable with her new family. It was time to celebrate in a modest way, and what better way than to invite a few friends for Sunday lunch? Unfortunately, we were all a trifle short of friends, Wick and Albert being the only two we could rustle up.

Roxanne and I were sent into town to give the invitations on Saturday morning. Tilda came, too, because she had a few things to do. Or so she said.

'A few things *not* to do,' said Roxanne. 'like not helping Minnie clean the house.'

Tilda said that as I had been helping Minnie, that ought to be enough house-cleaning for one day. How clean did a house have to be, for heaven's sake?

I shared Tilda's view, but I didn't say so. Minnie and I had been at it since six o'clock, and it was now eleven-thirty. It wasn't more *cleaning* that house needed, anyway, but a few more possessions: cushions and rugs and pretty plates set out on the shelves by the fireplace. Unfortunately, there didn't seem much likelihood of such luxuries coming Minnie's way. Mr Huggens didn't have any money to spare, or if he did, he wasn't going to spend it. And I didn't dare squander Otis Walkern's money on luxuries.

We three parted in the town, and I walked west towards Black Snake Creek and Wick's new hotel. I was not more than a few hundred yards from it when I saw an elderly slave ahead of me. He was barefooted, wearing a torn shirt and a battered hat pulled well down on his head. He was shuffling along so slowly, I rapidly caught up with him. In order to avoid a large puddle in the road, he suddenly stepped to his left and almost collided with me. His head swivelled round nervously, and our eyes met.

' 'Scuse me, ma'am. My eyes ain't so good these days. I didn't intend no disrespect, but – '

'William?' I asked, surprised to see the elegant St Louis barber dressed so shabbily.

He shook his head violently. 'Yo got de wrong man! I ain't no William. I'm Cicero. That be my name. I gwine work fo' my master back yonder.'

I looked all around. We were alone, not even anyone watching us from a window. 'You don't have to talk to me this way, William. Whatever is it, I won't tell. Mr Estes is just – '

The man – I was *sure* it was William – dug his bare toes in the dust and ran back the way he had come, darted in between two buildings and was out of my sight within ten seconds. It was quite a performance for someone who had seemed so old and decrepit.

A few seconds later, Wick came out of what would one day be the front door of his new hotel and began prodding a small fire he had built next to the road. When the fire was to his liking, he balanced a battered coffee pot on the embers.

'Wick!' I said, running up to him, and began telling him all about the man who had insisted he wasn't William.

'He *wasn't* William,' said Wick calmly. 'Do you want some coffee? William would never dress in the way you've described. I wish I had seen the man. He probably didn't look like William at all. How many times have you seen Willian in the last ten years?'

'There was a look in his eyes. He recognized me.'

'Carlotta, old William suffered too much misery when he was a slave ever to wear such clothes again. His fine coats and white linen remind him that he is free at last, and he intends to stay that way. You've frightened some poor old slave by accusing him of pretending to be somebody else, that's all. Say, why aren't you at Livermore's?'

'You remember Mrs Morgan from the *Spread Eagle*?' I took a sip of coffee from the mug Wick handed me and made a face. 'Your coffee is worse than Minnie's. Mrs Morgan came into the store a couple of hours after you left it. She was very surprised to see me waiting on people. After she left the store, Mr Livermore said he didn't have enough trade to keep me on.'

Wick frowned, rubbing his chin. 'I'm sorry to hear it. That will be Mrs Livermore's doing. Livermore doesn't act that way when he's left to himself, but his wife's got him under her thumb.'

'I don't care all that much. I've put an advertisement in the *St Joseph Gazette* offering my services as a school-teacher.'

'You won't get any replies,' said Wick. 'You should have known you wouldn't. This is St Jo, not St Louis. It's summertime – the kids are needed in the fields or the saddlery or the flour mill or whatever. Nobody sends their kids for schooling in the hot weather. Besides, this is frontier country. People don't think highly of book-learning. You don't need to know how to read in order to survive on the frontier. You need to know how to hunt. It's not brain muscles, it's arm muscles that count.'

'There are certain professions – '

'Most folks don't care about professions. Politicking is a different matter, of course. I've no idea how much you know about your birthplace, madam schoolteacher, but when Missouri became a state, half the men in the first legislature were illiterate. They managed all right. Besides . . .' He smiled slightly. 'You've chosen to keep the wrong company, and everybody knows it. No mother would send her children to be taught by any friend of Roxanne and Tilda!'

'I can't help being Belle's daughter.'

'No,' he said, suddenly angry, 'but if you hadn't got yourself tangled up with those two girls, nobody would have known who your ma was.'

'I've come to invite you to lunch tomorrow, but I expect you won't want to sit down with Roxanne and Tilda.'

He grinned broadly, feeling playful now, determined not to take me seriously. 'I would be happy to sit down at Minnie's table any day. You'll be there, won't you? I don't have to talk to the other two.'

On Sunday, there wasn't a cloud in the sky, and for once not even a hint of a breeze on the hill to take the heat out of the sun or stop your hair from sticking to the sweat on your forehead. We all got dressed up, and everybody said I looked just wonderful. Tilda had managed to buy herself a new gown too. New to her, that is. Nobody cared to ask her where she got the money for it. It was maroon and a trifle on the small side. By the time she was dressed and ready to walk to church, she was so hot her face matched the dress.

Minnie had seen to it that her men had clean shirts, polished shoes and slicked-down hair. Little Martha's dark hair had a natural kink in it. Minnie had held the child between her knees to make finger curls. These glossy brown sausages had been scraped into two bunches, one hiding each ear, and tied with white ribbon. Martha looked very pretty and happier than I had seen since the death of the first Mrs Huggens. She chattered incomprehensibly to her brothers as she hugged her father around the knees, hampering his search for his pocket-watch. She was not so happy when she realized that Minnie wasn't coming with us, but her father promised to carry her all the way.

It was ironic that Minnie, who loved going to church, was staying behind to cook, while Roxanne and Tilda, who didn't care for it, were forced to sit through a lacklustre sermon. Fortunately for us all, the preacher didn't seem to be in the mood to rail at us for more than half an hour.

In spite of the open windows, our small congregation suffered from the heat. The swish of fans all but drowned out the tired voice of the preacher. He only once shouted out about the devil coming to get us. I jumped and dropped my fan, because my mind had been wandering. Amos and Caleb were playing some game with their hands: making a fist, a flat palm or two fingers like scissors. I was so intrigued that when the moment came for us all to be threatened for our sins, I was taken completely by surprise.

Afterwards, Wick and Albert joined us. It was so hot when we were all walking back to the house that I longed for a shady spot to sit a while. Mr Huggens said he was too tired to carry Martha all the way, but the child finally settled happily enough on Wick's shoulders.

Minnie greeted us effusively, ushering us indoors, hugging the child as if she hadn't seen her for weeks, saying yes, the boys could take off their shoes and socks, and offering us all a nice cool glass of cider before we had properly got ourselves in the door.

Mr Huggens asked the men if they would like to see around the property. They readily agreed. Wick and Albert were given a brief inspection of the upstairs, then we all trailed outside to the backyard where the pigpen was still empty, but the hens were clucking in their caged run quite contentedly.

'Watch this,' said Mr Huggens. 'Whoo-eee!' he called, and the hens scrabbled to get into the henhouse, where they stayed for a few seconds before venturing out. Mr Huggens made his high-pitched call again. Again the chickens ran inside the henhouse, frightened for their lives. Chickens are not noted for their intelligence.

'Mr Huggens, you're going to run the meat right off their legs,' said Minnie. 'Give over calling at them like that. Sometimes he does that fifteen or twenty times,' she told Wick, which made him smile.

The fields of hemp were growing well, and Mr Huggens was able to discuss the crop's progress knowledgeably. Wick and Albert nodded from time to time, but I knew they had no idea about hemp, except that it was used for making rope.

'You're fortunate to be able to buy a spread like this,' said Wick. 'Much better than going West.'

'Oh, well,' mumbled Mr Huggens, 'I didn't buy it, you know. Carlotta bought it, but I'm going to pay her back one of these days, you can bet on that.'

Wick turned to me in surprise. 'That was a fine thing to do, Carlotta. And very sensible.'

'Place needs fixing up,' boasted Mr Huggens to Albert Jenkins. 'I expect if I'd a-done the deal, I'd of gotten the spread for less than a hundred and fifty dollars. That was the price you paid, wasn't it, Carlotta?'

'Yes, it was.'

I hoped Mr Huggens didn't have too many secrets to tell. He was embarrassing me, so I walked away and stooped to pull a few weeds from around some pole beans. This proved to be impossible, because of the tightness of my sleeve. Wick joined me just as I was standing up again.

'Joel says this is the first land he's ever owned. That man can brag on just about anything. I had to remind him he doesn't own this place. I hope I'm right. You did keep the deeds, didn't you?'

'I did. I was afraid he'd sell it all to get together some money to go prospecting.'

'You know, you're a good woman, Carlotta. I think I may have misjudged you. Joel Huggens can swagger around here all he wants, but I know you bought this place so that Minnie and the kids can have a proper home.'

'That's true' I said. 'But I also hoped it would pay for

itself with something left over, so that I could repay the money to Mr Walkern.'

'I keep forgetting you're a city girl. It will be some time before this spread produces anything. And you may find it's only enough to keep y'all in food and fuel. If I had any money. . .' He shrugged. 'But I don't. Come on. Minnie's calling us for dinner.'

There was a place for Minnie at the table, of course, but she wouldn't sit at it. She trotted back and forth from the big table to the kitchen at the back, which was like the inside of a stove on this hot day. The chicken, potatoes, hot biscuits, greens and milk gravy were delicious and plentiful. I knew there was apple pie to come.

Mr Huggens' table manners left much to be desired. Minnie was always on at him about them, and today with company present was no exception.

'Must you talk with your mouth full?' she asked, and whisked the cider jug away from him just as he was reaching for it. 'You've had enough cider for one day. Folks'll think you never do anything but drink.'

Mr Huggens reached for the jug again. There was a brief tussle, which he won. He poured himself a large measure, drank it with some bravado and poured another, all the time looking at Minnie to see what she was going to do about it.

Emboldened by his father's minor revolt, Caleb reached for the jug. 'I think I'll have some more, too.'

Mr Huggens repossessed the jug with one hand and gave the boy a swipe across the head with the other. 'You'll have more when I say you can.'

'Don't you always be hitting on that boy!' cried Minnie. 'Caleb, honey, you can't drink too much cider. You're only ten years old.'

Caleb stuck out his tongue at Minnie, which earned him a much harder slap from his father. Minnie was too slow to prevent it, although she tried. Martha began to cry.

170

'You know, Mr Huggens,' said Roxanne, who seemed determined to cause trouble between husband and wife, 'you can drink more than anybody I ever did see. Excepting Carlotta's ma. And she only drank real heavy when the pain got bad.'

'*What pain?*' I asked.

'Oh, the pain in her belly towards the end. You know – '

'Pass the biscuits, *please*,' said Amos.

Minnie had taken the crying Martha on to her lap, and was feeding her with a tablespoon. Mr Huggens, now in sour mood, said Martha would be spoiled so rotten she'd never be of use to any man as a wife.

'Hush your mouth,' said Minnie irritably. She may have understood about Mr Huggens' grief, but she was not giving any quarter today.

I wondered what Wick was making of this domestic scene, and lifted my eyes cautiously from my plate. He was having the utmost difficulty containing his laughter.

He turned to Albert. 'Have you come across any Black Widow spiders in these parts, Jenkins?'

Albert shook his head. 'No, I've never heard of them.'

'Small things, they are, but deadly. You've got to watch out for them. Their bite can paralyze your chest for a while. Make you think you're never going to breathe again.'

'I seen a big one, one time,' said Caleb.

'I seen a bigger one!' said Amos.

Wick smiled briefly at the boys. 'Interesting thing about the Black Widow spider is how she got her name.'

Albert was a quick-witted man. He caught the drawl in Wick's voice and was alert for whatever humorous remark was to come.

'Yes, sir,' said Wick coolly. 'She's only interested in babies, you see. But nature being what it is, she must have a mate. As soon as her husband gives her the babies she wants, she *eats* him.'

171

Now it was Albert's turn to try to keep from laughing. He looked at Minnie, then down at his plate. Now, pink-faced, he took up his tankard and drank heavily. I could see him quiver with suppressed laughter. Wick met my eyes with a bland expression. I thought it would be nice to give *him* a swipe across the top of his head. Minnie was doing the best she could. She didn't deserve to be laughed at.

'Mary, when you going to bring in that apple pie?' asked Mr Huggens. In the silence that suddenly followed, he realized his mistake. 'I mean to say, *Minnie*. Sometimes I forget.' His voice cracked. 'Seems like . . . well, we was married for eleven years. I got kind of used to having her around.'

I think we all noticed at the same time that tears were running down Mr Huggens' rough red cheeks. His raw agony breached the boys' bravado. They rose from the table and threw themselves at their father. He clutched a boy in each arm and buried his face in Caleb's hair.

With quiet dignity, Minnie stood up and began walking towards the kitchen. 'I think it's just too hot to be eating apple pie right now. Why don't we all go out and find us some shade under the pear tree. I'll take out some chairs and maybe a quilt. How would that be?'

We mumbled some agreement, rose from the table and left the three Huggens males to cry in peace, avoiding touching them as if their sorrow might become ours if we brushed against them.

I wondered how Minnie felt, seeing her new family grieving so deeply for her predecessor. She still had Martha in her arms, cooing to the child in that high voice that sounded so ridiculous to everbody but Martha. The first Mrs Huggens had been very sick for much of Martha's life. Minnie was the most loving mother the two year old had ever known. Minnie, therefore, had gained a daughter. I doubted that she would ever win over the boys. Or Mr Huggens, for that matter.

172

Wick and I sat on the quilt, leaving the chairs for the others. After a few minutes, the boys sprawled on the quilt beside us, saying that their father was having a sleep in the rocking chair. Albert began to entertain them with tricks of sleight of hand which had them roaring with delight. Tilda was hugely entertained as well. As for Roxanne, she behaved as if Albert was her possession. She was quite prepared to take the bows for him.

'You must be wishing yourself back in Boston, among refined people,' whispered Wick.

'No, I'm not,' I said without even thinking about it. 'I can't remember when I ever sat down to a table with ten people I could call my friends. The day hasn't exactly gone according to the rules of etiquette, I know. I've known people who knew just the proper way to act at the table, who could carry on a conversation on any subject you cared to name. But they weren't my friends. It's a bit wild in this house sometimes, but it's better than being lonesome.'

'Carlotta, I've been meaning to apologize to you for the way I behaved the other night. I shouldn't have kissed you.'

Why not?, I wondered. Hadn't he liked it? The last thing I wanted to hear him say was that he was sorry he had kissed me. But what could I expect? Wick wasn't the sort of man to say something poetic, like it had been a beautiful moment, and he would always treasure it.

'Sometimes a man can get the devil in him and do something really ugly,' he said so softly I could barely hear him.

Ugly? That kiss hadn't been ugly. *Had it?* I wanted to look at him, to read in his face if he really thought it had been ugly. But my eyes were cowards. I couldn't make them look up from the patchwork quilt, couldn't make them challenge him. So instead I said: 'I'm used to you, Wick. You don't have to apologize.'

He squeezed my hand, the one that was propping me up. I couldn't return the gesture without falling over. Besides, his hand moved away before I could react. Now, I did look up at him. He was watching Albert's antics again, smiling, a thousand miles away from me and that special moment under the tree.

Minnie looked a little peaked as she walked out into the backyard, accompanied this time by Mr Huggens. 'How about some apple pie now?' she asked heartily, and we all agreed that would be just fine.

The next morning I woke at six, as usual, dressed quickly and crept out of the bedroom, leaving Roxanne and Tilda still asleep. Minnie and I had hardly sat down at the table and taken our first sip of life-restoring coffee when Roxanne joined us, creeping down the stairs and making us jump with fright.

'Well, what in heaven's name – ' began Minnie. 'Has the sky fallen in, or ain't you feeling good? Come over here, child. Sit down beside me and have a cup of coffee.'

Roxanne's hair was combed and neatly arranged, and she was wearing her prettiest calico gown. She laid her bonnet on the table, yawned hugely, and took the mug of coffee eagerly, as if she really couldn't manage to start the day without it.

'I got a few things to do in town. I thought maybe while Tilda's still snoring her head off, you'd come down with me, Carlotta.'

'I suppose so,' I said. 'What sort of things?'

'Oh, I gave a few of my clothes to this woman I met, and today she's supposed to tell me how much she'll give me for them. I thought if I sell what I'm tired of, I could maybe buy me some more calico and make another dress. It's going to get mighty hot in July and August.'

I thought I understood her motive. 'Are you selling the green taffeta Albert bought for you?'

'It's in there,' she said. 'Y'all eating pancakes? I reckon I could eat a couple if you don't take too long to cook them, Minnie. Only, I don't want to be late meeting this woman.'

Roxanne had a young girl's appetite, and finished off all the pancakes that Minnie was prepared to make, washing them down with two more cups of hot coffee. Mr Huggens came downstairs about that time, grouchy as ever. He had a two days' growth of beard on his face that he proposed to shave off out by the pump. Whenever Mr Huggens appeared, I was ready to leave the house. I urged Roxanne to put on her bonnet, and she said, yes, there was no time to lose. She didn't like Mr Huggens either.

We walked down the hill at a fairly fast clip. Even at seven o'clock in the morning, St Jo was beginning to stir. Soon the stores would be open and greenhorns would be wandering around the town, seeing what they could afford to buy for the Trail. To my surprise, Roxanne said she was sorry to have rushed me out of the house. The fact was, it was far too early to see the lady she had in mind.

She suggested we find somewhere comfortable to sit awhile. That was how we found ourselves up on the cliff on a patch of lush grass with the magnificent river far below us winding its muddy beige way through the bluffs. Roxanne seemed disinclined to talk. She picked a few clovers, studying the little blossoms while I studied her. Then she began to make a chain, splitting a stem and slipping a new stem inside until she had a chain a foot long. When she had joined them up into a circle, she leaned over and placed it on my bare head.

'There you are, a crown for the queen. You are a sort of queen, ain't you, Carlotta?'

'I don't feel like a queen.'

'You are, though. Walking tall, the way you do, and looking down your nose at us all.'

'That's not true!'

'Yes, it is. Why, you're half a head taller than Minnie

175

and Tilda and me, and you always keep your chin up when you walk, and you don't talk like the rest of us. You don't never say "ain't". People just look at you different from the way they do at us. Sometimes it makes me sick. You thinking so well of yourself and all. Why, I feel more alone when I'm with you, than when I'm all by myself. You make me think of all the things I ain't never had, and won't never get.'

'I've tried to help you.'

'I know you have. I ain't saying you haven't. Trouble is, you make me feel bad about myself. You know, ashamed, sort of. I might as well tell you, I've been jealous of you ever since we met. You don't know how lucky you are. Living in the lap of luxury, as they say, in that fine house on Second and Walnut, then going off to Boston to be educated. Pampered and loved by your ma and your gran. My ma didn't give a tinker's cuss for me, and I never knew either of my grandmas. Don't expect they were much to talk about, anyway, especially my pa's mother. Probably glad I never saw her. Yes sir, you're real lucky. The rest of us just have to make do with what God sent us, which sure ain't much.'

'Look here, Roxanne, this kind of "poor me" talk won't do you any good. You are a very pretty girl. You are more intelligent than you know, and you could have a fine and happy life.'

'If I was to accept Bertie, you mean.'

'He loves you. That's worth more than gold.'

'No it ain't. It ain't worth nothing. I never met the man I could *like*, never mind *love*. I like you, though, and I guess I like Minnie pretty well. But I'm not going to have Bertie. I don't want to be tied to any man, especially not in this stupid little town. And not when I'm so young. Look, there's the *Oregon*, just pulling in!'

We watched the riverboat manoeuvre in to the landing, a smooth arrival that was a credit to her pilot. Roxanne leapt to her feet. 'Are we going?' I asked. 'I thought you said you didn't want to bother this lady until nine o'clock.'

'There ain't no lady. I'm leaving St Jo today on that packet. That's why I wanted you to come down here with me.'

'Leaving without Albert, is that it? Not even having the courtesy to say goodbye and tell him why you won't have him.'

'I'm not telling him nothing. And without Tilda! Fat, lazy, sneaky, no-good cow! You don't know her like I do, Carlotta.'

'You're making a mistake. All right. Don't marry Albert. But don't go away, either. You're only seventeen, too young to manage by yourself, if you plan to stay out of trouble. You don't want to go back to the life you had with my mother. Think, girl! There are better ways. You'll die young, penniless, friendless and diseased.'

'My, you are the cheerful one, ain't you? I'm leaving, Carlotta. What I don't want is to be lectured to by you. I can't abide being lectured to.'

'Where do you plan to go? Just tell me that.'

Roxanne smiled. 'Well, that's kind of up to you. I fancy spending the winter in New Orleans.'

'So you want some of Mr Walkern's money.'

'That's what I'm asking. You didn't think of it as Mr Walkern's money when you bought Minnie a whole spread, did you? I just want enough to get started, enough to keep me off the street as long as possible. Is that too much to ask of you? I *stole* it, after all.'

'Yes, but I'll be the one to pay it back. I'll give you fifty dollars.'

'Make it a hundred. Honest, Carlotta, I appreciate what you done for us. You spent a hundred and fifty on Minnie's house. You don't need to remind me it gives you and Tilda a roof over your heads, as well. I already know that, but I'm telling you I *need* a hundred dollars.'

I stood up and tore the clover chain from my hair. 'I

ought not to give you anything. I ought to make you stay here with me until you're twenty-one and have some sense. Roxanne, you're at the crossroads of your life. Try to think clearly. Where do you want to be in ten years' time?'

'I want to be rich. And I want to be free. I ain't never going to be a wife, waiting on some man and having his kids. I know where I want to be ten years from now, all right.'

'Then at least join forces with Albert. I expect his goals are remarkably similar to your own. Money and freedom. That way, you would be safe. There would be someone to protect you.'

'Someone to order me around, more likely. Are you going to give me that money or do I have to go out and steal another hundred dollars?'

I was tired of arguing. 'All right. We'll go to the bank as soon as it opens. You say that's the riverboat you want to board? The one owned by the fur company? But where are your things? Did you really give them to some woman?'

' 'Course not. They's all bundled up and hid under a tree down by Wick's hotel. I come out in the middle of last night, that's why I'm so sleepy this morning. The boat is supposed to sail at ten o'clock. That'll give us time to get to the bank, won't it?'

We didn't speak on the way to collect her possessions, each of us taken up with her own thoughts. I felt sorry for Albert, because he really loved this ungrateful girl. On the other hand, I didn't think he would be happy tied to such a flighty young creature.

As for myself, a hundred dollars was a small price to pay to get rid of one of my burdens, especially one who resented me. I had spent so much of Mr Walkern's money, a hundred dollars more wouldn't make much difference. The future looked so bleak, I dared not think about it. I could see myself spending the rest of my life in the penitentiary, while Tilda and Roxanne lived high on the hog. Minnie was different. Minnie would go crazy if she thought I was in trouble, but she couldn't help me.

As we neared the spot where Roxanne had hidden her clothes, we saw Wick just walking away from his property.

'You can tell Wick I'm going,' said Roxanne, 'but you're not to tell anybody else until I'm safely away.'

'Run on and get your things,' I urged, 'while I tell him the news.'

Roxanne picked up her skirts and ran down the road like a ten year old, giving Wick a wave and a saucy smile as she passed him.

He came up to me and straightened my bonnet, which I had put on rather hastily. 'What's up with her all of a sudden?'

'She's leaving on the boat that's just landed. She's going without Albert or Tilda, not even saying goodbye to them. It's her choice. I can't stop her.'

'You shouldn't try. Good riddance, I say. You know, I guess I've been mistaken about you, and I'm sorry for anything I've said to hurt you. You've got a heart as big as all outdoors. It's led you to take under your wing two no-good girls who never are going to amount to anything. It's funny. I know half a dozen men who owe their solvency to Belle's generosity. They knew they could always turn to her when they had gambled away every last penny. She gave them money because she had a big heart, even when her head told her it was foolish. You're Belle's daughter, all right.'

'No! How can you say that? She brought these two girls into the life. She ruined them. Well, maybe not Tilda, but my mother should not have corrupted young girls. What I've tried to do for them is to make up for her wickedness.'

'You mean you did it out of spite. I might have known. You're not really like your ma, I guess. That

179

grandmother of yours, with her Bible-spouting and her unforgiving heart, has ruined you. Belle was a warm-hearted woman with courage and a tremendous sense of humour. She was witty and wise in the things she said, if not in the things she did. And loving you as she did, she let you go when your grandmother came to take you away. Everybody in St Louis knew she cried her heart out when you left. Both times.'

I put my hands over my hears. 'I don't want to hear it! Stop trying to tell me she was a good woman. I know she wasn't. You think she's better than I am. You think being a whore is better than taking money from an evil man. But it isn't. She sold her body, and with it her soul.'

'I never said being a whore was better than being a thief. I know why you stole the money. To keep from having to sell your body. Maybe it was a brave decision. It was certainly a dangerous one. All I'm saying is: can't you love your mother's memory without condoning her deeds? She was famous. She made a name for herself.'

'She was notorious. She ruined her name.'

Wick turned to watch Roxanne walking towards us with her clothes in a small carpet-bag. 'That one's a dog,' he murmured. 'Full of fleas. No, that's not quite right. A puppy who's going to grow up and bite a few people one of these days.'

When Roxanne joined us, Wick solemnly put out his hand to shake hers. 'Well, Miss, I wish you luck. Where are you headed?'

'New Orleans.'

Wick frowned. 'Oh, yes? And what are you going to do for money?'

Roxanne shot me a quick glance. 'Carlotta bought Minnie a whole house. I don't see why she shouldn't give me enough to get started on.'

Wick smiled at me and lifted my chin so that it was impossible to avoid meeting his eyes. 'I hope you know what you're doing. You haven't heard the last of

Bullmouth or Walkern, I dare say.' He shook his head. 'And I can't help you. Never mind. This little . . . *lady* will be safely away from trouble. It's a wonder you can sleep nights, Carlotta.'

I wondered if he knew I did have trouble sleeping. Seeing him always upset me. All I ever wanted to do as each day dawned was to look at Wick Estes again. But every time I saw him, there was an atmosphere between us, a straining, angry words. Sometimes the words of accusation hung between us when neither had spoken.

On this day, he was wearing a brown soft felt hat with a band that was stained dark. Sweat glistened on his chest where his open shirt bared his neck, and his trousers were so dirty they could probably have stood up by themselves. He worked hard all day here at the hotel. I never saw any sign that he hated getting his hands calloused or his face sunburned. It seemed years ago since I had last seen him in a proper white shirt, cravat and jacket.

I did wonder what made Wick the sort of man he was. Why didn't he stay in Jefferson City and let his fancy family find him some pasty-faced girl whose daddy owned half the county? I decided it was all the contradictions fighting within the man that made him so fascinating. I couldn't read the look in his eyes as we stared at each other. Angry? Sad? Not indifferent; of that I was sure. Sometimes I thought he was as hungry for the sight of me as I was of him. Other times, I thought he would cheerfully strangle me and go off whistling.

'Are you coming, Carlotta?' asked Roxanne. 'I want to get to the bank the minute it opens. I don't want nothing to prevent me getting out of here. *And* I don't want to meet Bertie and have to make all sorts of explanations.'

'I'm coming.' A movement caught my eye and I looked past Wick. The shabby slave I'd seen before was coming out of the doorway of Wick's hotel! The man saw

181

me and darted back in. 'That's the slave!' I cried, pointing. 'That's him!. Go on, tell me it's not William.'

Wick took a pace backwards, away from me, as he glanced at the doorway. 'It's not William. That's Cicero, a slave owned by a friend of my father's. I've hired him to help me get this hotel built. It's not William, do you understand?' He raised his shapeless hat and scratched his head, keeping his eyes on me, daring me to argue. 'Good day to you, ladies.'

His attitude made me mad. If he had a secret he couldn't trust me with, then I didn't want to know it. I had secrets of my own. I turned round without a word, took Roxanne by the arm and led her towards the bank. It would be open in a few minutes. The girl was in a fine mood now, chattering as I had never heard her talk in the few weeks I had known her. She was happy to be leaving St Jo. Why should I worry about her any more?

When I had seen her to the boat, given her a peck on the cheek, and was preparing to walk back down the gangplank, she suddenly caught me up in a bear-hug that surprised me as much as it hurt.

'You know, Carlotta, I'm going to miss you. I never thought I'd say that, but it's true. Your ma used to talk about you sometimes. She was always bragging on you. I got so I just hated you.' She cocked her head to one side and studied me. 'You're very well preserved, you know that? I expect your skin's nice like that because of the sea air in Boston. Just the same, by the time I'm your age, I do hope I'm settled in life. When I'm twenty-three I might look real old, because of the way I've lived. I hope you don't end your life as a dried-up old spinster. I should have taught you a few woman's wiles so's you could catch Wick. You don't know how to treat that man at all.'

Some other time I would have been amused by her silly talk, but right now I had a serious question to ask her. I had been putting it off, but time was running out. It was now or never.

'You spoke of my mother drinking more than usual towards the end, because of a pain. What sort of pain was it?'

The smile faded from Roxanne's face. 'She was hurting real bad, Carlotta. And losing weight, too. Sometimes that old pain in her belly hurt so bad, she'd just sit there and cry with it. She didn't have long to live, if you ask me. I expect that's why she sent for you. But we all have to go some time, don't we?'

'Yes, some time, but she was only forty years old! Why didn't you tell me this before?'

Roxanne shrugged, indifferent now. The steamboat clanged its warning of imminent departure. 'She was dead by then. What difference does it make? Knowing about it hasn't made you happy, has it?'

I agreed it hadn't. There was nothing more to be said, so I walked down the gangplank and waved one last time.

I couldn't shake off the guilty feeling that I should have been by my mother's side when she faced her final illness. The thought of this terrible pain worried me. I had had bronchitis once. There had been pain every time I took a breath. When I was a little girl, I had fallen out of a tree and broken my arm. That was a pain, but not an unbearable one. What must it have been like, this pain of my mother's that made her sit and cry, that caused her to drink to oblivion? Maybe the fire had been a blessing, but had she died quickly? Painlessly? Visions of her charred body rose up before me, churning my stomach. I tried to shake off these unwelcome thoughts, tried to tell myself she was dead and beyond pain. An iron band clamped itself around my head; somebody tightened the screws. Why hadn't she told me she was ill?

'*Fool!*' I said to myself. Here I was blaming my mother for her own death. It wasn't her fault, any of it. I was blaming her for all sorts of things, because I couldn't

183

bear to think of her being alone and in pain. Wick wanted me to remember her as Missouri Belle: fat, sassy, gaudy and ready to fight the whole of St Louis if that was the way the town wanted it. I was beginning to have trouble remembering her clearly at all. Her face was blurred in my mind. And now, thanks to Minnie and Wick, I couldn't feel comfortable thinking about my grandmother either.

I walked along Market Street, nodding to a few people whose faces were familiar, aware all the time of the liveliness of St Jo. It was sure to be a big important town one of these days. It was proud of itself already. I could be a part of this town and its pride. I owned a house just a little way out of town. Minnie was there. Wick would probably live in St Jo now that he was building a hotel here. Minnie and Wick were the only people I had left to care about. I had to hang on to them.

There were greenhorns everywhere, cluttering up the streets, filling the stores, grinning their foolish grins, not knowing what misery was in store for them on the Oregon Trail. Running away from adult life, that's what they were doing, leaving others behind to work and wait and try to hold their families together. How I hated the sight of them, and the sound of their boastful voices!

I had no reason to stay in town this bright morning, so I turned my steps towards Minnie, towards my friend.

While I was walking, I tried to think of myself the way Roxanne did, as a lucky woman. I couldn't do it. Being the one left to tell Albert and Tilda that Roxanne was gone for good was a piece of very bad luck. I had read that in olden times, they used to kill the messenger of bad tidings.

13

A man I had never seen before was a few yards ahead of me, going through Minnie's front gate. He was hatless, his wet blond hair clinging to his scalp. Every step he took left a puddle of water, and Caleb – as still as death and just as pale was cradled in his arms. The boy had a six-inch gash on his forehead. Blood had congealed around it; a violent contrast to his white skin. Amos walked nervously beside the man, taking an extra step now and then to keep pace. His own dark locks were wet and dripped water onto his shoulders.

Minnie opened the front door. I saw her put a hand to her mouth as if to stifle a cry, and they all went into the house. I called, but she didn't hear me, and shut the front door before I could reach it.

It didn't take much effort to figure out that Caleb had been swimming in the watering hole, had dived from the cliff above and cut his head on the rocks at the bottom of the pool. Several boys had been hurt that way, and one had died the year before. Caleb and Amos had been threatened with dire punishment if they dived from the cliff. No wonder Amos looked so frightened!

I went around to the back of the house and entered quietly from the kitchen, standing unnoticed for some seconds in the doorway. Caleb lay across two chairs with a quilt of his mother's thrown over him. He was awake and said his head ached something awful. Amos sat on a low stool with his head in his hands, crying. Such desolate whimperings of despair! I pulled up another stool and sat down to comfort him.

'I'm sorry, Minnie,' whispered Caleb. 'I know Pa told me not to swim there, but all the boys was doing it.

185

There's this cliff, and you just have to show you're a man and dive off it.'

'You can't keep boys away from a swimming hole on hot days, ma'am,' said the man.

Now I could see that Caleb's rescuer was only sixteen or seventeen. His face had more freckles than I had ever seen on a person, and his forehead was sunburned and peeling unattractively. He had an ignorant, innocent face; a boy still, but with the shoulders of a man. With becoming hesitation, he accepted Minnie's offer of some cooling cider, but could not bear to hear himself praised for bringing Caleb home. I was returning from the kitchen with the cider when she asked him if he had dived in to save the boy. He wouldn't admit it, refused to give his name, and finished the cider I brought him in one gigantic gulp before leaving the house.

When I sat down again, Martha crept into my arms, her eyes huge. Normally the focus of Minnie's life, the child sensed that this was not the moment to demand attention.

Minnie pulled up a chair to sit by Caleb, murmuring soothing nothings, bathing his cut head with wet lint, and assuring the boy that she wouldn't let his father give him a licking for disobeying him.

I suggested fetching the doctor, but Minnie said why waste the money? She could do everything necessary for the boy. She was undoubtedly right. Within five minutes, Caleb was sitting up and boasting of his adventure. He was getting quite animated and full of himself when the door opened and his father entered. For some reason, Wick had decided to come with Mr Huggens, and now crossed the room to stand by me. Caleb suffered a dramatic relapse and laid back down on the chairs.

'I'll whup your hide!' bawled Mr Huggens. He was almost as white-faced as his son had been, a man who had endured more than his constitution could take in the last few days.

186

Wick stepped forward and patted the boy on the head. 'You showed a lot of backbone diving off that cliff. But sometimes it helps to have a bit of commonsense, too.'

'I'm sorry, Pa,' said Caleb, manfully facing his father's wrath. The boy was holding Minnie's hand, clinging to her for moral support.

'Damned fool!' said Mr Huggens, his voice breaking on the words.

Minnie stood up suddenly, and pulled Caleb to his feet. 'Look at you! I suppose you went swimming naked and they just put your clothes back on you without drying you off at all. And you, too, Amos. Let's go upstairs and get some dry things on the pair of you.'

She had them out of the room before the tears that had been gathering in Mr Huggens' eyes spilled over. He sat down, and Martha left me to scramble on to his lap.

Wick stuck his hands in his pockets and looked at me. 'One of the boys came down to the hotel to give us the news. Made a real good story of it. We thought Caleb was at death's door, if not actually dead. That's why I came along, too. It's a wonder Joel's heart didn't give out on him when we were coming up the hill.'

Mr Huggens blew his nose on a red handkerchief. 'I've had about all I can stand.'

Wick was still angry. 'I'm disgusted with that boy. You didn't need to know what happened right away, Joel. If there is one person in this world who can handle a boy's cut head, it's Minnie. Carlotta, I hate to ask when I'm a guest in somebody's house, but we sure could do with a long drink.'

I jumped up. 'Of course. I'll go and get some cider.'

Wick followed me out to the kitchen. 'She's done it,' he said softly.

'Done what?'

'You mean you haven't been taking any notice? Minnie has been trying to win over those boys ever since she met them. I expect they'll think of her as a mother

187

from now on. This little accident has been hard on Joel, but it's done the trick for Minnie. She's a very interesting combination of rough courage and cunning, don't you think?'

'You don't like her. You compared her to a Black Widow spider and laughed at her.'

'Minnie does make me laugh now and then, but I respect her. She goes after what she wants. Lots of people do that, of course. The special thing about Minnie is that all she wants is to look after others.'

I managed to find two mugs and filled them with cider. Wick picked them up and headed towards the parlour. 'Come on. Let's go back to Joel before he really does take a switch to those boys.'

Tilda came home for the midday meal and was just as upset about Roxanne as I was afraid she would be. Minnie and I were treated to a twenty-minute harangue that had Minnie's eyes glazing over. Tilda said so many terrible things about Roxanne that I wondered how she could insist she would miss her. Then I came in for my share of criticism, but Minnie, who had sat silent up to now, leapt to my defence with more venom than was absolutely necessary.

The two women bawled at one another for the rest of the meal. Tilda was so angry, she went back into town without offering to help with the dishes. I helped Minnie clear up, but when the chores were finished, I said I had better find Albert and get the telling over with. Minnie said I should remind him how lucky he was.

I might have known Tilda would make sure she was ahead of me with the news. Albert was waiting for me, leaning against a post outside the saloon where he gambled all afternoon and well into the night. He looked seedier than I had ever seen him. His fancy shirt was clean enough, but his brocade waistcoat had food stains on it, and one pocket was ripped where he had put his thumbs in so often. He was very angry and blamed me, because Roxanne hadn't liked him enough to stay in St Jo.

'I don't know what to do now,' he said morosely. 'I had my whole life planned out. Knew just what I was going to do from now on. Oh, what the devil! There's more fish in the sea. That little tramp kept me bobbing on a string. To hell with her. I don't need her.'

I left Albert as soon as I could. He was angry, but nowhere near as hurt as I had expected. Perhaps Roxanne would be better off without him. She had certainly valued his so-called love for what it was worth. In many ways that seventeen year old girl was older than I would ever be.

My mother was constantly in my thoughts. I thought about how she had run away at fourteen, probably bamboozled by the sweet-talking man three times her age that my grandmother had told me about. Then, when she was still too young to have any sense, he had abandoned her. Perhaps she had been all mixed up, just the way I had been after the fire, when the four of us hadn't known how we were going to survive. Instead of stealing twelve hundred dollars, the way we had done, she had gone on the streets. From then on, she never had a choice about the direction her life would take. I could just see that slim fourteen year old girl, alone and frightened.

I had been a party to stealing a lot of money, never mind the reason. If I didn't watch out, I could find my future was taken care of, too. I believed I was smarter than my mother had been. I was certainly older. If I was ever going to get out of this trouble, I had to do something clever. And I had to do it quickly.

Knowing all this, I didn't hesitate when I saw the *St Joseph Courier* was for sale. The rival newspaper, the *St Joseph Gazette*, was by far the more successful of the two papers. But the *Gazette* was overmanned. I was sure Mr Archer was getting good pay for editing it, because lawyers always made a lot of money, no matter what they did. Then too, the owner, Mr Ridenbaugh, would want his profit. And the staff they had! I had never seen so many people standing around in a newspaper office.

I didn't see why I couldn't lick the opposition hollow with a better written paper that had more guts to it. And I wouldn't be paying out any wages. I would be the owner-editor. Minnie, Tilda and the boys would help. We'd make lots of money, although my aim would not be to make a few dollars each week. My purpose would be to make the *Courier* such a threat to the *Gazette* that Mr Ridenbaugh would want to buy me out. I figured I could get him worried in about three weeks. Then I'd hold out for a good price, and have the money to pay off Mr Walkern before he had a chance to find me.

I opened the door of the small store and went in to speak to the proprietor, Mr Teel. The press was silent, the floor littered with printed paper, the corners of the ceiling almost hidden by dusty cobwebs.

'Business looks pretty bad, Mr Teel,' I said. 'But I suppose I could pay you five hundred dollars for everything – press, paper, ink and the rest of the lease on the office. How would that be?'

Mr Teel was at least fifty years old, a shuffling man with a noisy chest. He wheezed in and out a couple of times and said: 'You want to buy the *Courier?*'

'Yes, sir. Cash. Five hundred dollars. Take it or leave it.'

'I'll take it,' said Mr Teel and had a fit of coughing. 'Going to the gold fields. Going to get rich.' He gasped for breath, unable to say more.

'I wish you luck, sir. Now I'll go down to the bank to get the money. Don't you sell it to anyone else before I get back.'

Mr Teel gave a wheezy little laugh, and promised he wouldn't sell it to anybody, no matter how much he was offered.

I left and headed for the bank. I knew when I was being laughed at. I could have bought the paper for less, that was obvious. Still, Carlton, my one time fiancé, had managed to sell his flatbed press and the goodwill of his debt-ridden paper for a thousand dollars. I intended to make fifteen hundred when the time came to sell the *Courier*.

I was halfway to the bank when it suddenly struck me that this was the biggest purchase I had ever made. Minnie's spread had cost one hundred and fifty dollars. There would certainly be a lot less to show for my five hundred. But then, I calculated, the paper would make much more money. Besides, who would dare to sneer at the proprietor and editor of a newspaper? I was about to become respectable.

Tilda came trotting up to me as I neared the waterfront. I think she had been watching me for several minutes. 'Thank heavens I've found you,' she said urgently, pushing me into a doorway. 'Carlotta, we're in trouble. There's a man I used to know just come in on the riverboat from St Louis. Knows all about us taking Mr Walkern's money. We got to pay him off.'

I felt my heart begin to thud. 'Oh, God, not now, not when I'm so close to having my own newspaper! What do you mean, pay him off? I can't think straight. There's so much on my mind, Tilda.'

'He wants money to forget he knows where we are. Otherwise, he'll tell old man Walkern.'

'What's to stop him from asking us for money over and over?'

'He's going away tomorrow.'

'Then what's to stop him from going straight back to Mr Walkern and telling him where we are?'

'Oh, Carlotta, don't make it difficult. If he says he won't tell, he won't.' When I continued to look sceptical, she added irritably, 'He's a married man. I know a few things about him. What I told him is this. We'll give him two hundred dollars to forget all about it, because it's worth that to us. But if he ever asks again, I swear I'll travel back to St Louis and tell his wife and kids just what he likes to do in bed.'

I started to protest, but she rattled on. 'What we'll do, is you go to the bank and get the money. Then I'll go down to the landing and give it to him. If you want to, you can watch from a hiding place where he can't see you.'

I was in a panic. All I wanted to do was buy the *Courier*. I didn't want to be stopped by a blackmailer or anyone else. Tilda seemed so certain about what to do that I was ready to believe her way was the best. After all, by now I had spent so much of Mr Walkern's money, I didn't think another two hundred would matter. Halfheartedly I protested, saying I wanted to discuss it with Minnie.

'Don't you never get tired of worrying that poor woman? Give over, Carlotta. Let's you and me fix this business and be done. Come on, let's go to the bank. Do you want to get him riled?'

I most certainly didn't want to get him riled. We started walking towards the bank. 'I'm planning on buying the *St Joseph Courier*.'

She blinked at me. 'That only costs six cents.'

'The whole thing, press, paper and everything. I'm going to own the *Courier* and run it. You can help me.'

'Just as well I run into you when I did. Else there might not've been enough money to pay off this man.'

My head was whirling. I really wasn't thinking clearly. When I had the money, she carefully placed me in the shadow of a doorway, then walked down to the landing where a middle-aged man in a top hat, cutaway coat and pigskin gloves stood nervously tapping his cane on the ground. He looked very well-to-do. I hated for him to have any of Mr Walkern's money. I supposed men like this one got rich by taking advantage of every opportunity, picking up a few hundred dollars wherever they saw the chance, and not worrying too much about the rights and wrongs of what they were doing.

The man unsmilingly took the money, shaking his head at something Tilda said as he put it away in an inside pocket. She looked up in my direction and gave a very slight nod, which was our signal. I left my hiding place to complete the business that obsessed me.

Minnie said you could knock her over with a feather when I told her about buying the *Courier*. Mr Huggens said he had forgotten that I could read and write. I had forbidden Tilda to say anything about the blackmail, because Minnie had enough on her mind without hearing such worrying tales. Tilda showed surprising restraint at dinner that night, saying pleasant things about Minnie's cooking, and refraining from bawling at the children or baiting Mr Huggens.

I was at the door of the *Courier* office by half past eight the next morning. The *Gazette* was published every Friday. I couldn't hope to match that publication day, since this was already Thursday, but I would do the best I could. My first task had to be to sweep the place clean and see what exactly I had bought. Minnie came down about two hours later, loaded with old rags and a mop and broom. The children came, too. She soon had the boys helping to clear up.

Unfortunately, she never stopped complaining about Tilda's disappearance. 'She said she just had to get a few things straight,' moaned Minnie, 'and then she'd come on down and help. I should of known she wouldn't come. I thought it was funny she didn't complain about doing some good old-fashioned hard work.'

I also thought it was strange she hadn't complained, but I was too busy to dwell on it. Then, right on eleven o'clock, we heard the bell of a steamboat as it prepared to sail. I thought what a fool I'd been. Tearing off my apron, I called to Minnie that I just had to scc about something, and ran all the way to the landing. Sure enough, Tilda was there, hanging on the arm of the very man to whom she had paid the two hundred dollars. The *Gold Nugget* was ready to sail. Any minute now Tilda and the man would board, taking my two hundred dollars with them.

'Tilda, you dirty, rotten cow!' I screamed, brightening the day for half a dozen grinning roustabouts.

'Well, well. If it ain't – I mean, if it *isn't* Carlotta,' said Tilda, speaking in what she thought was a ladylike voice. 'Guthrie, my dear, I wouldn't normally introduce you to just any old trash, but you may recall having met Missouri Belle. This is her daughter, and she's *trying* to turn respectable. I've helped her out as best I could which is why my savings are down to two hundred dollars.'

'Tilda, if you want to keep your hair, you'd better come over here and have a word with me,' I gasped, out of breath from running so far. Tilda looked distinctly nervous, but she walked over to talk to me out of Guthrie's hearing.

We walked down the landing about twenty yards. 'If you don't want me to pull out every hair on your head, you'd better explain yourself. What's all this business about me trying to better myself? And since when did you plan to go with the so-called blackmailer?'

'I was just trying to drive you off before you said something out of place and spoiled everything. That's why I was rude. *I'm* trying to better myself here, Carlotta. Guthrie thinks he's poor, but he's just not as rich as he used to be. He was my best customer years ago. Wouldn't come to Belle's new place on the levee, used to send for me. He didn't know I was in St Jo. He came to sell up a business so he can live in Chicago until he's got enough money to pay off his creditors. He left his wife about six years ago. There ain't – aren't any kids.'

194

'So he never intended to blackmail us.'

'He don't even know about the money. Please don't tell him. He knows what I was. But, you see, I ain't seen him for six months, and he thinks I've become real ladylike. He says he'd be proud to have me on his arm in Chicago. You said you wanted something better for us – Roxanne and me – well, she didn't learn nothing. But I learned how to be ladylike, and that's all your doing, Carlotta. I been watching you. When I'm with Guthrie, I act the way you do. He thinks it's just dandy.'

'It wasn't very ladylike to make me think we were being blackmailed. I've been worried sick.'

'Well, I'm real sorry about that, but I had to have some money of my own. That's necessary in life, don't you think? You taught me that.'

'Why didn't you come to me and ask for it?'

Her eyes opened wide. 'Why would you give any money to the likes of me just for the asking?'

Guthrie was looking impatient. I took Tilda by the arms and shook her a little. 'You wouldn't understand, you silly girl, but I really care that you might fall on hard times.'

'Well, I sure could do with a bit more,' said Tilda happily, holding out her hand. I slapped it away.

'You've already had two hundred that I will have to pay back somehow. You've had more than anybody. I hope you're satisfied. Minnie didn't ask for anything. Roxanne asked for a hundred.'

'And you bought the newspaper for five hundred.'

'I'm hoping to pay back Mr Walkern with profit from the newspaper. I don't expect you to pay back anything. Goodbye and good riddance. I hope I never see your lying face again.'

She wasn't a bit put out by my harsh words. 'I never thought you liked me. Do you really like me? I never thought you'd do anything for me, at all. Nobody ever has before. Excepting your ma, of course. Oh, Carlotta!

195

If I'd of known, I'd of come right up to you and said I need two hundred dollars!'

I couldn't help smiling. She had apparently imitated my manners and caught herself a protector. He would give her greater security and prestige than she had enjoyed with my mother. She would live comparatively well. So perhaps I had done something worthwhile for her, after all.

'I wish you had asked, but you would only have got *one* hundred dollars from me. Tilda, I never hated you, please believe me. I wanted you to be happy and secure. I still do. I don't know this man at all. Are you safe with him? Will he treat you right?'

'Yes, of course he will. And if he don't, I'll leave him. I got my own money, you see. That's what it's for Carlotta . . .'

Tears welled up in her eyes. The tight maroon costume was already badly creased and damp under the arms. Her bonnet had seen better days on other heads, but I thought she had gained a certain dignity in the last twenty-four hours. Her pouting expression had taken on a new softness. Now that it was time to leave St Jo, she was quite distressed. We looked at one another for a few seconds and then embraced, both of us surprised by how much parting meant to us. Over her shoulder, I saw Guthrie's startled face, and smiled at him. Tilda and I had known each other for a little less than one month. I felt as if I was saying goodbye to a particularly irritating, but well-loved sister.

By the time I got back to the *Courier* office and Minnie, I had made up my mind that this newspaper would have to be the finest ever printed west of Boston. The only trouble was, I couldn't think of a thing to write. Minnie said maybe I should write about Tilda taking off with a man. And, of course, she said you could knock her over with a feather when I told her she and I were on our own from now on.

The *Gazette* made very dull reading: whole articles lifted from other newspapers in other parts of the country, the speeches of Thomas Hart Benton, letters from California and reports from the followers of some man called Fremont. There were market reports from St Louis, too. None of these things interested me. I *was* interested in the many advertisements. I couldn't hope for any advertisements in my first edition, but I must pray that there would be many in my second edition.

Four pages, six columns, eighty words to the inch made about twenty-four thousand words. I would have to write them all. There would be no time for pen and ink. My articles would have to be composed upside down and backwards right on to the type stick, line by line. Furthermore, Saturday was the latest day I could publish. I urgently needed whatever hard money I could raise from the sale of, say, five hundred copies.

The door opened and Mr Hays, the lawyer who had handled the sale of Minnie's house, came to the counter.

'I wish to place an advertisement in Mr Teel's paper, Miss Schultz. Do you work here now?'

This was not the time to say that the *Courier* was owned by a woman. I mumbled yes, and asked him what he wished to say in the announcement.

'It begins: *Negro For Sale*. Have you got that? Here is the rest, written out. Perhaps you will read it to me, so that I know there are no misunderstandings.'

'*Negro for sale*,' I read. '*The undersigned, Executors of Wm Williams, deceased, in pursuance of an order of the Buchanan County Court, will on the 18th day June next, at the late residence of said deceased (known as the "Missouri House" and situated on the road to Sparta) sell at auction to the highest and best bidder a negro woman slave, belonging to said estate.*
June 14

Benjamin Hays
Executor.'

197

He put a dollar on the counter, said: 'I believe that is exactly right,' and left.

I held the announcement in my hands and felt a lead weight in my stomach. As a child, I had been able to ignore the injustice of slavery. My mother and I knew several people who kept slaves and my mother disapproved. She refused to keep a slave herself. We thought that was sufficient. We thought we had fulfilled our moral obligations to oppressed negroes.

My years in Boston taught me otherwise. The citizens of Massachusetts despised slave owners. Many of them were active in organizations aimed at ending slavery. Carlton's opposition to this dreadful trade was one of the most attractive things about him.

Now, here I was, planning to make money out of the announcement of a slave auction. I needed the money, but I thought I knew how I could play my part in bringing to an end a practice that brought disgrace on the American people.

As the day wore on, more and more men came in to place advertisements. I took notices for farms for sale, harnesses, California Fixings, and medicines to help cholera and consumption. First-time advertisement squares cost a dollar, but a repeat run was only fifty cents. Some men expressed surprise that Mr Teel had taken on a female hired hand, others asked where he was. I said I didn't know, which was true enough.

Minnie said she had to go home. She had to start cooking. I thanked her for staying as long as she had, and wondered how I was going to manage without any help at all. Fortunately after four o'clock no one came in to place an advertisement. I had enough to pay for the paper and ink from the money I had received over the counter. Sales of copies would be all profit. Thirty-six dollars was a lot of money, but that was what I could earn if I sold all five hundred copies.

I was on the road to success, had found my place in the

world at last. I felt strong and proud. I was even able to laugh about the way Tilda had cheated me out of the two hundred dollars. I was free. She and Roxanne were gone, Minnie was happily settled. I could afford to think about myself. I would live right here in St Jo, and Wick would have to respect me, because I was a newspaper proprietor.

All through the long hours of the night, I set type. The point size was *agate*, the smallest size ever used on a newspaper, and hard on the eyes to handle. My back ached and my eyes felt as if they might pop out of my head, but I kept my spirits up by thinking that I was *a newspaper proprietor*! I wondered what Carlton would say if he could see me now.

At four in the morning, I dimmed the lamp and found a clean patch of floor on which to catch a few hours' sleep. What a slow business it was! Carlton's typesetter had been able to set type almost as fast as he could read. He had made it look easy. I was learning the hard way that there is a world of difference between knowing how to do something and being able to do it quickly and accurately.

So tired was I that I didn't wake on Friday morning until half past nine, and then only because Minnie was tapping on the window. Since I was faint with hunger, I was very glad to eat the bread and cheese and drink the cold coffee she had brought.

I returned to typesetting and eventually had pages one and four tightened up in the chase on the stone.

It was time to run off a proof to see if I had made any mistakes. I had been so busy setting type that I hadn't taken time to look over the press. It was a Franklyn, the flatbed type with a platen, and must have weighed going on for a thousand pounds. I inked the type, laid on a sheet of paper and brought down the platen. It was hard work. To print five hundred copies, the platen would have to be inked and pressed down a total of a thousand times. I was pretty sure I didn't have the strength to do it.

Lifting the sheet carefully, I stared at my very first effort. The impression was faint, but that could be corrected. I had two lines upside down. I could correct that fairly easily, as well. The trouble was, when the sheet was folded in half, page one was on the back and page four was on the front. Now that was a real problem! In fact, it was serious enough to bring the tears stinging into my eyes. You just couldn't have ST JOSEPH COURIER in big letters on the back and plain type with small headlines on the front. It was not a mistake I could forget about.

Besides, I had spent a lot of time and given a lot of thought to the editorial which was supposed to have pride of place on the front. I wanted everybody to know what I thought about slavery. Such a message must not be hidden away. It took me three hours to correct. Only then was I ready to run off five hundred impressions of the first side.

I stood on a stool. I fought with the handle of that press. I struggled every way I knew how. In the end, I recognized that I would have to get some strong man to run off the copies.

The only good thing that happened to me on Friday was that just about the time I was struggling with the press, the young man who had saved Caleb came in to say hello and ask after the boy. He had seen me through the window of the office and was intrigued by what I was doing.

'Roll up your sleeves, young man,' I said. 'You're about to find out.'

His name was Joshua Butts, and he was more than willing to help me run off five hundred copies. His father was a hemp grower who was having a hard time making ends meet, so Joshua was extremely pleased to receive a dollar for his efforts. He agreed to come the next afternoon to print the second side, pages two and three.

'What are you going to do now?' he asked.

'Well, you see how all the rows of type are held together in a sort of metal frame? I've got to get that type off the stone so that I can set up the next two pages.'

'That looks mighty heavy,' said Joshua. 'Here, let me lift it off for you.' He started to pick up the chase. The type was screwed very tightly into it, but there was no bottom. I had visions of all that type being scattered right over the floor. He actually lifted it up a little way, surprised by its weight, before I could stop him.

'Put that down, Joshua!' I cried. 'You might drop it; it weighs about two hundred pounds. And if the type falls out, I will never find it again!'

'Then what are you going to do, ma'am?'

'Unlock the chase, take out every single piece of type and put it back in its own special compartment on these two trays. Here, see how all the capital letters are in the upper case in the chest, and all the small letters are in the lower case? That's what I've got to do. I don't have enough type to set all four pages at once.'

'It's going to take you an awful long time to put back all those itty-bitty pieces,' mused Joshua. I agreed.

When I began setting the next two pages, I soon discovered that I didn't have nearly as many advertisements as the *Gazette* did. That meant I would have to write more copy.

To fill up space, I set up every poem I could remember. Then, I must confess, I read through the *Gazette* which had come out that morning, to see what stories I could copy. I did give them my own particular point of view. The emphasis in my stories was different from the *Gazette*'s. Mr Archer was apt to announce the deaths of thirty-five people in St Louis from cholera in a little item tucked away on the back page. I thought such a calamity needed more space. I wrote up the cholera deaths with all the powerful words I could find. Then, in articles placed around the announcement, I put every cholera remedy I could remember. It made a nice gruesome section.

The post office had taken some space in the *Courier*. *A List of Letters*, I called it. Ten inches of a double column of names of people who had letters waiting for them at the post office. If they didn't pick them up in three months, the letters would be sent to the general post office as dead letters. It was interesting to speculate why all these people had not come to collect their mail. Were they sick? Dead? Gone West?

The list started with *Atwood John* and I was three-quarters of the way through up to Renfroe, Charles C. when Wick came in to see me. He congratulated me on buying the *Courier*, which he said was the smartest thing I had ever done. I told him about my plan to sell off the paper in a few weeks, and that the first edition would be out on Saturday. He said he would come back then. I never looked up at him once while he was there. The post office was my biggest and best customer. I didn't want to make any mistakes on their advertisement.

I suppose it was tiredness that caused me to line up the pages wrong again. Page two was where page three ought to be, and vice versa. But on the inside, it didn't matter. I went home at four o'clock in the afternoon, and was almost too tired to eat. Minnie insisted on frying up some bacon and eggs before I went to bed early.

I calculated the five hundred second sheets shouldn't take more than an hour or two to print, so I didn't hurry down to the *Courier* office. Joshua Butts had promised to come over about half past ten to operate the press.

At eleven o'clock, I was still waiting for him, but quite a few other people were coming in to ask just one question. Was the *Courier* really owned, written and printed by a woman? The lawyer, Mr Hays, said I had better put out a good paper with a clear announcement of the slave auction, or he would demand his money back. Several men came in and tried to cancel their advertisements, but I said it was too late.

At one o'clock, despairing of ever seeing Joshua again, I began to print the second sheets myself. These were sheets that already had pages one and four on them, so that when I failed to get an impression of sides two and three, the whole thing was ruined. Since I had dismantled the chase, I couldn't print any more of pages one and four, so after twenty attempts, I gave up. There was nothing to do but wait and fret, because I didn't know how to get in touch with Joshua.

He arrived at four o'clock, saying his mother was very sick. Being anxious about my paper, it was all I could do to appear sympathetic.

By that time there was a crowd of men, mostly drunk, waiting to buy the first copy of a newspaper edited by a woman. I had to lock the door. Some of those men were getting dangerous, and besides they kept me from my work.

We had all sorts of problems; lines of type upside down or not printing at all. Joshua was willing to work hard, but I soon discovered he couldn't read, so there were certain tasks he just couldn't help me with. After a few hours, I put a sign in the window saying the paper would be on sale at eight o'clock that night. It wasn't all that common to sell newspapers after dark. But it was unthinkable to sell them on Sunday.

By the time I unlocked the door so that people could come in and buy the *Courier* there was a near riot going on outside. Twenty men forced their way in at one time, all demanding their copy and holding out their money to me. I had hoped that Joshua would help take the money, but he had left as soon as the last paper was folded, wishing to get back to his mother as quickly as possible. There was no sign of Minnie or Wick, so I just had to manage on my own.

As it turned out, I didn't have to work too hard. I sold

only fifty or sixty copies. Instead of each one buying a paper, the men stood outside, one holding up a lamp while half a dozen more strained to see what was on the page. Fifty copies weren't going to do me much good. I needed greater sales.

Still, I could congratulate myself on my achievement. No woman, I was sure, could have produced a newspaper entirely by herself. The printing of it required the brute strength of a healthy man. But I had done everything else. The paper was all my own work. It might have a few mistakes – it might be very faint in places, but I had written it and got it out in a matter of days.

In the future, I would be quicker. Maybe I would hire a boy, a printer's devil, to put away the type. And I would certainly have to hire a proper printer to set the type and operate the press. I would be the editor sitting at a desk, accepting advertisements. Instead of selling out, perhaps I would drive the *Gazette* out of business one of these fine days. Mr Lawrence Archer might be a lawyer-editor, but his paper was owned by Mr Ridenbaugh. I, on the other hand, was an owner-editor.

While these pleasant thoughts were brewing in my head, the mood outside was beginning to get ugly. A few men waved their fists at me through the glass. I heard shouts of 'Nigger thief!' which surprised me, because I had never stolen anything in my life, except twelve hundred dollars. Before I could get over my surprise and take cover, a half-brick crashed through one of the panes of glass in the window. I couldn't see any sort of signal, but the men seemed to have made up their minds all at the same time to come in after me. I didn't know what I had done to arouse their anger, but I wasn't given an opportunity to ask.

'To the river!' was the cry. 'Take the press!'

Hands were laid on me, great sweaty men with liquor on their breath took me by the arms and dragged me out of the the *Courier* office. I thought they were going to lynch me. I thought I might well be strangled before they came to a suitable tree, because there was an arm around my neck that cut off the air very effectively. Terror made me dumb. I couldn't speak, hadn't the strength to resist. Down the street we went, towards the river. I was carried along, my feet hardly touching the ground, in the very centre of a roaring mob.

Not much of what was going on around me penetrated my fear, but I did notice that people were standing around watching and smiling. Small boys, still out after dark, were joining the mob, learning new swearwords, learning how to be vicious to a helpless woman. No one cared what was about to happen to me. This was sport! Drown the lady editor was the cry.

The river had risen four feet just recently. I knew because I had read it in the *Gazette*, and copied it in the *Courier*.

I was lifted up by four men and thrown out from the bank about five feet, landing with a terrible splash. The water wasn't more than three feet deep at that point but it felt cold, and the current was strong. It sucked at my wet skirts, dragging me down, pulling me away from the shore. Instinct made me fight it. No one just lies in a river and waits to drown. I thrashed my arms, fought to pull my increased weight up on the bank. A boot on my shoulder sent me floundering backwards again. Still, I fought. Then, above me on the bank, two men lifted high one of the type cases and flung it as far as they could into the water.

I was peppered with *agate* letters, those little demons it had taken such an age to sort out. Now I stopped fighting. I had been struggling against my fate as long as I could remember. It was time to quit, to give up and let all the good people in the world destroy me. Why fight against destiny?

14

I was sitting in shallow water, my fingers clawing mud on the bottom. All I had to do was let go, give a little push, and my troubles would be over.

There were four or five lantern-bearers among the crowd of baying men. Harsh light glowed on drunken sweating faces, casting fantastic shadows, highlighting strong cheekbones, glittering in hate-filled eyes. Suddenly, the lights bobbed, then wavered wildly as the crowd split. Wick pushed his way to the front and shouted above the noise for the men to stand back. He laid his rifle on the bank and waded towards me.

'Dammit, Carlotta, help yourself!' he shouted.

I couldn't. I was exhausted. The current was tugging me away. He bent down, took one ankle and pulled, reached for an arm, clasped the back of my dress and hauled me to the shore. I lay there on the muddy bank like a netted catfish and gasped for breath.

'What the hell you think you're doing, Estes?' shouted a brawny man at the front. 'That whore's been writing things that would of got a *man* strung up! Let her drown.'

The brawny man rushed forward, both hands outstretched aiming at Wick's chest. Wick sidestepped and allowed the man's own momentum to carry him forward. Turning, Wick grabbed handfuls of belt and collar and helped his attacker in the Missouri river with a mighty splash.

There was a roar from the others – fifty or sixty men, maybe more, taking their sport the frontier way. They were like hungry wolves. I could see that Wick and I would be lucky to get away with whole skins.

Now that I knew I was going to live after all, a terrible

anger took hold of me. It welled up like a boil, the pressure inside me screaming to be relieved by some violent act. I wanted to kill, and Wick's rifle was lying right there to hand.

I pulled myself up, using the gun as a crutch, and stood before the mob, my fleet planted firmly about eighteen inches apart. I attempted to brace my quivering knees as I tried to take aim. My knees failed to cooperate and the Kentucky rifle was an awkward thing, very nearly as long as I was tall, and weighing about ten pounds. The slim barrel defied my efforts to raise it so that I could sight. My arms were shaking so much with the effort of simply holding the thing, that I couldn't aim higher than the toes of the nearest man.

When the men saw what I was up to, they began to holler and laugh and taunt me. They showed some sense, however, because they started to scatter, lifting their feet high, loving the thrill of the slight danger my erratic actions provided. Their contempt gave me new strength and steadied my hands. I shoved the stock tight into my shoulder and aimed at the heart of the loudest man, a young greenhorn with a low forehead and a large vocabulary of swearwords.

'No, Carlotta!' shouted Wick. He turned, grabbed the barrel and lifted it high. He had moved in quite close to me, but continued to speak loudly for the benefit of the men. 'I don't blame you for wanting to get rid of some of the slimiest vermin that ever crawled on their bellies, but I can't let you do it!' He leaned closer to speak directly into my ear. 'Besides, I didn't have time to load the gun.'

The fun was over. The greenhorn that Wick had thrown into the river knew when he was licked. He took off his boots, hopping around on first one foot and then the other, and finally limped off in wet stockinged feet. The mood of he men had swung right round. Now they were laughing goodnaturedly as they headed towards the saloons. Soon they would be drinking and bragging and congratulating themselves on having dunked a dangerous radical. Wick and I were left in the inky blackness of a star-filled, moonless night. Any minute now my knees were going to give out altogether. I leaned against Wick and closed my eyes. He didn't seem to mind that I was getting him all wet.

'How do you feel?' he asked quietly.

'Mean.'

He gave a short laugh. 'Mean and ornery, that's what you are. The most awkward woman I ever did meet. Come on, I've seen enough of the Missouri for one night.'

'What am I going to do, Wick? I can't make it back to Minnie's, I'm too tired. And I don't want to spend another night alone at the *Courier* office. I'd be afraid to stay. I expect they've wrecked the place.'

'They did their best. The door was standing wide open when I passed. They wanted to throw the press into the river, and wasted a few minutes trying to lift it. I guess it was too heavy for them. Anyway, it was more fun to pick on a woman than destroy a piece of metal. Come on, I'll take you back to my hotel. The walls are up, but the roof isn't on yet. There's a bit of a fire in the fireplace. You can get dried off and I'll walk you home when you're rested.'

'I'm lucky you came along.'

'You're *un*lucky not to have any commonsense. I sent a boy to buy a copy of the paper for me. He brought it back to the saloon where I was waiting. As soon as I read the first two or three paragraphs of the anti-slavery article you wrote, I knew you would be in trouble. I ran all the way back to the hotel, picked up my rifle and came to find you. For a while there, I thought they'd already drowned you.'

'Would they have let me drown?'

'The way it would have worked, they would have waited until it was too late before somebody stepped in to pull you out.'

208

'The Constitution guarantees freedom of the press. I had a right to say whatever I felt like saying in my own paper.'

'You exercised *your* freedom. Then they exercised *their* freedom of speech to object. You were a fool to write an anti-slavery article in this town. Why can't you just keep your head down and make something of yourself? You could have gone on publishing the *Courier*, and sold out to the *Gazette* for sure. Now, it's all spoiled.'

'They shouldn't have thrown me in the river. That's not their Constitutional right.'

'No, I grant you that, Carlotta. That's just their nature. You would do well to make a study of human behaviour as I have done.'

We were taking a circuitous route to avoid the men. Our pace was a slow one, because my wet skirts kept getting tangled around my legs. I felt as if my clothes weighed as much as the press. Arguing with Wick was a little awkward, because I was clinging to him for support at the same time. But I had to say my piece.

'If every time I ran away from the chance to speak out about what I believe, I'd be no better than those belly-crawling men. I don't go around preaching abolition on street corners, but when I found myself the owner of a newspaper, I knew I had a duty to do. Don't you believe in duty, Wick?'

'It's overrated. There's a time for speaking up and a time for staying quiet. You have to think things through. Sometimes the wisest thing is to do nothing. I hope you live long enough to find that out. Here's the hotel. The door's barricaded on the inside. I'll have to knock for Will . . . that is, Cicero.'

The black man I knew to be William opened the door, saw me and lowered his eyes, keeping his head turned away.

'Cicero,' said Wick. 'it occurs to me you might like to go get yourself something to drink. But first I want you to take a hammer and some nails and go to the *Courier* office and nail the door shut. A mob attacked Miss Carlotta, threw her in the river and wrecked her office, more or less like I told you they would when I came for my gun.' He laid a hand on Cicero's shoulder and said with added emphasis: 'Slavery is a ticklish subject in these parts. A woman nearly died tonight just for saying she was against it.'

'Yassuh,' mumbled Cicero, slurring his speech in a way that irritated me. I knew he could talk properly. 'You have to be mighty brave to talk against slavery in St Jo.' He took up his tools and made a great show of shuffling out. Wick barred the door behind him.

The floorboards had been hammered into place on the ground floor ready to be stained and polished, but I could see the stars through the joists and rafters above. The brick chimney had been completed and rose skywards. It had a fireplace on both sides of it, but the walls weren't in place yet.

Wick began stirring up the small fire that had been lit on one side. 'Get off those wet things of yours,' he said over his shoulder. 'You can put on one of my shirts. I just got two of them back from the washerwoman yesterday – they're in that tea-chest. Can you find them? It's lucky for you I've got a spare pair of work pants and boots, otherwise I might be a trifle mad at you for getting me all wet.'

I found the tea-chest and stood well away from the glow of the small fire to take off my wet things and put on the shirt. It left an indecent amount of leg exposed, but I didn't care about that. I crept forward and laid my wet things across the back of the only chair, and put my shoes on the floor, while Wick was out of sight changing his pants.

He had a few cooking utensils and supplies on the floor, but it was obvious he ate his meals in a hotel or inn somewhere. There were two piles of horse blankets on the floor. Cicero probably slept on one. I sat down on the pile closest to the fire and leaned back on one elbow as I pulled a blanket over my naked legs. The smell of horse filled my nostrils. I figured I would be covered in hairs when I got up.

'No need to put on your underthings to go back to Minnie's,' said Wick when he had changed clothes. He spread my yellow calico bodice and skirt out across the chair so that the heat fell full on them. 'We'll concentrate on getting your dress dry.'

I watched as he arranged my stockings daintily on top of the skirt. 'Soon your hotel will be finished.'

'Yes, it won't be long. I'm tired of living this way. I'm a bit short of the elegancies of life here, don't you think? I'll be in business in a few weeks. Of course, by that time the greenhorns will have gone away for the season but come next spring, I might well be a rich man, because men are going to carry on trekking out to find gold for years to come.'

'It is pretty rough here. Quite a change from the house on Second and Walnut. You've had a lot of bad luck lately.' I pulled a corner of the blanket right up over my shoulders. It was a hot night, but I couldn't stop shivering.

'I've had a lot of good luck in my time. I'm not complaining,' mused Wick. 'I'm going to heat up the coffee and put some whiskey in it. That should warm you up. Oh, damn and blast it!'

Wick had put the old coffee pot firmly on the embers, but the coffee came to the boil faster than he had expected. Gouts of liquid spurted on to the fire, while he looked around helplessly for something to protect his hand so that he could lift off the pot. One of my wet petticoats was handiest. He dragged it to the fire where it sizzled as it swept up ashes. He set the pot down with great haste and sucked his fingers. And the pot promptly branded the new plank floor.

211

It wasn't all that funny, but I laughed until the tears came. By the time he had a mug of coffee and whiskey ready for me to drink, I had shaken off my bad mood along with my fear of the men. Later, tomorrow maybe, I would mourn the loss of my newspaper. For the moment, I was content to be safe and dry.

'I'm glad you've found something to laugh about,' he said as he squatted down to hand me the drink.

Nothing had ever tasted so good, especially since I was drinking it on an empty stomach. The whiskey immediately oozed into my bloodstream and warmed me right out to my toenails. I drank it all and handed him the cup. Wick set it on the floor and moved over to sit beside me on the horse blanket.

'Scrunch up there, gal, and give me some room.'

Wick lifted a hand to pat my thigh just as I shifted to give him sitting space. He was sitting on my cover, which didn't move when I did. As a result, Wick's hand came down on bare flesh, and came up again as if it had been burned. Then, smiling warmly at me, he replaced his hand. Now I felt as if my thigh was on fire as his thumb gently caressed the skin.

'Six years I've been aching for you, Carlotta. Are you going to take me out of my misery?'

I licked my dry lips, and repeated the words I had spoken six years ago. 'I don't mind.'

Wick chuckled softly, but he didn't move closer. 'You were the sweetest little girl I had ever seen in your yellow dress. Like tonight.'

'That one was silk.'

'And cut low in the front. It showed off your little-girl shoulders and the freckles on your arms. I don't know what I would have done if Belle had said yes. What I mean is, what appealed to me about you was your youth and innocence. I don't think I could have destroyed that. A man goes to a brothel looking for experience, I guess.

212

But when I saw you, I knew I wanted somebody decent. Or nobody at all.'

'I'm a little older now.' I sat up so that I could lean against him. 'But I'm just as decent.'

'I know you are. I never doubted it, but I was afraid those girls might destroy what was special about you. Look at you. Your hair's come unpinned and the ends are wet.' He squeezed my hair and a few drops of water trickled down my neck. Pushing wet hair from my cheek, he tenderly kissed the place where it had been. I turned my head, and our lips met. Somehow, after a minute or two, we managed to stretch out side by side. He held me close and we didn't speak for a long time.

After a while, Wick raised himself on one elbow. 'We've only really known each other for a month. Have you thought about that? I made up my mind what sort of girl you were just from seeing you for a minute six years ago. Then when you came back to St Louis, you didn't say the things the girl of my dreams would have said. You didn't act the way I had decided little Miss Carlotta Schultz would act. That's stupid, isn't it? Making up a person. It took me a while to adjust. You can be pretty aggravating, you know that?'

I clung to him, covering his face with kisses. I did love him so! 'I'm doing the best I can just to be me. Don't you think I ever dreamed about the man who came to my mother's house all those years ago? But I had more to build my dreams on. She wrote to me once a month or so, and told me all about you every time.'

'Did she? Did she really do that? Good old Belle! She deserves more of your love, Carlotta. And my eternal thanks for keeping you safe. She might not have, you know.'

I sighed heavily. 'She knew she was dying, Wick. That's why she sent for me. I got there too late, and there wasn't even a letter or a will, only Mr Walkern saying she had intended to open a brothel out West and take me with her. That wasn't very loving of her, was it?'

'The trouble is, we didn't have the rearing of our parents. Sometimes they just don't turn out the way we want them to. But I don't want to talk about Belle right now.'

He pulled me into his arms again and kissed me. My whole body glowed with the feel of him. I loved him and knew that I always had. But there was more to my happiness. I had triumphed. I had made this man of good family forget his upbringing and fall in love with the daughter of a brothel-keeper. I had won! I would belong to him for ever. He would never leave me. I would one day be the wife of Wick Estes. Nothing could prevent it, so long as Wick wanted it to happen.

After a few minutes, he moved away a little and ran a hand through his hair. 'Aw, hell.'

'What is it?' I sat up straight, filled with a sudden dread. I watched him get to his feet and tuck in the loose end of his shirt. He picked up the bodice of my gown, and felt it carefully to see if it was dry.

'Here, you can put this on now.'

'Why? Why should I get dressed all of a sudden?'

'I've got to take you back to Minnie's.'

'You're mad at me. What have I done?'

'You've done nothing. It's just that I'm not going to treat you like one of Belle's girls, that's all.'

'You mean kissing me didn't mean anything. You were just thinking about kissing any old whore.'

'No, dammit! I don't mean that at all. Why must you put words in a man's mouth? What I'm saying is, what we were about to do isn't right. I hadn't thought things through.'

'Tell me what you mean. You don't want to be kissing Belle's daughter, is that it? You like telling me what a wonderful woman she was, but you don't want to have anything to do with her relative. That's it isn't it?'

214

He looked bleakly at me as I sat on the blankets. 'Carlotta – '

There was a loud knocking on the door. 'Massa Wick?' croaked a voice.

'Give me five minutes, Cicero!' called Wick.

'Yassuh,' said Cicero. There was knowing laughter in his voice.

'Cicero thinks we've been up to something.'

'I don't care what he thinks. Will you get dressed before I lose my temper?'

My dress and stockings were more or less dry; but the shoes were cold and wet. We made a neat bundle of my underclothing. I didn't speak, didn't make a sound. My head was all mixed up, and my body was throbbing with frustration. There was so much I wanted to say, but I was afraid my words would destroy what little understanding there was left between us. I thought I knew what was troubling him. He did love me in his fashion, but he could never imagine himself committed to a whore's daughter. He was reminded of Belle and everything she stood for whenever he came close to me. The ghost of my mother was haunting us both.

We were ready when Cicero returned. There followed the old charade wherein Cicero/William pretended to be an ignorant slave, and I pretended not to know that he was a successful barber and property owner in St Louis.

We walked halfway up the hill before Wick said his first words. 'How are Minnie and Joel getting along?'

'All right, I guess. He's a weak man. I don't like him. But at least he married her.'

If Wick thought I was trying to make a point, he didn't let on. 'That's true. I guess she's happy enough. A woman always wants a ring on her finger.'

'And you think that's stupid.'

'I didn't say so. Here we are.' Wick strode ahead to unlatch the gate.

Minnie opened the door on the first knock. 'Where

215

have you been, Carlotta?' She sounded like a mother. Not *my* mother who probably wouldn't have been curious, but like the sort of mothers good girls have, which is why they're good girls right up until the day they marry.

'Some men broke into the *Courier* office and threw me in the river.'

'I know that. We heard all about it. We heard Wick pulled you out, too. Albert came by to tell us.'

'He should have let you drown,' added Mr Huggens helpfully. 'After all them things you wrote about abolition and all.'

'I took her to my hotel to dry off,' said Wick. 'What's the matter, Minnie? Worried about her reputation?'

'Somebody has to be. What's that you're carrying, Carlotta? *Petticoats*?' She flung a worried glance at Mr Huggens.

Wick and I looked at each other for a long time. 'I'll come over tomorrow, Carlotta.'

I could see the pain in his eyes; I hoped he could see the pain in mine. Slowly, he reached out, lifted my chin and very deliberately kissed me on the mouth right there in front of Minnie and Mr Huggens. It was too late. My joy, my passion were dead. The kiss tasted of nothing at all. I thought he did it not because he wanted to kiss me, but because he wanted to tell Minnie and Mr Huggens something that he didn't intend to put into words.

'You coming for Sunday lunch?' asked Minnie with her head tilted to one side, her sharp eyes studying him. She was asking him if he intended to court me properly.

Wick was silent for a long moment, and I held my breath. 'That I am, ma'am.' Now he smiled. Not at me but at Minnie. He bent and kissed her on the cheek, which drew a grudging smile from her.

When he had gone, she gave me a little hug, but I pushed her aside. 'I'm not counting my chickens,' I said.

'Very wise. Be a bit standoffish, that's the way.

216

Somehow, I don't suppose you been playing hard to get tonight. Let's get that dress offen you, it's caked with mud. I'll put it to soak right away, and wash everything tomorrow morning.'

'Tomorrow's Sunday,' I reminded her.

'Sunday starts when I say it does. I wish I'd known what you was writing in that paper but that small print is hard on my eyes, so I didn't look too careful.' She helped me out of my bodice and skirts. 'Ticks! Look at that!' She began picking the little black insects off me. I found one in the crook of my arm.

'Will they do me any harm?'

'Awful critters.' She crushed each one under her heel. 'They'll crawl around on you for a day or maybe two and then dig themselves in. Once they get their teeth into you, it's the devil to get them off. You can break them right in half, and still they won't let go.' She looked up at me. 'I don't think they can swim. You didn't get them from the *river*. Being in the woods might do it. Where these ticks are, you'd have to of been lying around on the ground for a while.'

I smiled at her fondly. 'We walked through some wooded parts to get to Wick's hotel. Nothing happened, Minnie.'

She gave me a disbelieving look and carried on examining me for ticks. Her disbelief didn't bother me. I wouldn't have believed such a tale either.

'Minnie, what did you have for supper? Have you got any cold potatoes? I'm so hungry I could eat a horse.'

Minnie straightened up and met my gaze. 'Nothing happened, huh?'

The next morning, I woke to the sound of the pump-handle going. I looked out of the window and saw Mr Huggens at his morning ritual. He stuck his head under the spout and gave the handle one downward thrust which drenched his head. Then he soaped both hands and scrubbed his face, working his way up to his ears, leaving them glowing bright red, before he finally reached the back of his neck. Mr Huggens had one of the cleanest back of necks in town. I had my doubts about the rest of him.

Wick came into the backyard and ducked under my dazzling white petticoats which were blowing on the line.

'I thought I'd come up to walk to church with Carlotta,' he said to Mr Huggens.

Mr Huggens dried his face and hands. 'You sure are sweet on that girl, ain't you? Well, I'm right glad she's found a beau. I'd like to see her settled somewheres else.'

'Is that a fact?' asked Wick, sweetly. I knew that tone of voice; it spelled trouble. 'Anxious to get her moved out of her own house, are you?'

'Well, sir,' spluttered Mr Huggens, 'I just want to see her happily settled, that's all. I'll pay her back for this place. You can bet on that.'

I left the window and scrambled into my blue dress as fast as I could. No point in leaving the two men alone together any longer than necessary.

Every day was hotter than the one before it. This Sunday was so hot the sun beat right through my bonnet and cooked my hair. It was unfortunate that the blue gown had tight long sleeves. By the time we reached the church, I was ready to claw them off to get a little fresh air on my arms.

The church was made of wood and open to the rafters, and was surprisingly cool when we entered. It soon warmed up when every seat was taken. I had a feeling it was going to be a long morning.

The heat made us all fidgety. The boys seemed to get on everyone's nerves, and Martha whined all the way back up the hill. Mr Huggens' temper was always short; today it seemed to be at snapping point by the time we reached the house. Minnie had stayed behind to cook, as usual, and this time she had company: Albert Jenkins.

218

This Sunday lunchtime was very different from the last one when the two men had eaten with us. I wouldn't have thought Roxanne and Tilda could have made such a difference to our enjoyment.

As soon as dinner was over, Wick suggested that he and I return to the *Courier* office to see how much damage had been done.

'We won't ask you to come with us, Jenkins,' said Wick smoothly. 'I know you want to sit a while and talk to Joel.'

I hadn't helped Minnie clear away the dinner dishes as I usually did, but I didn't dare ask Wick to wait. He wasn't in a waiting sort of mood. We went down that well-worn path at a pace that left me puffing.

'Aren't you going to speak to me at all?' I asked.

'Not out here. We're not going to the *Courier*. We're going to my hotel.'

William let us inside, not bothering to hide his face from me this time. 'Hello, Miss Carlotta. I'm mighty sorry I had to deceive you by calling myself Cicero.'

'You didn't deceive me at all, William.' I looked past him to the horse blankets where a black boy was crouched down. 'I'm just sorry you didn't feel you could trust me.'

'We have to trust you now,' said Wick. 'Come over here and meet Mary Benson.'

The 'boy' was a woman in her middle years, small and a little stoop-shouldered, with a wrinkled face and a few teeth missing. She was barefooted, wearing a shirt and pants, and could have been any age from forty to sixty. Her hair was jet black, but I later learned that she put boot blacking on it.

Mary Benson stood up. 'How do you do, Miss Carlotta? Mr Wick says you may be able to help me out.'

'I'll do anything I can. Just tell me what you want.'

Wick offered me the only chair. William and Mary

Benson sat down side by side on a makeshift bed, while Wick leaned an elbow on the brick mantelpiece.

'I'm going to start at the very beginning, Carlotta,' he announced. 'You will have to be patient. What's happened in the past makes sense of what is going to happen now. Five and a half years ago, I was a very hot-headed young man. I didn't like to be aggravated by anybody, and what's more, I knew exactly how everybody else should run his life. Being so stubborn could be troublesome. Do you mean to say your ma didn't tell you about me getting into trouble?'

'She only said that you were getting rich and had opened a hotel. She didn't even tell me that your hotel was her old house.'

'In that case, you don't really know what sort of man I am.'

'A good man,' mused William.

'Amen,' said Mary Benson.

'A stupid man! Look at the trouble I've caused. My mother's father left her a large farm in Jefferson City five years ago. The estate included eight slaves: Mary here, her four brothers and her three children, a girl of eleven and two boys, nine and fifteen. My parents changed overnight with that inheritance. The money turned their heads. My father started building a fine white house almost as big as Thomas Jefferson's, and began talking about going into politics.

'When I was a boy, we had managed to live quite comfortably without slaves, and I hated his keeping the slaves that came with the estate. My father was not concerned about my opinion.'

'We was well-treated,' said Mary generously, 'but I was unhappy, because Mrs Estes' father had already sold my dear husband down the river.'

'I had heard,' continued Wick, 'about a young man who stole his own father's slaves and set them free. I made up my mind that was what I was going to do.

Figuring out how to do it was the hard part. As you know, Jefferson City is almost in the middle of the state, a long way from the western border here, where just crossing the Missouri river would mean the slaves would be safe. It's also a long way from St Louis where crossing the Mississippi river would put them in Illinois which is a free state. And there's no river from Jefferson City leading north. The slaves would have been caught in no time if they had tried to travel north by land. I – '

'You was clever, Mr Estes,' said Mary. 'We all said it was a clever plan.'

'Considering the heartache I've caused you, I don't know why you're willing to speak to me. My father was so ambitious, I thought I knew how to get him to part with some of the slaves. I told him a very important man in St Louis would like to hire out a woman and four strong men for a week to get some work done. I pointed out that doing this man a favour could be beneficial to Pa's political ambitions. It was winter at the time. There was hardly any work to be done, so Pa said he'd rent out the five; Mary and her four brothers. I offered to take them to St Louis and keep an eye on them.

'Pa sent along his white overseer. We chained up the slaves and took them under guard down the Missouri to St Louis, arriving just as it was getting dark. I said we couldn't take them right away to the man who was hiring them, so I had arranged for us to spend the night in a warehouse. As soon as we got there, I came up behind old Bill Buckle and hit him on the head and tied him up. When I had got all of the slaves across the river into Illinois, I came back and released Bill. Mary and her four brothers went to the First Presbyterian Church in Galesburg, and all five got away to Canada on the underground railway. That is to say, they travelled at night from one safe house to another.'

'Oh, Wick, I'm so proud of you! You must be very happy, Mary.'

221

'Happy and sad Miss Carlotta,' said Mary. 'I couldn't take my three children. My girl, Daphne, was left to do all the housework and cooking, and her only eleven years old. I didn't know what would happen to John. My youngest boy, Freddie, he was so sickly that I hated to leave him most of all.'

'You see.' Wick stuck his hands in his pockets. 'Mary only agreed to leave with her brothers, because I told her I would see to it that her children joined her in Canada in the spring. I went back to Jefferson City with Bill and told my father exactly what I had done. We had one hell of a fight. I had freed slaves worth at least four thousand dollars. He disinherited me and said he never wanted to see me again. He made me get out of the house there and then, but I wouldn't leave town. Two days later, he wrote me a letter saying that he had been betrayed by his own son, but if I didn't want him to have slaves, he'd get rid of them.

'I took the next packet bound for St Louis to tell William to get word to Mary that her children would be joining her. When I got back to Jefferson City, I heard that Pa had *sold* the three children to a slave dealer, who had taken them down the river to pick cotton in the South.'

'Lot of money,' said Mary. 'Fifteen hundred dollars for them three children.'

Wick smiled sadly at Mary. 'They were all sold to different owners. This brave lady has never stopped trying to find her family and free them. Time and again she has crossed back over the border from Canada and travelled dressed as a boy all over the South. Sadly, Freddie died about six months after being sold.'

'I never did see my husband again, Miss Carlotta. 'Course, he wasn't really my husband, because the law says slaves can't marry. But he was a husband to me and in the eyes of the Lord. He died before I found out he was living in New Orleans.'

222

'You went all that way?' I exclaimed. 'It was so dangerous.'

'Yes, ma'am. Travelling at night. Always a chance some slave dealer would catch me and sell me again. But I have to do it. John is safe. I found him in Mississippi two years ago. We almost didn't make it back to Canada, but finally we won through. William has always helped me when he could, getting information and all, like he does for lots of folks. But we're not related, or anything.'

Wick leaned against the bricks. 'William turned up here a few days ago, as you know. He didn't choose to tell me the reason for this charade, but I took him in. Of course, he didn't dare come to St Jo dressed like a gentleman. They'd've strung him up.'

'Didn't know Mary would turn up this morning,' said William. 'Didn't know if I should ask you for help. You was pretty cut up when your pa didn't want to know you. I thought maybe – '

I leapt to my feet. 'The girl slave! The one who's going to be sold tomorrow.'

'Yes'm. My daughter, Daphne.' Mary Benson took out a red handkerchief and blew her nose. 'I've had a terrible time finding her. She's grown into a beautiful young woman, they say. She's nearly seventeen now, and I'm mortal afraid some wicked man is going to buy her for his own evil reasons.'

'And you want me to help?' I asked. 'Oh, Wick, I'm so proud you trust me. How are you planning to get her away?'

'I'm hoping to buy her. Then I can just take her to Illinois as my slave. Mary can meet her in Galesburg.'

'But you haven't any money!'

'No.' Wick smiled at me. 'But you have. Walkern's money. I wouldn't borrow it for myself, but I'll borrow it to buy Daphne. She's unlikely to go for less than eight hundred dollars, you see. The price in souls is going up all the time. That's why it's so hard to free slaves just by buying them. Freeing them all would cost hundreds of thousands. Lucky for Daphne you've got Walkern's money.'

'But I haven't got any money.'

'*What?* What about the two thousand dollars you took from Walkern? What do you mean you haven't got any money?'

'There never was two thouand dollars. Please believe me, Wick. I'm sure Bullmouth stole some of it. I've just got one hundred and sixty-eight dollars left out of the twelve hundred dollars that we put in the bank when we got to St Jo.'

Wick ran both hands through his hair as if trying to pull it out. 'You damned fool! Couldn't you even hold on to *stolen* money? What the hell have you done with twelve hundred dollars?'

'We had to pay our boat fare. I paid one hundred and fifty dollars for the Huggens' smallholding. As you know, I was quite glad to get Roxanne off my hands. She wanted a hundred dollars. After all, she was the one who actually stole it! I admit Tilda tricked me. I thought she was being blackmailed and gave her two hundred dollars before she left with some man. I paid five hundred dollars for the press.'

'Seems you've been cheated every which way,' said Wick. 'That press was never worth five hundred dollars. Three hundred at the most.'

'Your father is the one who should pay. He's evil! Selling children! It's all his fault. I'm surprised you spoke to him in such a friendly way on the landing at Jefferson City.'

'It was the first time we had seen each other for five and a half years. No matter what he's done, he's my father and I love him. Loving's not easy sometimes, but some of us don't forget what we owe our parents.' He scrubbed his face with his hands, while the three of us were silent. 'Besides, I can't get money from him for an auction that's going to be held tomorrow afternoon.'

'I'll sell the press.'

'Who would be fool enough to buy it now?'

I squeezed my eyes shut. Mary had been so brave for so many years. William had endured the insults of the townspeople when he could have been living safely and in comfort in St Louis. Wick had defied his family to save five slaves all those years ago. Now it was my turn. I was needed, but had to fail those who looked to me for help.

'I'll offer the press to Mr Archer at the *Gazette*. I can get some money that way.'

'If we can't get together eight hundred dollars, it doesn't matter how much we can raise. We won't be able to buy her.'

'What about the bank? A loan, maybe, on this hotel.'

'I've borrowed every penny they're going to lend me. If William here had just trusted me sooner.'

'Mr Wick!' protested William. 'When I came here it was to find out what I could. I was as surprised as you were when Mary came into town.'

Mary stood up and I could hear her joints protesting. 'They told me in St Louis you was here, William. Nobody had any money to give me. I didn't even know if Daphne was somewhere around here. I just heard a rumour. And I surely didn't know her master was going to up and die, and the executors was going to sell her. Now there's no time left. We got to find some other way.'

'Yes,' I said. 'We'll steal her away, but we'd better do it tonight.'

'You're not getting involved in this,' said Wick coolly. 'If you had the money, I would take it from you. Anything else will be done without you. Just keep your mouth shut.'

His words wounded me deeply. 'If you don't trust me, there's nothing I can do about it. I'll leave you three to your plots. I wouldn't want to interfere or spoil your chances of helping Daphne. I'm going to the *Courier* office to clean up the mess.'

'I fixed the front door, Miss Carlotta,' said William. He dug into a pocket for the key and held it out to me.

'Thank you, William. I appreciate it. When will I see you, Wick?'

He looked distracted. 'I don't know. I'll send word to you. I beg of you, don't make trouble. We've got enough of that already.'

I said goodbye to William and Mary Benson. Both of them were as preoccupied as Wick. I hated feeling so useless, but this was no place for me. I left, and I think the three of them hardly noticed.

15

The Printer's Devil has the tiresome task of dismantling each page of set type and returning every individual letter to its assigned compartment in the correct type-case. Removing the copy line by line and returning the letters of a sentence can be fairly speedy, especially if the Devil is very experienced. He doesn't have to look too carefully at what he is doing, because he reads the line and then separates it letter by letter. It sometimes happens, however, that the whole line of type slips through his fingers. In that case, each piece of type must be picked up from the table or the floor and *read*. What usually happens when type is dropped is that the Devil says: 'Aw, hell!' and throws all the pieces in a box, to be sorted at some other time.

The *Courier* hell-box was four times the size of the one at Carlton's printing house, and full to the brim. Since I had lost an entire type-case in the river – *agate* capitals, as it turned out – I thought I would sort the hell-box to see how much type I had to sell to Mr Archer. Pages two and three were still locked in the chase. As they wouldn't be so hard to sort, I decided to leave that task for a later time.

An hour later, I gave up. The jumbled type in the hellbox was impossibly small, and *non pareil* (the next size up from *agate*) was so similar to *agate* that I couldn't see the difference at all. I decided Mr Archer would be offered the press, and could make his own decisions about type. I was about to lock up and go home to Minnie when there was a knock on the door. It was Wick, wearing a sassy smile just as if he had never been mad at me. The sight of his good humour blackened my mood considerably.

227

'How are you getting along with the cleaning up?' he asked cheerfully.

'I've been trying to sort out the type, but it's impossible.'

'Come on now, Carlotta. It's not like you to give up. I'll help you.'

He deserved to be taught a lesson. 'All right. Here, take this box. First you pick up a letter. Then you look to see what it is. Then you put it in its special place. See, the letter is written in pencil by each compartment. Just put away all these pieces of type while I get on with something else.'

Wick reached into the box and came out with a handful of letters. 'These little things? You have to put *each* one back? It can't be done.'

'That's what I just said, isn't it?'

He dropped the letters back into the box and took me by the shoulders. 'Forget about it. I don't think Archer's going to buy this business anyway. I came to say I'm sorry I spoke to you so roughly back at the hotel. I'm a rough man, little darling. I say what I think. Thank the good Lord you're not one of those simpering women who faint when a man frowns at them. You do understand my plain speaking, don't you? All the same, I apologize for being so offhand.'

'You don't trust me.'

'I think you're a mighty fine woman.'

'But you don't trust me.'

He gave a massive, exasperated sigh. 'I don't want you to get mixed up in this business. Stay away from Mary Benson and William, and forget about the girl. I expect you to do what I say, Carlotta.'

'Why should I? What right have you to order me about? Tell me that.'

Wick went red right up to his ears. I was surprised he got so mad. I thought I was giving him an opportunity to tell me he loved me and wanted to marry me. He could

228

have cleared the air between us right there and then. Instead, he said: 'I'm a damned fool,' and walked out of the *Courier* office.

Five minutes later, I went home to Minnie. 'He doesn't want me,' I said, blinking back the tears. 'He doesn't want to be tied up with Belle's daughter.'

'I tell you,' said Minnie fiercely. 'Sometimes I get sick to death of hearing you go on about your ma. Nobody thinks about her as much as you do. You're boring that man with all your talk of Belle. Try to be nice to him for a while.'

I felt there was more than a grain of truth in what she said, which didn't make it any easier to hear. I went up to my room and lay down. After a lot of hard thinking, I decided Wick and I would sort out our differences as soon as this business with Daphne was over. Then I would be nice. I'd smile and do whatever he wanted me to, so long as it didn't interfere with any plans I already had. And I'd never mention my mother to him again.

I assumed the slave girl would be stolen away that night, and couldn't think about anything else for the rest of the day. Sunday dragged on for ever, made frustrating by the fact that I couldn't tell Minnie anything about what was happening. The next morning, I got up bright and early and walked down the hill with Mr Huggens. Wick was at the hotel, but didn't speak to me. William was there, too, avoiding my eyes. There was no sign of Mary Benson, but I knew she hadn't left St Jo. If a slave had been stolen on Sunday night, the town would be buzzing with it this morning. Wick might need every penny he could raise.

The press was no longer any use to me. Nobody would ever buy a newspaper from me in this town. I thought if I could sell it, I might have a little money to contribute towards buying Daphne. I assumed that was what Wick planned to do, if he could. Stealing her away was very dangerous. He would surely have done it on Sunday night if it had been possible.

Mr Archer jumped to his feet, grinning broadly, when I entered the *Gazette* office. 'Why, if it isn't the lady editor! I'm very glad no harm came to you the other night. Folks in this town can get pretty riled with abolitionists.'

'Folks in St Jo haven't heard about freedom of the press.'

Mr Archer leaned on the counter that separated us. 'They know about freedom of the press, Miss Carlotta. They also know they like their women to stay at home. Why, what would happen if women started doing men's work? We'd have the men staying at home cooking and washing and having babies!'

'Mr Archer, I didn't come here to be the object of your wit. I came to sell the *Courier* press. Will you make me an offer?'

'No. If you had read the latest edition of the *Gazette*, you'd know that we have an old press for sale here. You could have bought ours real cheap. We've got a new press and don't need that old thing at the *Courier* office. I'm afraid you'll just have to hang on to it, although I have a feeling you aren't going to be putting out any more editions of the *Courier*. That should teach you not to meddle in something you don't understand. Good day to you, ma'am.'

As I left the *Gazette* office, I saw Wick crossing the road wearing his fine coat and beaver hat. I figured he was going to the auction.

That afternoon, along with half the citizens of St Jo, I went out to Missouri House, which was set back a quarter of a mile from the road to Sparta, to see the slave auction. I had the foresight to hire a horse early in the day. Latecomers to the stable were going to be disappointed, Mr Smithers told me. At least I had given myself two full hours to practise riding the horse, much to the amusement of the nag's owner. I was advised to ride straddling, because that way I was much more likely to stay on. Mr Smithers didn't want his horse to return to the stable on its own, which he said was very likely if I fell off.

Missouri House was a fine, white-painted two-storey mansion with a deep porch. There were five steps leading up to the front door, where the slave could have stood to be seen by all. That didn't suit Mr Hays, however. He had set up a block in front of the house in the full glare of the sun. There stood Daphne, bare-headed and wearing a simple drawstring skirt and short-sleeved shift. She was bare-footed, her wrists and ankles weighed down by manacles and chains. She was also full-breasted, paler-skinned than her mother and very beautiful. No wonder her mother feared for her safety!

A large crowd had already gathered. I walked up close to the slave and overheard someone say that the auction would take place in about half an hour. Meanwhile, the girl was forced to stand out in the cruel sun, sweat beading her forehead. She looked down on us with hate-filled eyes. A slight movement, a tensing of muscles and the chains clinked softly.

She was looking beyond me and had evidently seen something that agitated her; Wick, probably. I moved away from the auction block as quickly as I could and tried to lose myself in a group of women who were gossiping in the shade of a large oak tree.

From my vantage point, I could see Wick arrive. He joined a cluster of about twenty men, those most likely to bid. He seemed relaxed and talkative, content to be neither at the back nor right up next to the block. Somebody had brought along a jug of whiskey, and Wick smilingly took a swig from the jug when it was offered.

Mr Hays, who was no fool, chose to conduct the auction from the shade of the porch. 'Gentlemen!' he called, and the slave lost her icy dignity and began to look distressed. 'What am I bid for this fine specimen?

231

This excellent house servant who can cook and clean and do fine needlework. Will somebody bid eight hundred dollars?'

'Four hundred!' said Wick.

'Five hundred!' said a dusty, hard-looking man at the front.

A toothless old farmer standing next to me bared his gums and said: 'That's Jones, the dealer. Dirty, no-good, egg-sucking son of a monkey. Pity decent folks has to do business with him.'

'Six hundred!'

Somebody else had entered the bidding. I scanned the crowd and found a fat man in a beaver hat.

'Seven hundred!' said Wick.

'Eight!' said the fat man.

Wick turned, looking very briefly at someone over to my right, and shook his head slightly in a helpless gesture. I craned my neck to see who it was and saw Albert Jenkins. It must have been Albert who had loaned money to Wick. I was not surprised that the gambler had managed to save so much in such a short time. The greenhorns lined up to lose their money to him. I had to revise my opinion of the man. I didn't think much of Albert, but Wick had known he could be trusted.

After a few more bids, the fat man bought the slave for eleven hundred dollars. It was a staggering price for a female slave. The crowd was agog, and the slave dealer turned away in disgust. I guess he knew he couldn't make a profit on such an expensive female slave.

The fat man seemed surprised to have let himself be run up so high, but he quickly waddled forward to pay the auctioneer. As the crowd began to disperse, I saw the girl look in desperation at Wick, who gave her a very slight nod. He began sauntering over to the auction block. I pushed my way through the crowd to stand behind the block, in the girl's shadow where I could hear what was being said.

The fat man was half a head shorter than Wick and twenty years older. He needed a cane to support his weight. The sun had gone behind black clouds and rain could not be far off. It was an exceptionally hot, oppressive day, one which was apparently trying the fat man to his limit.

'I drove you up pretty good,' said Wick with a smile, 'but you ran clean out of my pocket.'

'Worth it,' puffed the man, wiping his face with a handkerchief. He took off his hat and wiped the inside of the brim.

Wick took out a cigarrito and lit up. 'Are you leaving town today?'

'Yes. Going to Platsburg in Clinton County.'

'Why, I'm going that way myself! On to Kingston, in fact. I'll ride with you, if you don't mind.'

The fat man scrutinized Wick suspiciously. 'You don't want to dawdle along with me. I've only got one horse. She's going to have to ride behind me.'

'My friend, you're going to have one tired horse by the time you reach Platsburg. I tell you what – I've got three horses with me. She can ride on one until our ways part.'

'That's mighty nice of you,' said the fat man cautiously. 'No hard feelings, I trust. It was a fair auction.'

Wick laughed softly. 'No hard feelings, sir. I can buy me another nigger any time.'

His suspicion allayed by this callous remark, the fat man beamed. 'I'd appreciate the loan of a horse. And the company would be welcome, I do admit. I couldn't expect much conversation from *her.*'

From my place behind the slave, I peered towards the shady grove where my horse was tethered. I had a pretty clear idea of what Wick now intended. My horseback riding was lamentable, but I intended to go along with him. I moved around the block, and Wick saw me for the first time. He gave me a look that could have made hell

233

freeze over. I ignored him and looked up at the slave. She was the colour they call yellow, so tragically beautiful that I felt the tears pricking my eyelids. She had scarcely moved since she first stepped on to the auction block. Sweat oiled her face and bare forearms. The scorching heat had weakened her, but the taut mouth and alert eyes told me she had missed none of the implications of Wick's offer to the new owner. When the moment for escape arrived, she would be ready.

I took the stopper out of my water canteen and offered it to the girl, who gave Wick one terrified look before drinking greedily. The fat man was dumbfounded.

'Madam, I hope you aren't one of them abolitionists. Get away from my slave.'

'Excuse me, sir,' I said as humbly as I could. 'I just thought it's a hot day, and this here slave is a fine specimen. You don't want to arrive home with her all dried up like a prune. What would your wife say?'

'My wife!' exclaimed the fat man, his face going redder than ever. 'Well, you know. My wife doesn't know anything about this little transaction.'

He mumbled the words to Wick. I wasn't meant to hear them. He tried to assume the air of a man of the world and gave Wick a rather sickly grin.

Wick smiled in a friendly way. 'So you've come to St Jo where nobody knows you to buy just what you're looking for, is that it? You sure did buy yourself the best. I envy you and that's a fact.'

'Well, yes. I'm not likely to be passing this way again, you see.'

The legal formalities were taking some time. Wick took me by the arm and walked me towards where the horses were tethered. 'Madam,' he said loudly. 'Do allow me to help you mount. You must want to be on your way.'

'No, sir, I'm in no hurry. It's a long way back to town. I thought I'd rest awhile.' I tried to prise Wick's fingers from my upper arm, but he held on like a leech. I didn't like the expression on his face.

He bent close and whispered in my ear so vehemently that I could feel his hot breath. Of course, I knew he was mad at me even before he spoke. 'Get yourself the hell out of here and don't come near me or that girl again. What are you trying to do, get us all killed?'

'You aren't looking after her very well,' I murmured. 'I'm only thinking of her. She might die before you ever get her to a place of safety. I had to give her a drink of water.'

'Well, she's not as dumb as you. She'd rather go thirsty than have that fat fool catch on to what we're up to. Go home, Carlotta, before I get real mad at you.' He gave me a little push to send me on my way. But I wasn't going.

When it came time to depart, the fat man was reluctant to allow Daphne's legs to be unchained. Wick was quiet and reasonable in his argument. The girl would do best riding straddled. There was no danger. She knew she couldn't run away. The new owner reluctantly fished with pudgy fingers in a waistcoat pocket and removed the key which the auctioneer had given him.

One of Daphne's ankles was bleeding where the manacle had rubbed away the skin. With splendid dignity, she refused even to look down as blood oozed over her ankebone. Accepting Wick's helping hand, she stood on the auction block, put one foot in the stirrup and slid cautiously on to the horse's back. I saw immediately that she was no more experienced a rider than I was.

I had no idea how far they would have to ride before William and her mother rescued her. In the meantime, she would be alone with the two men. I put myself in her position and knew that she would appreciate having another woman along. I didn't give a tinker's cuss for

Wick's opinion at the moment. He was only a man. He didn't understand.

I could see Albert Jenkins lounging against a tree, out of earshot, but clearly more than passingly interested in what was going on. I ran up to him. 'Come on, Albert. Wick's going with the man and the slave. I want to follow them, but I need an excuse. You'll do. We can be travelling together.'

'He's leaving town with my money? Let me get my horse.'

I knew Wick would hate to have the two of us trailing along, but I saw no reason to tell Albert that. I fetched my horse and led him to a log which I stood on to mount. It was a pretty undignified mounting, but I made it. The animal had been fed and watered. I had seen to that when I first arrived. I now guided the poor beast to where Albert was mounting up.

He was scathing about my animal, and didn't want to take me along. He said the way I rode, he'd be for ever picking me up off the ground. I had faced up to Wick, so Albert's fussing didn't bother me at all. We followed about twenty yards back, and I was grateful for Albert's advice about riding a horse properly. I really did feel safer because of his instruction. And besides, it kept his mind off the angry gestures Wick was making towards us. Anyway, Albert had no intention of turning back until he had his money. He had been glad to make it available to buy the slave, but since Wick clearly didn't need it, he was damned if he was going to let Wick ride away with it.

'I don't know when I might see him again. He's playing such a dangerous game, he might end up in the penitentiary or dead,' said Albert casually. 'And then how would I get my money back?'

When for the third time, Wick fell behind and gestured for us to go away, Albert said he was tired of this business. We would ride forward. Wick could give him his money and he'd be on his way. I could do as I pleased, said Albert, but he strongly advised me to travel back to St Jo with him. It seemed to Albert that Wick wasn't too pleased to see me.

'Mind if we ride along?' asked Albert when we caught up to them. Wick said through gritted teeth that he didn't see how he could stop us. Albert turned his attention to the fat man who soon fell victim to the gambler's charm.

The afternoon wore on. The slave and I were beginning to tire badly. Several times, Wick asked Albert if he and his whore were planning on travelling far. I gasped the first time he said it, but I didn't back off.

'I thought she was an abolitionist,' muttered the fat man, just as if it was impossible for a woman who had made herself a slave to men to be opposed to slavery for black people at the same time.

Albert said he would ride along until a convenient moment came to complete his business with Wick. Wick wasn't about to stop and hand over a lot of money in front of the fat man. The man who had said he loved me growled under his breath and looked at me with hatred in his eyes as we all rode on in silence.

Late in the day, the fat man looked heavenwards at the low, black clouds. 'It's going to rain. I got a cape for myself but I didn't bring anything for her. I do hope she don't sicken and die before ever I get her home. What I mean is, to the place where I'm taking her.' I thought he sounded quite exhausted. His horse didn't look too happy either.

When the rains came, they did so with great force, accompanied by a sharp drop in temperature. It seemed like it was raining lead-shot. Daphne and I began to shiver. The fat man put on his cape. The rest of us tried not to mind that we were getting soaked.

Wick said we had better ride on until about eight o'clock before trying to find a tavern in which to spend the night. Albert said he hoped he didn't drown before then. The fat man and I were too tired to say anything. Daphne sat on her horse straight as an arrow and gave us all a lesson in raw courage.

Twenty minutes later, with water running off his cape in torrents, the fat man said we really must stop at the very next settlement or town we encountered. Or better still, we should turn back to the one we had passed through about threequarters of an hour ago.

'It will make for a long journey tomorrow, my friend. I think we should press on,' said Wick. 'There's quite a decent town about ten miles ahead, I'm almost sure. Can't think of the name of it just at the moment.'

'I don't know.' The fat man wiped his face with a well-padded hand, a gesture of extreme fatigue. 'This is awful heavy rain. The slave is soaked through. I got to look after her. I got to protect my investment.'

'I can make it,' said the girl. They were the first words she had spoken all day.

'I think you and your lady friend better turn back,' said Wick to Albert. 'She's not got anything to keep her decent or dry. We don't want to walk into some genteel tavern with you and that whore. My friend here is a respectable man.'

'I agree, but I'm a trifle short of the readies,' replied Albert, giving Wick a meaningful look.

Our pace slowed as the path turned into a dangerous quagmire. Daphne was having some difficulty managing her horse whenever it foundered in a deep rut.

'You ride ahead!' shouted Wick to the fat man above the noise of the rain and wind. 'I'll take the nigger's reins and lead her horse. I know what my animal is capable of.'

The fat man kicked his beast in the ribs. 'We should have stopped. I'm not a well man. I know we should have stopped back there apiece.'

Wick edged his horse between Albert and me and

238

reached inside his leather coat. 'Here's your money, Jenkins. I appreciate your loaning it to me. Will you take this baggage back to St Jo for me? I told her not to get involved. She's nearly spoiled everything.'

'Wick, please!'

'I thought you had some sense, Carlotta. I see now I was mistaken. You're a glory girl, aren't you? Wanting a few thrills, that's you. You don't care how much danger you put that poor child in, so long as you get your fun. What sort of game do you think this is? Get the hell out of here. And while I'm gone, try to grow up and get a little humility.'

'I was thinking of Daphne, alone with two men. She needs me to come along.'

'You must be the biggest damned fool that ever wore a skirt. She doesn't need you. She needs to be out here in the wilderness with the rain and the wind for cover, and that lecherous old man thinking about anything but her running away. There's nothing you can do for her. Her mother is a real woman. She can take care of Daphne.'

'Don't be too hard on her – ' began Albert.

'Shut your mouth and ride!' snarled Wick.

Leading Daphne's horse, he trotted forward to catch up with the fat man. It was getting dark. I could hardly see them by the time they were fifty yards ahead of me. I was aware of a furtive movement in the woods to the right of the path.

The next minute the fat man had fallen from his horse and lay in the mud. He hit the ground with a terrible thud. It's a wonder he didn't break his neck. I saw three people, one so small she could only have been Daphne's mother.

'Come on!' said Albert. 'We can't get mixed up in this.'

'But I want – '

'You want to be in at the kill. Estes just as clearly doesn't want you. Come on, Carlotta. There's going to be murder done this night.'

239

I saw Wick dismount and come forward towards Mary Benson. Someone came up behind him and hit him on the back of the head. He dropped in the mud like a stone. I cried out and urged my horse forward.

Albert reached over and grabbed the reins, jerking so hard on the poor horse's head that it reared up and almost unseated me. 'Leave him be! He won't be hurt badly. Don't you see what they're doing? Estes and the fat man will both be robbed. That way, no one will suspect Estes had anything to do with the slave getting away.'

We trotted back towards the settlement we had passed almost an hour earlier. For a long time we rode in silence, but after a while, Albert tried to console me, telling me Wick was just mad and worried, saying Wick hadn't wanted me to risk my life.

'No,' I said. 'It was more than that. It was thinking I had mean reasons for wanting to come along. It was thinking I had no place. It was thinking I should do whatever I'm told. My mother used to say the only thing men are good for is telling a woman what she ought to do.'

'Your mother didn't make a magnificent job of deciding for herself what she should do.'

'She did all right,' I said. 'A man told her to run away with him. After that, she made the decisions. She lived high on the hog. She slept until she felt like getting up. She ate everything in sight, and there was always plenty on the table.

'It seems to me I've got to get myself sorted out,' I continued. 'I'm not going to spend the rest of my life asking for permission to breathe.'

Albert said, yes, sure. He understood. He said it with that maddeningly superior tone of voice that men use when they haven't anything sensible to say. He knew Wick and I would sort out our differences one day soon. We were made for each other. Anybody could see that.

I didn't answer, but I disagreed in my heart. I was beginning to see that winning a man was not the most important thing in the world. Winning one's self-respect, now that was important. I knew then that Wick and I were destined to go our separate ways. I had grown up in the seconds it took Wick to tell me I needed to. I could decide things for myself. I could decide that I didn't need Wick or Minnie. I could go on alone, making a new life, getting myself respected for being Carlotta Schultz. I would never again let a man put his face up to mine and tell me that I was a fool. The next man who tried would get his head blown off. I thought about buying a gun. I'd have to teach myself how to shoot, because I was damned if I was going to ask some man: 'Please, could you tell me which end to put the cartridge in?'

My thoughts were black on that long, wet ride. Albert left me in peace. He had his own thoughts, I guess. Maybe he was thinking about Roxanne who wouldn't have him, because she thought she could look after herself without anybody's help. Smart girl, Roxanne. She had taught me a thing or two.

We looked like a pair of wet rats when we finally arrived at the tavern. Fortunately, Albert had eight hundred dollars in his pocket and innkeepers have a nose for money. We were readily given separate rooms for the night. I suspect we were charged twice the going rate, but at least no one made any unfriendly remarks about us.

We slept soundly and in the morning set off for St Jo, a disreputable-looking pair in crumpled clothing. As we entered the town, Albert pulled his hat low over his eyes, ashamed to look so down-at-heel. The rain had ruined his fine clothes.

'Do you suppose Wick went directly to St Jo?' I asked.

'No, he won't be back for a day, perhaps two. He bought those three horses with some of my money. He'll probably give the horses to the others and walk back.'

241

Coming in to town, we turned a few heads. Some of Albert's friends shouted out lewd remarks as we passed them. Albert answered cheerfully with a wave and a smile.

I slumped in the saddle. I had tried to win myself a good reputation in St Jo, but it was no use. To protect Mary Benson and her daughter, I had to let all these roaring boys think I had been away for a night of love with Albert Jenkins. What made me mad was that their opinion of Albert was higher because of what they thought he had been up to. They now had no opinion of me at all!

The owner of the stable was furious that we had kept our horses for an extra day, but Albert soothed Mr Smithers' feelings with his smooth tongue and some of his money. When we had walked back to Jules Street, Albert turned to shake my hand.

'I must say goodbye, Carlotta, for I shall be leaving town today. St Jo is an interesting place. I've enjoyed my visit to the frontier, but there's nothing left for me now. The Mississippi riverboats are the place for me. Comfort and rich men, that's the ticket. Try not to be too angry with Wick. He's a good man. I wish you well, Carlotta. Stay out of trouble.'

He gave me an impulsive kiss on the cheek, and I said goodbye to yet another friend. With Wick no longer around, I had only Minnie left. Much as I wanted to see her, I wasn't looking forward to explaining where I had been for twenty-four hours.

'Out of town with Albert Jenkins?' asked Minnie in amazement. 'Weren't you even with Wick?'

'Wick's gone away for a while. I'm going upstairs to change my clothes. We got caught in the rain last night.'

'Tell me you've not gone off your head,' said Minnie, following me to the foot of the stairs. 'Tell me you haven't taken to the Life, after all.'

I couldn't tell her anything. I went upstairs to my

bedroom and lay down on my feather quilt. Not even a bedstead! A few short weeks ago, I had a room with proper furniture, a fiancé and the prospect of a home of my own in Boston. Ever since Carlton had disappeared, my life had been turned upside down. It surprised me to have to admit it, but I didn't regret coming West. I didn't regret having slept in a tent or on the floor of this house or being thrown in the river – well, come to think of it, I did regret that. I certainly didn't mind being thought a bad girl if it could help a runaway slave. I had grown up, all right. And I had grown to hate the man who told me I should.

The day passed somehow. Minnie kept giving me strange looks. She knew I was keeping a secret from her. She couldn't think what it might be, nor why I wouldn't tell her what was troubling me. And because I couldn't tell her about the slave, I found it next to impossible to talk to her about anything. My mouth wouldn't open, words wouldn't come. By dinner-time, she had given up on me and didn't address a single remark to me during the meal.

Mr Huggens came home and sat down to dinner in all his dirt. He told us Wick Estes had gone to a slave auction the day before and had not come back. Nobody knew where he was. And, even more surprising, Albert Jenkins had left town. Mr Huggens said he had been told to keep on working on the hotel, and the bank would pay his wages.

Minnie gave me a swift quizzical look, waiting for me to say oh, yes, that's what I've been up to; something to do with slaves. I said nothing, avoiding her searching gaze.

The boys came home and spoke of their adventures, and the other boys they had met. Their father said to shut their mouths as he had a headache. We dined in almost total silence, except for the sound of Mr Huggens eating. Before I had finished doing the dishes, Minnie had all three children in bed.

Mr Huggens took three chairs outside and lined them up against the back of the house. He leaned his chair back on two legs, and we sat in silence, watching the daylight disappear, listening to the chirping of the crickets, slapping at the mosquitoes, catching tantalizing glimpses in the gloom of lightning bugs flickering their little lights.

'Well . . .' said Mr Huggens on a yawn. He got up from his chair, stretched, and went inside. Presently, the glow of a lamp reached us through the back window. A few minutes later, he returned with two corncob pipes, saying he knew I didn't smoke, but hoped I wouldn't mind if he and Minnie did. They lit up and sucked noisily, getting their tobacco glowing.

Minnie coughed. 'What in the name of goodness am I smoking?'

'Hemp,' said Mr Huggens. 'Ain't you never smoked hemp afore?'

'No, don't believe I have. Stinks a bit.'

'Keep puffing. Makes a real nice smoke. Settles the nerves.'

It certainly settled Minnie's. The two of them began to talk, comparing stories about their previous marriages, the good times and the bad. Minnie giggled a lot. Sometimes, I just couldn't see what was so funny. Darkness came and still they sat. The lamplight falling through the back window lit Minnie's hair and gave her a halo. They seemed to have forgotten I was around, but after half an hour of feverish talk, they fell silent. We heard the crickets again. Their chirping was an incessant yet soothing accompaniment to our separate thoughts.

'Well . . .' said Mr Huggens again as he stood up. He turned, so that the lamplight fell on his face as he looked down at Minnie. He was not irritable tonight. His expression was soft, intent, eyes catching the light, gleaming, twinkling. 'Reckon I'll get me an early night.'

Minnie was staring into his face. I couldn't read her expression, but I could guess at her thoughts. I could imagine the slight smile that made her look young again, the dark eyes with their heavy lids drooping.

'I'll be up directly,' she murmured, and knocked the dottle from her pipe.

Mr Huggens leaned forward and squeezed her shoulder. Nothing more, just a firm lingering pressure close to the column of her neck. The air was electric with unspoken emotion. For a split second, I thought the crickets had stilled their chirping. All I could hear was a roaring in my ears.

I wished I was in bed. I was a Peeping Tom, an unwanted third party, observing an important moment between two people who had earned their right to privacy. This still moment was for them both an ending and a beginning. Minnie's life was on course, her future already plotted. Companionship and loving, hard work and poverty. The two of them were together, well matched. By contrast, I had never felt so utterly alone in my life.

When Mr Huggens had shuffled indoors, I offered to lock up and put out the lamp when I had lit my candle. Minnie nodded and stood up, smoothing her calico skirt, untying her apron strings, folding the apron into a neat square with loving hands.

There was no denying that Minnie and Mr Huggens were more comfortable with each other than Wick and I had ever been. The children provided them with a common purpose. The need to care for their family would keep them together, give them an unending source of mutual pleasure and interest. They didn't ask much of each other. That was the secret. I felt rootless, without a single tie binding me to Wick. And, of course, I had never got the hang of Wick's mental processes.

The next morning, Minnie's serene face at breakfast quite took away my appetite. I dawdled over a second cup of coffee. Then, as soon as Mr Huggens was well on his way to work, and I could be sure I wouldn't have to walk with him, I told Minnie I had things to do at the *Courier* office. I wanted to get away from her private happiness, and ran straight into my private nightmare.

16

A covered wagon had apparently run over a dog just before I arrived at the waterfront. Its young owner was kneeling beside it in the mud, covering his face as he cried heartbrokenly. No one stopped to comfort him; wagons continued to roll on to the ferry. Animal noises and smells made the landing an unpleasant place to be. No wonder the passengers just now disembarking from a packet looked bemused.

One neatly-dressed man seemed familiar, although I was certain we had never met. He was tall and fleshy, but far from being fat. He looked bad-tempered and had an imperious way about him.

Mr Livermore arrived at the landing, seated on the box of an open wagon. He was probably waiting for supplies to be unloaded from the packet and was startled when the familiar-looking man tapped him on the knee.

The stranger was probably asking a question. Mr Livermore scratched his chin as his eyes wandered across the scene on the landing. Suddenly, he straightened and pointed at me. The man nodded and walked briskly in my direction. I was too terrified to move, although I still didn't know who he was. I knew he must have come from St Louis. I knew he meant trouble.

'Miss Carlotta Scultz?'

'Yessir.'

'My name is Walkern.'

My blood froze as I blinked at him. Now I could see the family resemblance. This man must be the son.

'The Walkern name does mean something to you, doesn't it?'

'Yessir.' I didn't know what else to say, and there was nowhere to run to.

'My father, Otis Walkern, died about two weeks after the fire. I believe you owed him some money.' He looked around with distaste. 'Is there somewhere we can be private? I don't wish to discuss this business in front of the world and his dog.'

I suggested we walk towards Wick's hotel. I didn't know where else to take him.

'I'm sorry to hear of your father's death. I hardly knew him – '

'He died just about a week after you and your cohorts stole two thousand dollars of his money from the pocket of Mr Boyd.'

'Bullmouth Boyd stole eight hundred dollars of your father's money before we stole the rest!'

'A regular thieves' convention! That does not surprise me. Everything about this enterprise was unsavoury. I am ashamed my father ever entertained such a despicable money-making scheme. It is sadly true that we don't know what our parents are capable of. He was such a stern man, for ever lecturing me. Imagine the shock I sustained when, on going through his papers after his death, I came upon the contract he had with you. I summoned Mr Boyd and soon heard the whole story, or his version of it. The whole enterprise is disgusting. Beneath the dignity of a Walkern.'

'He forced me into it. He had come to a similar agreement with my mother, you know. He says he had already given her two thousand dollars, but it must have gotten burned up in the fire.'

'I don't want to hear about it. Besides, there is no record of any money given to your mother by my father.'

'Perhaps he had some money tucked away that didn't appear in his accounts.'

He started to deny the possibility, but thought better of it. 'As I have said, nothing would surprise me.

However, any understanding he had with your mother is finished. They are both dead. I am merely concerned with your contract. Under other circumstances, believe me, I would have put the law on you. As it is, I am only too aware of the scandal such an action would bring. Therefore, I propose to return your contract.'

'Oh, Mr Walkern! Thank you! Thank you, sir. To be relieved of the burden – '

'I have it with me.' He reached inside his coat to pull out the piece of paper that had haunted my dreams for weeks.

'You see,' I said eagerly. 'We, my friends and I, just couldn't do what your father wanted, so we took the money and came here to make a fresh start in life, live decently, you know, but, well, we've had, that is, *I've* had – ' I gasped for breath – 'but what I mean to say is, I'll pay back the whole twelve hundred dollars. You can bet on that.'

'In that case, there is no difficulty. You give me the money and I'll give you the contract. No one else need know anything about it.'

I stopped abruptly and put a hand to my stomach. The sick feeling was coming back. I wished there was somewhere to sit down.

'I haven't got the money, sir. Not right now, I haven't. But I plan to pay back every penny.'

'And how, exactly, do you plan to do so?'

'I don't know. It's very hard to find the sort of work that pays well. A respectable lady has . . .' His expression was hardening. He didn't want to hear excuses. 'I guess,' I said slowly. 'I could go out to the gold fields and set up a hurdy-gurdy house like your father wanted. That would make money pretty quickly.'

'Yes, but then you would be so far away, I could not be sure of ever hearing from you again.'

I noticed that he didn't say he disapproved of my doing such a thing in order to pay him back. He was

249

simply concerned with the practicalities. 'Mr Walkern, you're just going to have to trust me. Now, you can call the law and have me put in the penitentiary, if you want to. But then I'll never be able to pay you back, will I? And there's the scandal. Or, you can trust me to get myself out West, go into business and send back regular payments.'

Mr Walkern nibbled at the head of his cane, wrestling with what was left of his conscience. 'I don't believe I wish to hear details of how you plan to repay me. I just want to know when the first payment can be expected.'

'You'll receive the first five hundred dollars one year from today. California is a long way off, after all. I've got to get there, earn the money and send it back. That all takes time.'

Mr Walkern returned the contract to his pocket and turned round in the road. 'I guess there is nothing else to discuss. I will return to St Louis immediately. I suppose you, of all people, will know how to . . . er . . . set up in business.'

'It doesn't take much talent,' I said wearily. 'Any damned fool could do it.'

Time had run out for me. I had to get out of the United States. Young Mr Walkern didn't fool me. He wasn't a nicer man than his father, he was merely a bigger hypocrite. I didn't intend to open a hurdy-gurdy house anywhere in the world. I knew, therefore, that I wouldn't have five hundred dollars to send to Mr Walkern in twelve months' time. My only hope was to travel beyond the laws of the Republic.

San Francisco would do. Out in California, so I had been told, men sang a song that went: '*Oh, what was your name in the States?*' There were so many men in the Far West who had left the States for one reason or another and changed their names, that people had made a song out of it. I would change my name, too, when I got out there. I had no choice.

I had known for the last twenty-four hours that sooner or later I would have to take to the Oregon Trail. I had hoped to sell the *Courier* first. I realized after talking to Mr Walkern that I was just daydreaming again, not being grown up.

I went up the hill to tent city and asked to be shown the way to Captain Martin who, I knew, was taking a party of men to the gold fields. His was the last party left in St Jo. There was a lot of talk around town that the captain was leaving it too late to get going. Now I was grateful for the broken wagons, shortage of funds and sick men that had delayed his departure.

The captain was a red-eyed man who hadn't shaved for a day or two or, I imagined, changed his clothes since coming to St Jo. He laughed in an ugly sort of way when I said I wanted to join the train.

'I'm not going to the gold fields,' I told him. 'I'm going to San Francisco. I intend to take my printing press and my type-cases and some ink and paper. I'm going to set up the *Courier* in San Franciso. The press is heavy, but it's mounted on a big old wooden frame. I can leave the frame behind. Just the same, I won't be able to carry my printing things as well as supplies in one wagon. If I could put my supplies in somebody else's wagon – '

'You crazy?' asked the captain. 'We all know who you are, what sort of women you came into town with. Nobody here's going to want you along, lessen you perform the service God put you on earth for.'

I straightened my shoulders and looked at this self-styled captain so hard and for so long that he eventually lowered his eyes as the smart grin faded.

'Captain, for a long time now, everybody has been trying to drive me into the mud. I'm getting sick of it. I'll pay you a dollar a day, the same as everybody else, and I'll buy a gun and keep it close by so that no man gets the wrong idea. But don't you go thinking things about me. I'm a newspaper owner and lady editor, and no damned belly-crawling, egg-sucking son of a monkey is going to turn me into a whore!'

Captain Martin smiled and looked around to see who else was listening to this eccentric woman spouting nonsense. He didn't say anything. He just sat there chewing tobacco. I could see his jaws working. When he turned his head and spat brown juice a yard out onto the dusty ground, I gave up on him and started back to Minnie's.

I had gone a fair way and was in woodland, well out of sight of tent city when two young men caught up with me. The sight of them sent my heart throbbing painfully in my chest. They were handsome and they were brawny with forearms as big as my thighs. I looked around, but nobody could see us. Feeling a little nervous, I backed up against a tree.

'Miss Schultz,' said the blond one politely. They couldn't have been more than eighteen or nineteen years old. 'We heard what you said to the captain. We'll carry your supplies for you. Maybe help out on the cost of getting you a rig, on account of we want two wagons when we get to California.'

'Oh, yes? And what do you want in return?' I dug my nails into the tree bark and wished I had left myself space to run. These two lads were a head taller than I was, and so powerfully built.

'Is it true your ma was Missouri Belle?'

'Yes, but I'm not – '

'You're not a green girl, that's the important thing. You wouldn't be hoping to go West if you were. We think you might understand,' said the dark one. 'Hyram and me, we're friends.'

My eyes opened wide as understanding dawned. They were risking a lot by telling me. 'I see.' Respectable women didn't know about such men as these, but I had learned of their existence at an early age. I relaxed. They wouldn't harm me. 'So you want me to be a sort of decoy. Make the other men think you've got a girl.'

'That's it!' said the blond one. 'If the others find out about us, our lives won't be worth a red cent.'

I extended a hand. 'It's a deal. Meet me down at the *Courier* office in three hours, and we'll discuss how we're going to do this.'

'But why are you going?' asked Minnie when I told her my plan to start a newspaper in San Francisco. 'You always said you hated the idea of going on the Oregon Trail. You always said people were crazy to go. Wait for Wick. Wait till he comes back.'

'I'm finished with Wick. It's over. I guess I've known all along that I have got to prove to myself that I can make it alone. He can't insult me and get away with it. I won't be sent away like a naughty girl. I don't want to see him again.'

Minnie smiled in the same way that Albert had done: superior, as if she knew some secret I wasn't in on. 'Carlotta, honey, you got to take the rough with the smooth. Men can be handled. *Have* to be handled. Look how I handled Mr Huggens. Got him tied up legal before he got over his grief and decided he didn't want a new wife. And he's happy enough. I'm giving him what he wants. Now, if sometimes a man has had too much to drink and gets a little mean, why you just think how much worse off you'd be on your own, and you put up with the cussin' or the slap. Mr Huggens ain't exactly what I'd of chose in a perfect world. But if you can't get what you want, you got to want what you get. You got to let men think they make every important decision. But there's ways, see, of getting what you want. Women's ways. Don't give up on Wick. He's your best chance of happiness.'

'Oh, Minnie!' I put my arms around her and gave her a warm hug. 'It can't be that way for me. I'm different. I won't put up with it. I don't think any man is my best chance of happiness. I'm going to San Francisco.'

At first Minnie tried to talk me out of it, then she began to calculate. 'Let's see. The wagon train won't make more than twenty miles a day, and then only when everything goes well. At a steady pace, Wick can ride five miles an hour. With a change of horses, he could go even faster. If he wants you, he'll come. There's no doubt about that. And my guess is, you'll take him.'

'For his money?' I asked drily. 'Because he'll keep me, so I won't ever have to think again?'

'Well, there is that to it. You can't deny there is that to it.'

'I'm not hanging around here for Wick or any other man. I'm going. One day I'll have all the money I need.'

All the same, I didn't get away until Thursday, the twenty-first of June. Minnie came to the ferry landing to see me sail away. By that time, we had stopped telling each other our secrets. We were almost like strangers, divided by our different views on men and women. Minnie said I was cursed by my mother's attitude to marriage, and look what happened to her. I didn't answer her back. I wanted to part on friendly terms, so I held my tongue. She met Hyram and Eli and told them to take good care of me. They were so polite to her that she seemed a little happier after that. We cried a little, and told each other to write. We had been friends for just a few weeks; I had a feeling I would never see her again.

Fifty wagons, a hundred and fifty men and I rolled off the ferry and set off on the Kansas territory side of the river. The party had buried four men in St Jo, all dead from cholera. I had the wagon that had belonged to the dead men. The prairie schooner and six yoke of oxen cost four hundred and twenty dollars, which I didn't have, of course. Hyram and Eli bought the rig to carry the press in. I was very grateful to those boys. Without them, I would have been stuck in St Jo, still dreaming about getting away. My supplies cost me very nearly every penny I had. I tried not to think what would happen to

254

me in San Francisco, before I could get the paper to start making a profit. I wouldn't even be able to raise a little money by selling the rig, because it didn't belong to me.

On the Trail, our day began at four in the morning. Hyram and Eli expected me to cook for them, and that was fair enough. After all, nobody asked me to take my turn at sentinel duty during the night. We set off at six each morning and rode for four hours. Every day a party of hunters would set out on horseback looking for food. They rode five or six miles ahead of the wagons. The land was flat and treeless. On clear days we could see a long way ahead, but sooner or later we always lost sight of those men and wondered what they might run into.

At the nooning place, we didn't unyoke the oxen, but we did set them loose from the wagons so that they could graze. Again, I had to make a fire and cook. The men were always hungry, but sometimes I felt so tired I didn't want to eat, much less cook a meal. Afterwards, everything had to be gathered up, the oxen harnessed to the wagons, the livestock collected, before we set off again.

By eight o'clock each evening, we had drawn the wagons into a circle, settled the animals, eaten the evening meal and were ready to sleep if we could.

I counted the days ahead, calculated the miles left to go, and tried to keep up my spirits. Above all, I prayed for good health. Travelling overland on the Trail was infinitely worse than I had imagined it would be. The backbreaking hours sitting on the box and driving the oxen gave me time to think, and my imagination ran wild. Sometimes I felt like pulling my hair out with worry about what I was travelling to. Even the men were tired and drawn. I was exhausted by the third day out and never got enough rest. I hadn't known how much I loved trees until we rode into territory that had not one in sight for mile after mile. The prairie grass was waist-high on me, and tough to walk on. But the wheel ruts of all those rigs that had gone before meant that the wagon jolted so much, I soon got a headache if I rode on the box. The sun blinded us all.

We buried two men on the tenth day. Everybody was silent that day, fearful of the future, unable to stop thinking about who would be next. By the time we had been on the Trail for three weeks, we had stopped counting the gravestones erected by travellers who had gone before us, or the dearly beloved possessions that had been abandoned. I was getting so tired, I came to accept that I couldn't make it to San Francisco. Not the whole four and a half months, not the whole two thousand miles.

It was on a bright hot day when we had stopped by a small stream for our nooning, that some of the men shouted they thought someone was following us. The men stood ready with their guns in case it was an Indian war party. There was a lot of excitement when we were able to see the lone rider and knew he was a white man. I was afraid it was Mr Walkern, or someone he had sent after me. Despair sucked the strength out of me as I watched the man riding ever closer. I couldn't fight any more. If they wanted to put me in the penitentiary, so be it. At least I wouldn't have to worry about where my next meal was coming from.

When I saw that it was Wick with five or six horses, I was so surprised that I had to lean against the wagon to keep from falling down.

I told myself I was glad he had come, because I had a few sharp things to say to him. But the familiar face, shaded by a big hat, the easy way he sat in the saddle gave my heart a lift. Every man in the train had treated me decently. I couldn't complain. However, there are times when a familiar face is the finest sight in the world. I left the shelter of the wagon's shade and started walking towards him. Our eyes met and held. Somebody said: 'Aw, I'm going back to my grub. He's just some feller come for Carlotta.'

256

Judging by the set of his mouth, Wick wasn't too happy to see me, but I knew he had come all those miles for no other reason. I put my hand on the horse's neck as he dismounted.

'It's good to see you, Wick.'

'You could have seen me just fine if you had stayed in St Jo. I wouldn't have had to ride like a madman to catch you up if you hadn't run away. What in the name of God possessed you to take the Trail? It can't have been anything I said, because you know I didn't mean it. Aw, Carlotta, don't cry.'

He pulled me into his arms and squeezed me until I had spots in front of my eyes. He smelled of sweat and dust and horse. His red shirt was hot from the sun and his chin had at least a day's growth of beard on it. I tried desperately to remember why I was mad at him, what I had thought was so all-fired important. No use. My heart sang and the tiredness dropped away from me like a cloak. I held on. I think there was an ironic cheer from the men. I heard Wick laugh, and because I had my head on his chest, I felt the vibration of it, felt his laugh inside of me.

'Mr Walkern's son came to St Jo. I had to get going.'

He held me away from him so that he could study my face. 'Is that why you left?'

'I left because you treated me badly. I left because you talked to me as if I didn't have any proper feelings. When there is no respect, there can't be love, Wick.'

His arms dropped to his sides, and I almost wished I hadn't spoken. But no, there was a special feeling between us, like a magnet that would always draw us together. Better to say my piece now and clear the air.

'I cussed you out in front of Albert and for that I apologize most humbly. But if you love me, you'll understand how much I love you. I'd have said anything to keep you from getting into slave trouble that night. Folks in Missouri hate slave stealers more than any-

257

thing. If they had caught me, they would have strung me up as sure as shooting. I couldn't have that happen to you. Love is a terrible pain in the neck, Carlotta. You have to understand that you can't do whatever you want to do, whenever you want to do it, because you scare me half to death. Like coming out here.'

'I was scared for you, too, but I understood that I had to let you go ahead and do what you could for Daphne. I've thought of you dead and I've thought of you in jail. Like most women, I've kept my fears to myself. Don't ever treat me that way again.'

We were out of earshot of the men, but I could feel their eyes boring into my back. They must surely be able to sense the tension that was keeping Wick and me from reaching out to one another. He hooked his fingers in his belt and glowered at me. I glowered back, standing my ground, determined not to win this or any other argument with one of Minnie's women's ways.

'I went to Walkern's office in St Louis,' he said in a low voice. The information was a flag of truce. There was to be no more discussion about the night Daphne escaped. 'He said he'd seen you. I paid him the twelve hundred dollars.'

'Where did you get the money to pay off Mr Walkern?'

He grinned at me, thinking he had turned my mind to other things. 'Now, there's a story. Have you got any coffee? I've been swallowing dust since sun-up. I've ridden that horse right down to his knees. We both need a rest.'

We walked over to the buffalo-chip fire and sat down on the trampled prairie grass. I found a mug and poured some coffee for him.

'Mary Benson, William and the girl got away safely. They didn't take our horses; they had some of their own hidden in the woods. They turned ours loose, and I managed to catch all of them in about an hour. They took our money to make it look like both of us had been

258

robbed. That blow on the head sure did catch me by surprise. I had some money in my boot, and so did the fat man, so I guess we didn't suffer too much. He was anxious to get home. The last thing he wanted to do was start a ruckus about the loss of a slave like Daphne, because his wife was not what he called the accommodating type.

'I made my way down to Independence and took a packet to St Louis, where I saw William. He said they had made a raft and floated all the way, travelling by night. Mary and her daughter had only just got safely into Illinois when I reached St Louis.'

'Why did you go to St Louis? Why didn't you come back to St Jo?'

Wick looked aggrieved. 'I figured I'd better do something right, because you were awful mad at me. The things you told me about Belle bothered me. Of course, I didn't know you would take some fool notion into your head. I thought you would trust me and wait for me in St Jo so we could sort out our difference of opinion. It's lucky I did go to St Louis. My insurance money had come through and was sitting there waiting for me. William found a buyer for the hotel, so I completed that deal. I made a thousand dollars profit on the hotel, believe it or not. Now, here's the best part. I went to see Lyman Gray, your ma's lawyer.'

'My mother had a lawyer? I thought she died penniless and in debt – why, Mr Walkern told me so!'

'You see, Carlotta, you are always too hasty. I knew she had used him in the past, so I made some enquiries of my own. I went to see him in his office, told him I was your husband and had come for your inheritance.'

'Did he believe that?'

'He sure did! You've inherited two thousand dollars, among other things.'

I laughed out loud for the first time in weeks. 'That will be old Mr Walkern's money.'

'Maybe, but there's no record of it. I used some of it to pay off your debt and get the contract back. Seems you signed a promissory note for Bullmouth – he gave it up without too much of a fight. Your ma left a will which I've read. She's left you three acres of good building land within the city limits. She also left you a letter, which I haven't read.'

My hand shook when I reached for the letter. My mother was never one to waste time in writing; there wasn't much on the single sheet of paper. She spoke of her love and her desire to leave me something. It was clear she didn't know if she would last until I arrived in St Louis. Finally, she said she was sorry she couldn't tell me who my father was. It could be any one of half a dozen men, she said, in her characteristically forthright way. Better not to speculate. Better for me to forget all about it.

I had always hoped that I would one day discover the name of my father. It was too late for that now, but the disappointment was not too great. She had loved me, after all. She had left me some money – I didn't dwell on how she came by it – and she had left me land. If you can't find gold, the next best thing is to own land. Gold and land beat working for a living every time.

'I'm asking you to marry me, Carlotta,' said Wick, breaking in on my thoughts. 'I love you. I'll try to be the kind of man you want. I'm willing to compromise.'

'I'd be proud to marry you,' I said. 'Will we live in St Louis? We could build ourselves a fine house, and I'm going to put up the finest tombstone money can buy to mark the passing of Missouri Belle.'

I moved closer so that I could wipe some dust from his cheek. He took my hand and kissed the back of it. 'Better rest up overnight. You look thin and tired, but I have to tell you the return journey is going to be every bit as hard. Fortunately, it won't take three weeks. Minnie said you brought your printing press along – but you

260

won't be able to take it back home. We can't use a wagon. We'll have to ride and I've seen you ride, so I don't think we can travel too fast!'

'It doesn't matter about the newspaper fixings. The wagon belongs to two men I'm travelling with, that is, cooking for. They can have the press. Did Minnie tell you about them?'

'She sure did. I think I know their type. Never thought I'd be grateful to two men like that. I presume you knew what you were doing joining up with them. Here comes a fancy-looking young man. Is he one of your friends?'

Wick and I were on our feet by the time Eli reached us. The two men solemnly shook hands, sizing each other up. 'I'm told you're Wick Estes,' said Eli.

'That's right. What can I do for you?'

'Be our wagon-master and lead us to safety in California.'

'No!' I cried.

Eli turned to me. 'Carlotta, Captain Martin is dead and there's not another man in the party who's ever been this far West. Estes has done it before. All we're asking is for him to take command. He's here, after all. I presume you were both planning to go on to California, Estes.'

I stepped between the men. 'No, we weren't. We're going back to St Jo tomorrow. I never really wanted to come. I thought I had to, but now I find I don't. You take the press and sell it in San Francisco, Eli. Wick, tell him you won't do it. Why don't you say something?'

'You're mighty late in the season. It might be a good idea to turn back. Wait until next year and get away early.'

'We're not going back,' said Eli. 'None of us has the money to wait a whole year. We've got to get where we're going as fast as possible. I beg you. Stay with us and lead us all to safety. I've heard about the Donner party. I don't want to be somebody's dinner. We could get caught in the snow! Besides, nobody knows the way.

261

We're depending on you, Estes. I think it's your duty to help us.'

'Duty can be overrated,' I said, but neither man was listening to me.

'You've come a damned fool way. Captain Martin doesn't seem to have been a capable man for the job. Are you an officer of the train?'

'No, sir. Hyram and I didn't think they wanted men of only eighteen. We knew we couldn't get elected, so we didn't put ourselves forward.'

'That's the trouble with elections. The right men don't run, and the wrong ones get elected.'

Eli grinned. 'You don't have to worry about that. There won't be an election. We appoint you.'

'Wick, say no.' I begged.

'No,' said Wick. 'You get every man jack in the party to meet me at the lead wagon. I want their votes. Any man doesn't vote for me, and I don't take the job. I want to know they're with me. I want to see the roster of pickets. I've seen the corrals you've been building of a night, and I don't like them. Indians have been watching this train. Any day now, they may decide to start a prairie fire and stampede your cattle. I swear I've never seen so much livestock travelling on the way to the gold fields. What are you men? Prospectors or farmers?'

'I'll go tell them you're coming,' said Eli. 'I think you've still got to convince one person you're doing the right thing, but I reckon she don't have a vote.' Eli walked off, and I grabbed Wick by the sleeve.

'How could you, Wick? How could you do this to me? I hate travelling in a wagon train. I want to go to St Louis and build a fine house. I want to see your hotel in St Jo when it's finished. There's so many things I want, and none of them can be found west of Missouri.'

'I know. I'm disappointed, too. But, in a way, it's your fault I'm not leaving these damned fools to their fate. You made me understand about caring for others. Why,

262

do you know, if Mary Benson had asked me for help just one month before I met you, I would have said I didn't want to get involved. You've saved me from my bad nature, darling. Now you're going to have to put up with my sense of duty.'

'I want to get married. I had thought maybe – '

'I want to get married, too, you foolish girl. Don't you know I love you? Do I have to keep saying it out loud? I love you, dammit and I'm asking you to be my wife. But there is just no way we can get married out here on the prairie. I tell you what, as of this moment, I consider you to *be* my wife. There now. Do you feel married?'

'Oh, Wick!' I didn't get to say anything more. He kissed me, squeezing me so tight, my feet left the ground. 'I guess so,' I managed to say at last.

'When we get to San Francisco, we'll build a house and set up a newspaper. Or maybe we'll go back to St Louis. I've given up on guessing what the future holds. Cheer up, Carlotta. I'll see you don't get too tired on the trek. We can think of the weeks ahead as our honeymoon.'

'A hot, dirty, bone-wearing, dangerous, boring honeymoon.'

'Oh, come on, now. Not boring,' said Wick before he kissed me again. He knew I couldn't resist his kisses, knew I couldn't argue any more. Eli called to him, and after a second or two, he released me to stride off towards the lead wagon without a backward glance for his new wife.

I watched him go with tears in my eyes. Some compromise! If you can't get what you want, want what you get, Minnie had said. There were some women strong enough and with enough trailcraft to strike out on their own for St Jo. I wasn't one of them and I knew it. I had gotten this far with the help of two men. Only Wick could take me back to St Jo, and he wasn't going to do it.

'Well, Ma,' I said out loud. 'Before you died, you tried

to give me a little security and comfort, but I'm going to have to settle for love and adventure. Will it do? Are you happy for me? If only I could see you one last time to tell you Wick and I are going to be together. That would tickle your funny bone.'

I thought I heard her chuckle. I thought I felt her presence. Then I remembered how she looked. I could see her as clearly as if she were standing beside me. Missouri Belle, all dressed up in black satin and a froth of expensive lace that never quite concealed her cleavage. She always wore a smile, and rouge. On hot days, her whole face would go red, but she didn't care. She would give a sassy push to those yellow curls, settle the feathered hat, adjust her parasol and say: 'Strut, Carlotta, we're high-stepping folks! Let 'em stare. I can pay for my own liquor and never say thank you to any man. Strut, girl! You're the daughter of Missouri Belle.'

Here I was in the middle of nowhere and too tired to strut. It seemed to me that ever since Carlton had run away from me, my whole life had been directed towards the West. I was being sucked by forces greater than anything I had ever known towards new frontiers. God knows I had fought against it!

Perhaps now was the time 'to accept my manifest destiny, to stop fighting and embrace the challenge of a new, unsettled life. I had thought I wanted the comfort and culture of St Louis, but I just might surprise myself and excel at helping to start a new town like San Francisco. Wick's voice and mine would be heard when the state of California joined the Union.

One thing was certain. I was beginning to feel proud of myself; a present from Wick and my mother. Why, I was a decent, God-fearing woman who could square up to anybody and set a fine example. California would be lucky to have me. And I was lucky to have Wick! With him by my side, everything was going to be all right.

264